VIRAGO
MODERN CLASSICS
65

Winifred Holtby

Winifred Holtby (1898–1935) was born in Rudston, Yorkshire. In the First World War she was a member of the Women's Auxiliary Army Corps, and then went to Somerville College, Oxford, where she met Vera Brittain. After graduating, these two friends shared a flat in London where both embarked upon their respective literary careers. Winifred Holtby was a prolific journalist and novelist. She also travelled all over Europe as a lecturer for the League of Nations Union.

Her first novel *Anderby Wold*, was published in 1923, followed by *The Crowded Street* (1924), *The Land of Green Ginger* (1927), *Poor Caroline* (1931), *Mandoa! Mandoa!* (1933), and *South Riding* (1936), which was published posthumously after her tragic death from kidney disease at the age of thirty-seven. She was awarded the James Tait Black Memorial Prize for this, her most famous novel.

ANDERBY WOLD

Winifred Holtby

virago

VIRAGO

This paperback edition published in 2011 by Virago Press
First published by Virago Press in 1981

First published in Great Britain in 1923 by John Lane at the Bodley Head Limited

The moral right of the author has been asserted

*All characters and events in this publication, other than those
clearly in the public domain, are fictitious and any resemblance
to real persons, living or dead, is purely coincidental.*

All rights reserved.
No part of this publication may be reproduced, stored in a
retrieval system, or transmitted in any form or by any means, without
the prior permission in writing of the publisher, nor be otherwise circulated
in any form of binding or cover other than that in which it is published
and without a similar condition including this condition being
imposed on the subsequent purchaser.

A CIP catalogue record for this book
is available from the British Library.

ISBN 978-1-84408-791-4

Typeset in Goudy by M Rules
Printed and bound in Great Britain by
Clays Ltd, St Ives plc

Virago Press
An imprint of
Little, Brown Book Group
100 Victoria Embankment
London EC4Y 0DY

An Hachette UK Company
www.hachette.co.uk

www.virago.co.uk

TO
DAVID AND ALICE HOLTBY
IS DEDICATED
THIS IMAGINARY STORY OF
IMAGINARY EVENTS ON AN
IMAGINARY FARM

'Felicity is a continual progresse of the desire from one object to another, the attaining of the former being still but the way to the later ... so that, in the first place, I put for a generall inclination of all mankind, a perpetuall and restlesse desire of power after power which ceaseth only after death ... and there shall be no contentment but proceeding.'

– HOBBES. *Leviathan*, I, 11.

Contents

I

FULL SUZERAINTY

When Sarah Bannister's dogcart bowled along the High Street of Market Burton, its progress was observed by several pairs of eyes, peeping discreetly from behind lace veiled windows.

'Look, Lizzie, Sarah Bannister's got a new bonnet.'

'My word, she'll be late if they don't hurry.'

'This is the fourth year she's worn that black coat of hers. She made it in 1908, from some old stuff of her mother's.'

Everybody in Market Burton knew that Mrs Bannister and her husband were driving to a tea-party at Anderby Wold. Everybody knew that the party had been arranged to celebrate the final clearance of the mortgage from the Wold Farm. Sarah knew that they knew. Their furtive glances were not lost upon her; but she accepted all remark as a tribute to her highly respected personality.

It was a good thing, she thought, that her neighbours at least referred to her as 'Sarah Bannister.' Her sister Janet, and her sister-in-law Tilly, might be known familiarly as 'Mrs Donald' or 'Mrs Richard,' as though their only claim to recognition lay in the identity of their lord and possessor. But no one could think that of Sarah. Anybody looking now at Tom's shrinking figure on the seat beside her might have guessed that he only crept through life like the shadow cast by the flame of his wife's vitality.

Sarah bowed severely to an acquaintance in the road. It was no use being too familiar with the wife of a retail grocer. Of course, as Mrs Bannister, she had no claim to social superiority. Tom's father had come to the town as a cattle drover sixty years ago, when farmers sold by private agreement. It was only during the last ten years of his life that his 'Now then, gentlemen!' had become a commonplace of the Saturday market, and he had risen to respectability as a dealer of some repute. But as a former Miss Robson, Sarah had a position of importance to uphold in the East Riding.

The dog-cart passed the red villas and square, tree-encircled houses skirting the town, and began to mount the steady ascent of the Wolds. The December air was keen with frost and the wheels spun through fringes of ice along the puddles. Sarah drew more tightly round her the thick black coat she always wore when driving.

'You don't get stuff like this now, Tom,' she observed, affectionately fingering her collar. 'Not with all your newfangled electric factories and German dyes. My mother used to buy wool from a packman who came round the Wolds from the West Riding somewhere, and beautiful stuff it was too. When she died, her wardrobe in the best bedroom was full of gowns not a bit the worse for wear; but, if I died to-morrow, there wouldn't be anything worth keeping except a few bits I had from her like this cloth.'

Her husband made no answer. Long ago he had acknowledged the superiority of his wife's intelligence, and considered that her judgments required neither criticism nor confirmation. He felt ill at ease, perched on the high box-seat, the foot-rest advanced to its nearest hole to accommodate his short legs. Sarah's lower seat seemed to emphasize her mental superiority.

'You're letting the reins slip down, Tom. It's a fault I'm continually having to find with your driving – let alone with other things. How do you expect the horse to know it's being driven unless you drive it? You seem to think the Almighty arranged the world on purpose to save you trouble.'

Tom gathered up the reins obediently. It was useless to resent Sarah's criticism because, whether right or wrong, she had too much respect for her own judgment to acknowledge an error.

He liked a visit to Anderby; but his pleasure was always spoilt by the consciousness of Sarah's disapproval. Sarah didn't seem to like Mary. It was a pity they couldn't get on. Of course it was bad luck for Sarah that John should leave her after they had lived together for forty-two years. Still, what was a man to do? He was sure to marry one day and Mary was a fine woman even if her father had been a wrong 'un. Besides, she had been a Robson even before she married John, and that should count a good deal with a family which tended to despise every one who entered its ranks by marriage instead of by birth, as Tom knew only too well.

Noticing the uncompromising angle of Sarah's bonnet, Tom

decided he was doomed to an uncomfortable afternoon. His wife cast a discerning eye across the Wolds and sniffed with meaning.

'Young Swynderby's got a fine crop of turnips there – pity they say he drinks too hard to see them.'

The cart splashed on between bare, blackened hedges and chequered slopes of plough land and stubble. There were eight miles of undulating road to cover, but Sarah had no desire for the journey to end. Enjoyment was the last thing she expected from any party, but a festivity at Anderby Wold was almost too much even for her endurance.

John was, of course, everything a man should be, as Sarah frequently assured him. She ought to know, for after their mother's death she, as the eldest sister, had taken complete charge of his upbringing. She had packed his tuck-box with crab-apple jelly and plum loaves, when first he went to Dr. Deale's Academy for young gentlemen at Hardrascliffe. She had marked his linen and darned his socks and bound his hands when the blisters broke after his first heavy harvest forking in '81. When as a young bachelor he first began to farm on his own at Littledale, she had gone to keep house for him.

Of course she knew him better than Mary could. For years she had understood him with his alternating moods of obstinacy and indecision, far better than she understood herself. His orderly mind was like a familiar room, of which she held the key. She knew the thoughts from which his words arose as well as she knew the shelves from which her cups and dishes were brought to the table.

But now – it was all different. In looking for John, she found Mary.

'I do wish you'd tuck the rug in at your side, Tom. There's such a draught round my legs. Of course, if you want me to be crippled by rheumatism, there's an end of it. I've no doubt I should live somehow, and perhaps it's as well to get used to being uncomfortable before we go to that house of Mary's.'

Anderby Wold was Mary's house. Littledale had been John's – John's and hers. He belonged far more to that solitary farm among the hills than to Mary's bustling place on the village street. John never had a word to say for himself at Anderby. The place bore the imprint, not of his personality, but Mary's. Mary had no right to marry him, just to make use of him. Of course it was easy to bully John, with his slow, kindly nature. He never would stand up for himself. But Sarah had managed him properly. When she had wished to visit her sisters at Market Burton she had delicately steered John to a confession of wanting to go himself. Mary simply went out and ordered the dog-cart.

'I've no patience with these newfangled ideas at Anderby,' she continued. '"Hygiene" Mary Robson calls it. "High fiddle-sticks" I say. We were healthy enough before. My father died when he was ninety-two, and would have lived long enough then if he hadn't fallen out of the Upper barn when they were woolpacking.'

'He was a fine old man,' remarked Tom, seeking as usual for uncontroversial ground.

'No finer than most of us Robsons,' snapped Sarah. But she remembered one Robson who had not been fine. Mary's father, Benjamin, had always been a most unsatisfactory person. Drinking and betting were bad enough, but there were other tales of servants hurriedly dismissed and governesses who would not stay. Of course it was a pity his wife had died when the girl was born; but she had been a queer, dowdy sort of creature, fond of books and no use in a house. Probably she would never have prevented the deepest disgrace of Ben's career – the mortgage that imperilled five hundred acres of land that had been farmed by a Robson since the sixteenth century.

'Who's building that house over there, Tom?' she inquired.

'Oh, it's Sam Burrard. He's putting up a house so as not to have to drive out from the town to farm every day.'

Sarah frowned.

'Why didn't you tell me? You never tell me anything worth hearing. It's just as well Sam is building himself a mansion in this world. From all accounts he won't get much of a one in the next.'

In a quarter of an hour they would be at Anderby Wold. That was where Ben had died over ten years ago, and where John had called to see if he could do anything for Mary – eighteen-year-old Mary, left alone to cope with her father's debts. Oh, but she was clever! She knew that John was capable of managing two farms as well as one. Six month's tribute had been paid to decorum before she had married him – poor John being too guileless to understand her cleverness. And, for the hundredth time since the marriage, Sarah had to enter John's house as his wife's guest. It was hard.

The road rounded the summit of the hill and tilted towards the valley, two miles away. There from a cluster of leafless trees rose the welcoming smoke of Anderby Wold.

Well! Mary had everything now. Sarah wished her joy of it.

The thought of her husband driving placidly by her side, without a thought for her discomfiture, goaded Sarah to fury.

6

'Tom,' she exclaimed, 'I wish you'd use your handkerchief. There's a drop on the end of your nose!'

Tom and Sarah were the last of the family to arrive. Sarah had declined Mary's invitation to midday dinner, because she had made her Christmas puddings on the fourteenth of December ever since she was old enough to hold a wooden spoon, and nothing short of a sale or a stack fire would induce her to postpone the ceremony.

Their host and hostess stood in the porch to receive them, and Sarah alighted stiffly, passing a large white handkerchief across her lips before she came forward and kissed her brother.

'Well, John,' she remarked, 'I suppose I am to offer you my congratulations.' To Mary she extended a more formal hand. 'Well, Mary, I see you have a houseful. Has Uncle Dickie come?'

'Yes. We made him come last night so as not to be too tired for to-day. You're cold. Come in and take your things off.'

'Thank you, I will. It was a very cold drive.' Sarah sounded aggrieved, as though Mary were responsible for the weather.

They went upstairs. Mary's room always annoyed Sarah. The queer books, the vase of chrysanthemums, the fire in the grate, all looked as though they were trying to make it a little better than anyone else's.

'I can't think what you want a fire for at your time of life, Mary. What with coal strikes and everything and firing such a price.'

'Oh, well' – Mary slid to her knees on the hearth-rug and knelt there fingering the poker – 'I thought you would probably be rather cold after a long drive, and you know what the drawing-room fire is when the men get round it, backs to the mantelpiece, heels on the fender, and sixteen stones of John or

7

Toby between us poor women and any ghost of heat. We have to do something.'

The poker slipped from her fingers and fell clattering into the grate. Sarah did not know that when she was not present Mary rarely fidgeted. She thought to herself, 'I don't know how John stands it. She's never still for a minute, and just think of a woman married ten years sitting about on the floor like that!'

The youthful ease of Mary's movements flaunted Sarah's sixty-three years in her face.

'I'm sorry you didn't get over in time for dinner. You'd have liked to see the spread we gave the men in the front kitchen. They had roast beef and Yorkshire pudding and apple pie and cheese. It was a business, but Anne and Louisa helped me, so we got through.' Mary sighed with satisfaction.

'I should have thought it would have been better to make a bit of money to set aside for a rainy day instead of spending all this as soon as your debts were paid. If you are not careful, you'll be your father all over again, Mary. Was this John's idea?'

'Well, as a matter of fact, it was mine. But John was perfectly willing. The men have helped us more than anything and it's only fair we should show them we appreciate it. Are you ready to go down?'

They might as well go down. Sarah had not come to John's house to wrangle with his wife. Anyway, it was no use criticizing Mary since she was so obviously convinced of her own perfection. They descended in silence.

The family was assembled in the drawing-room. Sarah rustled forward and greeted with varying degrees of formal familiarity her uncle, brothers and cousins. She kissed each of the women with distaste.

Mary had grouped them carefully – Aunt Jane, Uncle Dickie, Richard, Sarah's brother, his wife Tilly, who talked at intervals to nobody in particular, Anne and Louisa Robson, relegated to the window-seat as became undowered spinsters. Sarah could hear them now whispering together over a quarrel they had begun in their cradles and saw no particular reason for ever finishing. On the sofa Janet, whose profitable marriage with Donald Holmes had been her unique contribution to the world's welfare, laboriously displayed a London-made satin gown to her relations.

'Janet's getting fat,' thought Sarah. 'She doesn't wear as well as the rest of us. That's what comes of living in hotels and such and lying in bed till all hours. No wonder she's always suffering from nerves.'

She moved across the room to Mrs Toby Robson, the solicitor's wife. 'And how are the girls?' she asked. 'I suppose they'll be getting measles again this spring as usual?'

Mrs Toby's four unattractive little daughters possessed the sole talent of acquiring infectious diseases.

'It's to be chickenpox this year, and mumps next. I asked.' Ursula, the winner of North Country Golf Championships, whom Foster Robson had introduced into the family, replied before Mrs Toby could collect her wandering wits.

'Oh, indeed.' Sarah did not like Ursula.

She sat very straight in her chair, and drew from her velvet reticule a half-knitted sock. Presently she found Mary at her side. 'That's pretty wool. Are those for Tom?'

'Yes. I always make them myself. The things you buy in shops nowadays are useless – shrink up to nothing in the first wash.'

'I know. I knit John's too. I'm just making some for him now.

Look, I've got a new stitch for double heels. They're so nice to wear with heavy boots.'

'John does not like double heels. He has such tender feet. From a boy he blistered easily.' Sarah announced this distinction proudly.

'Oh, he'll like these. They are of the softest wool.'

'Has he worn any yet?'

'Not like this, but he's going to this spring. I got the wool at Dobbin's in Hardrascliffe, four shillings a pound. It's lovely and soft – it couldn't hurt.'

'I think you will find that it will, Mary. I've known John's feet longer than you have and his skin won't stand double heels. We Robsons are delicate in our skins. Of course if you want to save yourself the trouble of darning—'

The colour rose to Mary's face. She looked angrily at Sarah for a moment, then her knitting-needles clashed in the silence. After a little while she left the room.

Sarah watched her smile at one relation and then another on her progress to the door. It was ridiculous, the way she behaved, as though she were a queen holding a court. Well, nobody was likely to bow down to Mary, unless one counted the villagers, who were said to make an absurd fuss of her.

Sarah hoped she had gone to see about tea. Really with Mary you never knew. She might just as easily have gone off to drive old Mrs Simpkins in to the hospital, or to sit up all night with a sick cow. She would think nothing of leaving all her relations in the drawing-room, thirsting for tea. Poor John! Double heeled socks indeed!

The gong boomed through the house.

2

THE TOAST

Sarah felt more comfortable when tea was served and the family established round the table. The meal was correct according to the best Robson tradition. All the food was rich, substantial and self-satisfied. The roast chickens, plump and succulent, were flanked by a dignified ham of Anderby curing. The butter oozed from luscious golden tea-cakes. On the sideboard lay a second course of tarts and cheese-cakes with filmy pastry. Plates of spiced bread, black and sticky, surrounded the huge cake.

Under the influence of warmth and rich food Sarah's irritation disappeared. She allowed Violet to pass her plate for another helping of chicken. Violet's hands were hot and red, but Sarah had come prepared for imperfections, so that was easily ignored. It was harder to overlook John's forgetfulness when he carved for her a slice of breast. Ten years ago he would never have forgotten she preferred brown meat.

Across the table Ursula chatted with Toby Robson. 'But,

my dear man, it's ridiculously easy. I always drive myself. Foster prefers a Humber of course, but I think an American car so much lighter. Mary, don't you like my new two-seater best?'

'I really don't know anything about cars, Ursula. Ask Mr Holmes, he knows far more than I, and I haven't seen your two-seater yet.'

No, thought Sarah, Mary would know nothing about motor-cars and, knowing nothing, would decide that there was nothing to know.

Tilly, Richard's wife, helped herself to a third cheese-cake and wistfully regarded the netted frill of a doily on the plate before her.

'Do you get these doilies up yourself, Mary?' she asked. 'I always find netting goes so badly when you iron it. I do wish you'd tell me what to do.'

'Yes. We do all our own laundry work. I ironed those myself. It's simply a matter of careful starching, and then pulling them away from under the iron.'

Possibly she was right. Mary was a good housekeeper. Sarah impatiently speared a pat of butter and began to spread it on her bread. Was it never possible for half an hour to pass without some one asking her advice? And accepting it when given as though it were as reliable as the Bible? No wonder the girl's head was turned. And really there was nothing so extraordinary about her. Why, she wasn't even good-looking!

Yet, watching her tall figure, broad-shouldered and long-necked, her wide mouth with its faint indication of complacency, and the sudden upward thrust of her chin when she wished to emphasize a statement, Sarah knew well enough wherein lay

Mary's attraction for John. Her finely shaped hands were unusually muscular. Every easy motion of her arms or body suggested that behind it lay a reserve of strength. Her gentleness seemed to be compounded of restricted energy rather than weak emotion. All the qualities which John had admired in Sarah he found softened by youth in Mary.

Sarah looked towards the head of the table where John sat behind the chickens. He was a fool to sit like that quietly carving or looking up occasionally to catch Mary's eye with his shy smile. Why couldn't he get up and say something for himself? Once he got started he had as many wits as any of them. It was only because Mary was convinced he couldn't talk that he never did.

'John,' Sarah asked suddenly, 'why didn't you show that shorthorned bull of yours at York? You know there was nothing to beat it from the North Riding.'

'We are not going to begin showing yet,' interposed Mary, ignoring Uncle Dickie's unfinished anecdote. 'It's too expensive. We're going to start when we get a little capital laid by.'

'I asked John,' commented Sarah, and said no more. But she mentally registered Mary's spasmodic extravagance over the men's feast and her meanness over the show as another grievance against her.

Uncle Dickie resumed his narrative. He was enjoying the society of his hostess. Prompted by her smiling responses he had passed from one story to another, sometimes abandoning one before he reached its climax. But as Mary knew them all by heart that did not matter much and was perhaps more entertaining. He had told the story of the bull-pup at Highwold and the gardener's son, and of the ghost seen by Sir Michael Seton's great grandfather ... or was it great grand-uncle? He was not quite sure ... getting an old man, and Mary must not expect his memory to be as good as once it had been ... well, perhaps great-grandfather of the present Sir Charles ...

Mary accepted each tale serenely, dispensing appropriate answers with the same unflurried precision as she dispensed second cups of tea to their rightful owners.

Ursula leaned forward and picked a cocoa-nut bun from the plate before her. She bit off a little circle with her white teeth and ate it slowly before she turned to Toby Foster.

'Why *does* Uncle Dickie tell all those awful old chestnuts?' she asked.

Toby cocked his head. Being the only professional member of the family he had a reputation for wit, and felt that something good was expected of him.

'Because, my dear lady, I expect he has learnt that in the telling of stories, as in other things, it is more blessed to give than to receive.'

Uncle Dickie was only deaf enough to ask people to repeat phrases whose repetition might embarrass them. The fear that he might miss any of the good things of life haunted him ceaselessly. He stopped suddenly and turned round.

'What's that? What's that? Some one mention me? Hey?'

The family was silent till Mary turned to him smiling. 'Cousin Toby was only saying – though I don't think you were meant to hear – that you were one of those people who have learnt that it is more blessed to give than to receive.'

'Stuff and nonsense!' Uncle Dickie threw out his chest like a cock-sparrow. The room was warm; the meat had been tender; Mary enjoyed his stories. After all, in spite of his eighty-seven years, he was still an entertaining companion. It occurred to him at last that his family's declared affection might arise from appreciation of his good qualities rather than from expected enjoyment of his bank balance.

Under the table-cloth he groped for Mary's hand with his knotted fingers.

Sarah, noticing the gesture, sniffed.

One of the famous Robson silences held the company spellbound. Then John, prompted by a sign from Mary, went to the side-table, and the pop of a cork closed the incident.

'We thought we would have some champagne to-night as this is a rather festive occasion,' said Mary. 'We don't often have an excuse.'

'Splendid! Just the thing!' Toby licked his lips and winked at Ursula, intimating that he and she stood apart, belonging to a world where tea and champagne were only mixed at wedding-breakfasts. A faint smile quivered at the corner of Ursula's mouth.

Sarah felt more convinced than ever that Mary was leading John to ruin.

The glasses were filled and the guests paused. Then Aunt Jane, sitting at John's right hand, became aware with awful certainty that her husband was about to make a speech. She turned to John in fluttering horror.

'Oh, John, your Uncle Dickie's going to make a speech. Do stop him. He always says something dreadful, and it upsets him so that he can't sleep for nights afterwards.'

But to John the effort of initiative, especially concerning his own relatives, was intolerable. He shook his head and said nothing. Uncle Dickie rose slowly to his feet.

'We have come together,' he began without further cere-mony, 'on a most auspicious occasion. Ten years ago our little lass here was married to John.'

'Little lass!' thought Sarah. 'Why, the woman's five feet ten at least.'

'Not but what ten years is a short enough time for a man and his wife to live together without quarrelling. Our Jane and I have stood it for three score. But, when John crossed over the hedge from Littledale and hung up his hat in Anderby as you might say, things weren't exactly plain sailing.'

He paused and ran his fingers up and down the table-cloth awaiting further inspiration. His wife coughed apprehensively.

'There was some matter of a mortgage what had to be paid off. And a bad business it was too.'

'Hear, hear!' commented Donald Holmes. Then realizing that emphasis on this point was undesirable, he relapsed into stifled silence.

'A bad business for those that had less sense than these young folks. But I understand that now the final payment has been made. I'd hoped to see them comfortably settled before I went, for John is a good lad and Anderby a fine farm, and now it seems that nothing is wanting to make us happy but a young Robson to hold it after they're gone. But I've no doubt—'

Jane had suddenly choked and looking up Uncle Dickie caught sight of Sarah's grim perturbation and Mary's crimson-flooded cheeks.

'I've no doubt that we – John – I was saying –auspicious occasion—'

His flow of eloquence was checked, but he remembered his carefully considered peroration and raised his glass.

'I want you to join with me in drinking their health. Ladies and gentlemen, I give you John and Mary Robson of Anderby Wold.'

They drank in awkward silence until Toby, glad of an excuse to cover Uncle Dickie's lapse from tact, broke forth into a lusty carolling of 'For he's a jolly good fellow!' And the company caught up the chorus. Even Anne and Louisa, their cheeks flushed by the unwonted champagne and their emotions slightly beyond control, joined in with their creaky sopranos.

Foster called upon John to reply. He looked helplessly round the table until he met Mary's encouraging smile and then rose slowly to his feet.

'I can't make a speech,' he said, 'any more than the gardener could who was invited to dinner at Edenthorpe Hall because he fished young Master Seton out of the lake. He had to reply to Sir Michael's vote of thanks, and he hummed and hawed till his wife came to the rescue. "Now, Sir Charles," said she, "you mun excuse our John. 'E ain't used to speechifying. Any talking that's done in our 'ouse – *ah* does it"!'

He sat down suddenly, his large form shrinking abashed behind the ham. His confidence deserted him as rapidly as it had arrived.

'Get up, Mary,' Toby called, knocking on the table with his fork. 'Come along! Your man's given you away. You'll have to do it.'

Mary rose.

'I'm not much of a speaker either,' she began, but to Sarah her low clear voice betrayed no self-distrust. 'I can only say thank you all very much for your kindness and you, Uncle

Dickie, for your good wishes. John and I could never have managed if you had not stood behind us and given us confidence. It mayn't seem much to have done, but we are pleased to-night because Anderby is safe. And – and we thank you all for coming and hope you'll often come here again.'

She paused and smiled at her relations round the table. 'She doesn't hope we'll come here again,' Sarah was thinking. 'She doesn't care if she never sees us again. She cares for nothing but her farm and that people should think she's a wonder!'

Mary concluded:

'I don't think I can wish you anything better than the old toast, 'Ere's tiv us, all on us. May we niver wan! nowt, naun on us. Nor you, nor me, nor ony on us – nor me neither!'

The last dog-cart had rumbled down the darkness of the road; the last guest had been escorted to bed with candles and hot whisky, before John and Mary stood alone together in the drawing-room. The fire had burnt low. A heavy scent of tobacco, chrysanthemums and hot whisky hung about the room. The clock on the mantelpiece struck twelve thin, tinkling notes.

Mary knelt on the hearth-rug and swept the fallen ashes beneath the grate. There was a green line round the handle of the hearth-brush where Violet had omitted to rub away the brass polish. For a moment this absorbed Mary's attention. Then she turned to her husband and said:

'Well John, I think that went off all right, don't you?'

'Oh, ay,' responded John without enthusiasm.

'John – I—' She rose, and began to straighten the chintz covers on the sofa. 'I've been wondering – I mean – you know I'm sorry about Uncle Dickie – I mean that he should have to

18

say – all that about a young Robson to carry on here – I mean – I wonder somethimes how much you mind—'

'Oh, that's all right. Don't you worry, honey. It can't be helped.' John turned slowly from her and left the room. In passing the silver table near the door he knocked over a small vase. Always in the drawing-room he seemed to occupy more than his fair allowance of space.

The door closed. Mary went forward and picked up the fallen vase. It was a flimsy fluted thing, a wedding present from Anne and Louisa. Mary held it in her hand while she listened to John's footsteps on the mat, on the tiles of the hall, on the stair carpet. One stair creaked. They must get a new board there, she thought. At a turn of the stair he hit his foot against a brass rail that rang jangling through the house. Then she heard him in the room above, now by the window, now sitting down to throw off his shoes, now by the bed. It creaked and groaned. Then there was silence.

She knelt again by the fire, holding her hands above the glowing ashes.

Well, that was that. It had been a long day, and even her vitality could not stand unlimited exertion. Still, it had been worth it. Mrs Holmes's toupee, Sarah's hastiness about the socks, the hole in the best linen sheet – all these were only echoes and shadows from another world. The only real and solid thing was the knowledge that the mortgage was paid. Nothing else mattered. She was prepared to sing her *Nunc dimittis* for the consummation of her life's work, forgetful that over forty years of her three score and ten still remained in which all sorts of things could happen. This was her hour of triumph in which she tasted that unfearing gladness which gives no hostage to defeat.

The ashes crumbled and collapsed. The room was growing cold. She rose and began to move dreamily about the room, straightening chairs and tables, and flicking cigarette ends from the ashtrays into the fire-place.

Because of the mortgage she had lived for twenty-eight years on the Wolds under the shadow of their reproach. In her lonely childhood the fields of Anderby had assumed for her a more definite personality than any of the people whom she knew. Land was, after all, the thing that mattered most. That was why she had been so miserable when her father brushed aside the foreman's suggestions of improvement with a curt 'We can't afford it. So there's an end on't.' That was why she had laboured for nearly a whole day, trying to stuff up the cracks along the cowshed wall with bits of mud and straw because she was sure the Wolds must despise such shabby buildings.

And then that haunting fear that one day 'They' would suddenly swoop down upon the farm and carry it away as the jinns in the fairy book carried off Solomon's palace ... and the restless uncertainty that seemed to stand between her father and any joy of possession ... All this, he had constantly explained with increasing emphasis as the farm grew more dilapidated, was not his fault, but the result of the mortgage.

Well, there was no need to lie any longer, as eight-year-old Mary had lain, with the bed-clothes drawn up round her ears to shut out the voice of the wind howling along the corridors, because it might be the voice of the mortgage, come at last from the dark sky to carry off 'every stick and stone, lassie, every stick and stone.' Her father had said that this would happen, and he must know.

He must know – must know what? Why, of course, that a

bowl of water placed in the middle of the room prevented it from reeking with stale tobacco for days after a party. She must go and get one.

Mary rubbed a drowsy hand across her eyes. She must have been half asleep, sitting in the big arm-chair while the room grew colder and colder. Wearily she rose and walked towards the door.

Then she stood still.

Out in the hall she heard a faint rustling sound. It could not be a mouse. No one would be walking about now. It must be ever so late. She looked at the clock – half-past two.

A click as though a door shut. The dining-room door. Some one was up. Not John. She would have heard him move. Who then?

She stood hesitating, the handle of the dining-room door in her hand. It was strange to wait again like this, wondering whether one ought to go on into the dining-room because Father was there and the whisky bottle and that was an undesirable combination . . .

Well, it couldn't be that now anyway. She opened the door and walked across the hall.

The dining-room door was ajar. A strip of light wavered against the darkness.

All this had happened before. If she entered the room, Mary was sure that her father would look up from the table and swear softly at her intrusion.

Of course he couldn't. He had died over ten years ago. Mary had seen him die, crying aloud that the mortgage, the mortgage, the mortgage had got him at last, and that she alone was left to fight it.

Her breath came quickly. There was a scraping sound, and somebody sighed heavily. She pushed open the door and went in.

Janet Holmes, in a voluminous quilted dressing-gown, knelt on the floor near the sideboard. Seeing Mary, she rose to her feet with greater alacrity than the Harrogate specialist would have thought possible but unfortunately in her haste she dropped a china biscuit jar that fell against the corner of the fender, breaking in a hundred fragments.

'Oh dear, oh dear! How you startled me!' she gasped.

'Is anything wrong?' asked Mary severely. The jar had been a relic of her mother's lifetime. It was old Spode, and Mary loved dearly the twisting blue flowers on its glazed surface. She regarded it ruefully.

'Oh dear! I'm so sorry. But you did startle me so. It just slipped out of my hand. I hope it was not of any great value, though with these things it's not what they cost, is it? It's the things they belonged to – I mean, you know since we went to the Grange – late dinner – my digestion – the doctor at Harrogate said "Now, Mrs Holmes, always take food one hour before retiring," and I thought perhaps a biscuit—'

'Oh, I see.'

Ten minutes elapsed before Mrs Holmes could be consoled for the omission of late dinner, Mary's inopportune appearance, and the destruction of the biscuit jar. Mary escorted her to her room, and then returned to gather up the fragments.

Fingering the broken pieces reverently, she forgot that the jar had been cracked before and only remembered it as a beautiful thing that had once been hers. The thought of possession was comfortable and satisfying. Mary's mouth curved in a soft little smile. Anderby was hers. The mortgage was paid. That was worth anything; worth unlovely dresses made in the village, worth the constant strain of economy, worth the ten year's intimacy with a man whose presence roused in her alternate irritation and disappointment.

'Nothing is wanting to make us happy except a young Robson.'

Mary brushed together the crumbs from the hearth-rug and straightened her back.

Well, worth that too, perhaps.

She looked round the shadowy room – ghostly dark beyond her feeble candlelight. The smile flickered again across her face.

'May we never want nowt, nawn on us,' she whispered.

3

THE KINGDOM

While Uncle Dickie was proposing his toast in the Robsons' dining-room, another party was in progress up the village in the smoke room of the *Flying Fox*. The *Flying Fox* was a cosy little inn, not frequented by strangers like the *Eden Arms*. The men who now sat there, smoking and talking, were old habitués.

On the highbacked settle near the fire-place sprawled Ezra Dawson, the Robsons' shepherd, a great soldierly figure in corduroys. A drooping eyelid marred his handsome face, half obscuring his twinkling left eye in a perpetual wink. He was holding forth to a young farmer who stood sheepishly near the table.

'Noo, lad, tha may be a clever fellow.' The men on the far bench snorted incredulously. 'Ah'm not saying tha is, but taking it for a parable like. Tha may be a clever fellow, but if tha marries a fool she'll ruin tha. And if tha's a fool and weds a clever lass wi' a good hand for pastry, who feeds lads well and keeps in wi' gentry and dealers, tha's fair fettled up and mebbe'll find tha self a rich man some day.'

'Then mun I marry a clever woman?' asked the boy.

'Noo, lad, ah wouldn't go so far as to say that. If tha' marries a good for nowt, 'un she'll ruin tha, but if tha weds a clever lass folks'll give her all credit and call thee a fool.'

Bert frowned anxiously.

'Then what am I to wed?'

'Stay single, Bert,' advised another voice from the doorway. It came from a short, red-bearded man who had not yet spoken. 'Stay single an' tha'll never have cause to rue.'

'But if ah'm single ah'll have to get a housekeeper. Our Liza says she can't stay with me much longer.' Bert was genuinely anxious to profit by their counsel.

'Noo then, Shep,' laughed another, 'who'd you say he ought to get as housekeeper, a clever lass or a fool?'

Dawson turned slowly.

'Nay lad, did'st ever hear tell of a clever housekeeper?'

Bert scratched his head but failed to recall such a phenomenon.

'You see,' explained the shepherd gleefully, 'all clever housekeepers marries their masters. Y'can't get round women. They scores all ways.'

'Ah'm not denying they scores,' said the red-bearded woman-hater. 'What I asks is – why do we let 'em? Because we're fond fools! That's why. Take any man you like an' any woman you like and set 'em to do t' same job, and ye'll find t' woman fair beat before they've been at it ten minutes. Talk about women's reets – if they had their reets they'd all be shut up in their houses wi' their bairns!'

'Missus been a bit pawky to-day, Eli?' inquired Dawson with a quizzical glance at the fiery orator.

The company nodded in sympathy. They knew the humour of a wife's tongue when the wind was easterly and the Christmas rent due, and another addition to the family expected. Eli Waite's domestic troubles had been a welcome topic at many similar gatherings, so, though he was unpopular and suspected as an extremist, to-night his audience was inclined to be gracious. But Eli disappointed those who hoped to hear further details of the Waite household. He changed the conversation.

'There's rare goings on up at t'Robsons tonight they say.'

'Ay,' replied Dawson, taking another drink. 'T' family stayed on to tea, and health drinking and the like. Violet let me see table when I was up salting bacon this after' an' giv'd me a bit o' t' cake.'

'And a drop o' whisky ah'll be bound,' laughed old Deane. 'Noo then, Shep, tell t' truth and shame t' devil.'

'Ay. Mebbe a drop o' whisky. Allus keep in wi't women ah says.'

'Ugh,' growled Eli. 'Ye talk o' women, Dawson, but ye'd any of you sell your souls for a bit o' dinner up at Mrs Robson's. She knows how t' manage you all – coals an' Christmas pudding – an' then there'll be no grumblin' about wages at Martinmas.'

'Tha eats dinner there tha'sen fast enough, Eli, when tha's chance.'

'Ay. Chance is a bonny thing.'

Eli turned upon the Shepherd. 'Chance is a bonny thing wi' you, Shep, and Mary Robson – going following her aboot like a gawking lad, as if tha' hadn'twenches enoughwi'out your master's woman.'

'What's that?' Dawson's one eye suddenly opened.

'Ah only said tha' hadn't much self-respect, sucking up t' gentry,' said Eli, retreating hastily.

'Ay. Tha'd better only say yon. Ah thowt mebbe it was a matter o' summat else.'

'So did I, indade,' broke in a sharp Irish voice from an obscure corner. A little, black haired man came forward and placed his glass on the table. 'If you have anything to say about Mrs Robson at all, you'll just have the goodness to step outside the door and repate it to me, slow and careful.'

'Ah've no call to answer for my words to a drunken Irish harvester who stays beyond his times.'

'Noo then, Mike,' interposed Dawson. 'Doant take on. Eli didn't mean nowt. 'E's been like a bear wi' a sore head ever since his missus hasn't been well like. Anderby air don't suit him like that out at Market Burton, does it, Eli?'

'I'll thank you to mind your own business, Misther Dawson!' began Mike O'Flynn.

But Dawson rose slowly and laid one hand on the little man's shoulder.

'It's my business as much as your'n, lad, that no one here speaks words like them there o' Waite's, what I wouldn't care for Mrs Robson to hear. Ah've known her since she was a little lass, an' used to ride her pony up to Sheepfold as pretty as a circus girl. Eli's a stranger like, an' don't know what we of Anderby does.'

'Then it's me who'll tell him quick enough bedad, if he clacks his foul tongue again.'

'Doant be a fool, Mike.' Dawson's deep voice rose from a cloud of blue smoke. 'Waite won't say no more. Ye see, it's like this here, Eli. Mike was sick two years ago last harvest up at

Littledale, and Mrs Robson went up at night an' sat poulticing him an' the like for long enough.'

''Twas pneumonia I had,' broke in Mike, unwilling to surrender to another the pleasure of telling this story. 'Like to die I was, and seeing the gowlden gates half opened an' she came to me like an angel from heaven.

'"Is it the praste you'll be wanting?" says she. "Now what should I want with a praste when 'tis the angels themselves have come to look after me"? says I. But she only smiled and sent for Father Murphy from Hardrascliffe, and for three days an' nights she hardly left me side an' me with a pain like hot iron across me chest, an' me voice like the creaking o' the pump when 'tis oiling it needs.'

'Ay. That's all very well for Robsons, but all folks ain't like that, nor all farmers either. Mrs Robson 'ud give away her last coat if need be; but ah've just come from a talk wi' Ted Wilson – him as is gardener for Willerby's up at Highwold.'

The speaker was a lean, melancholy man who had been fidgeting by himself with a draughtboard in the corner.

'They're new folks, ain't they?'

'Ay. Wust turn old Granger ever did to Anderby was dying like that an' letting Willerby take his farm.'

'I thowt Willerby was a decent, quiet sort o' chap. 'E doant say much, but 'e could do worse nor that.'

'Nay, but yon's not trouble.'

Dawson took a pull at his pipe and hazarded grimly:

'It's a woman ah'll be bound.'

'Ay. I said to Wilson, "'Ow'd ye come on wi' missus these days?" Ah says. And he gives me one o' them there slow, considerable looks like, an' says, "She doant like rattens getting in among 'er chickens." 'E does fowls up at Willerby's does Wilson. "Well," ah says, "nor does other folks, but it's all fortunes o' war." "It's. fortunes o' war when it's other people's chickens," says 'e. "But it's danged carelessness o' some one else's when they're your own. Missus is a bad loser," 'e says. "Why, she bain't mean, is she, Ted?" ah says. "*Mean?*" 'e says. You know that way 'e has o' waiting to let you get one word well chewed before 'e gives you 'tother. "Oh no. She's not mean. She'd only steal t' shroud off her mother's corpse, an' then take on because it wouldn't wash!"'

'Ay,' murmured Dawson sagely. 'There's nowt so queer as folks.'

'Except women, Shep,' jeered Waite.

'Then what wages will they be giving up at Willerby's?' asked Bert Armstrong, feeling that as the only farmer present he ought to show a decent interest in the affairs of his new neighbours.

'Same as anyone else's. Same as Robson's. But when you get no bits o' beef, nor packets o' tea, nor nursing if you're sick, you can soon tell t' difference. Ah can tell you, Wilson says 'e won't stay after Martinmas unless things tak' up a bit.'

'There you are,' pronounced Shepherd triumphantly, removing his pipe from his mouth to give greater effect to his words. ''Tis t' woman again. Get a bad'un and a good farmer's nowt. Get a good 'un and t' farmer don't count.'

'If you think so much o' them, Shep, why have you never married yourself?'

'Ah've never yet found a lass wi' a bit o' brass who'd have me. If ever ah does find one wi' same mind as myself, ah'll away get wed.'

'Tha mun have her rich then?'

'Oh ay.' Dawson knocked the ashes from his pipe and prepared to depart.

'But if she turns out a bad 'un?' pursued Bert, in quest of information.

'Well then, she'll still have 'er brass, and a fat sorrow's better t' bear than a lean sorrow.'

The company stirred and smiled. Old Deane in the corner shook his head.

'Ay. But you don't find 'em like Mary Robson growing on every hedge bottom,' he said.

Outside, the wind tore at the stacks and hedges in a shrieking hurricane. It snatched at Mike's hat, and whipped the sleet across his face. He had left early, for work, interrupted that day, began next morning at six, and the long nights were short enough after back-aching days in the sheepfold.

As he passed the railings of Mary's garden he heard through a lull in the storm the clop, clop of hoofs on the road before him, and Sarah Bannister drove past in a flurry of black shadows and yellow carriage lights. Upstairs in the Wold Farm, a single light burned and Mike, thinking it to shine from Mary's room, sighed sentimentally and murmured a paternoster for her soul's salvation. Neither his experiences as a soldier in India and Africa nor the indifference of his fellow workers on the farm had robbed him of a simplicity which somehow confounded the Mary of Anderby with the Lady of Sorrows.

Unfortunately for his pious intention the light before his shrine was only a candle carried by Violet into the spare bedroom where Foster and Ursula had decided to spend the night rather than face the violence of the storm.

4

THE QUEEN

Next morning Mike's devotion met with its reward, for as he rode along the village street, swinging his legs from the shaft of a turnip cart, he saw Mary emerge from her garden and turn towards him along the road.

Mike was whistling a tune as he rode, for after the storm the morning air was radiantly clear. In its cold clarity the sweeping curves of the Wolds, the filigree tracery of black branches against the sky, and the sturdy outline of the Norman church on the hill were as boldly defined as in an etching. From every blackened twig on the hedgerows trembled a lucid drop of moisture. There was a salt sting in the wind from the sea six miles away.

Mary seemed part of the freshness and gaiety of the morn-ing. Mike watched her as she strode forward along the path, loving her buoyant, confidant movements and the sheen of her brown hair, like wet beech leaves below her small fur-trimmed cap.

She smiled at Mike. Her smile caught the sunlight and dazzled him.

'Well, and how does Becky go?'

Becky was the old mare who drew the turnip cart. Mary condescended to share with Mike the delicious intimacy of a secret that, left to herself, Becky would go as far as the *Flying Fox*, but there would stop, trained by Mike's predecessor to unbreakable habit. Such jokes gain point by frequent repetition.

'She goes well enough till she has to stop for her "usual,"' laughed Mike. 'Oh, Mrs Robson, we're wishing it was married you were every day after the foine dinner we had yesterday.'

'I'm very glad I'm not, Michael. You've no idea what a lot of work it makes, or how much washing up there is afterwards. And people about the house to get cleared away – and – oh, lots of things.'

'Indade, it's lucky they are to have the chance of staying.'

'It's not lucky for me. Here am I only just going up to decorate the Christmas Tree and late as it is because of everything. Still, there's fifteen years before our silver wedding . . . '

She smiled a gracious dismissal and passed on.

It was good to be alive, she thought, and good to be queen of so fair a kingdom, and to have worshipping subjects like Mike O'Flynn who paid her homage in the street. In no place sooner than in a village does philanthropy bring its own reward and Mary, pleased because her subjects' gratitude was swift, forgot it might be also transitory.

Everything had gone very well. Perhaps she had been a little too prompt in speeding her parting guests. Uncle Dickie had looked almost hurt when she bustled him into his carriage. But then such a busy person as Mary would never have time for anything if she always stopped to consider other people's feelings. There were so many really important things to be done. The Christmas Tree was important. She had superintended its decoration ever since she was fifteen. There was literally no one else who could do it properly.

Then it was a singularly pleasant thing to do. All the way up the Church Hill Mary was repicturing former trees and former decorations. She always felt a little awed by the tall, tapering tree, standing darkly green against the whitewashed walls of the schoolroom. Still untouched by frivolous hands its regal austerity retained something of the frosty stillness of pinewoods on a starlit night. For a moment – this silent dignity; then with the arrival of noisy helpers the scene became one of riotous carnival. For they carried boxes of coloured balls, bales of scarlet and yellow bunting, baskets laden with glittering tinsel, trumpets painted silver and vermilion, dolls in vivid muslin dresses, stars and medallions, tops and skipping ropes, and tumbled them in festive profusion over baskets and chairs. They tied the oranges on first and the tree was rich with the gold of alien fruit, then the stars and balls and spangled disks, and finally the gaily tinted candles in fragile metal stands, till the tree stood in many-coloured splendour ripe for its fantastic harvest.

She entered the school.

The room was in a state of chaos. All the desks lay piled at one end, so that the door would hardly open. At the other a group of women surrounded the tree.

The door squeaked as Mary pushed it open. Mrs Coast, the schoolmaster's wife, set down a basket of coloured balls and came forward to greet her. She was always a little more afraid of life than usual in Mrs Robson's presence, half admiring her, half abashed. Mr Coast did not like Mary, and where Mr Coast disliked Mrs Coast must not admire.

'Well, this is good of you, Mrs Robson,' she said quite sincerely. Mary generally managed to impress other people with the immensity of her goodness. 'We were just saying "Now I wonder if she'll come, being so busy with everything."'

Miss Taylor, the assistant schoolmistress moved rapidly out of Mary's way, accidentally stepping on two china ornaments in her transit. Her plump arms were almost bursting from her flannel blouse in their exuberant eagerness for work. She beamed upon Mary.

'Yes, I'm sure,' she broke in. 'Little Hal Stephens met me this morning with his mouth full of mince-pie and said "Have you been to Robsons', Miss Taylor?" and I said, "No Hal." So he said "Then you'd better go. Mrs Robson's been getting married again and there's lots of good things to eat. But you know I still saw the old Mr Robson about. What's going to happen to him now there's a new one?"'

Every one smiled, recognizing that Miss Taylor, for very love of living, had to say something however silly on every occasion. Only the young ladies from the Glebe Farm were not quite sure that this was a proper subject for a joke.

'Oh yes,' said Mary, drawing off her gloves and beginning to string thread through the oranges. 'Hal came up with a note from his mother, and we had so much stuff left over from yesterday I just gave him some mince-pies. He's a good little chap and ever so useful his mother says.'

'His brother works for you, doesn't he?' Mrs Coast made a desperate effort to entertain her distinguished helper. If only Mr Coast was not always remembering that time when Mrs Robson persuaded her husband not to sign a testimonial of recommendation. Even if he was applying for a new post then, and Mrs Robson had spoilt his chances, she was a very nice woman.

Mary replied serenely.

'Yes, he's third lad and John says he is going to be a very smart boy. We might put some of these oranges on now, don't you think? Lily, would you mind getting the steps? Your legs are younger than mine, my dear.' Mary was mounted on the steps, an orange hanging from each hand, the boughs of the tree swaying round her in a curtain of feathery green, when the vicar entered the room.

'Good afternoon, Mr Slater,' she called. 'Have you come to help us?'

'Good afternoon, Mrs Robson – Coast – afternoon, Miss Taylor. Well, Lily, Gerty, how are you, ha? How are you? Most kind of you to come, Mrs Robson – so busy – most kind. Cold weather for the time of the year. Yes, very, ha?'

The vicar came forward firing off little staccato sentences as he threaded his way cautiously between the boxes, baskets and kneeling girls who strewed the floor. Miss Taylor held out her hand towards him, then realizing that she was alone in her action withdrew it and giggled, the blushes chasing one another in rosy waves across her face. She had been a farmer's daughter before she became a teacher, and now her appearance was reminiscent of churns and milk-pails rather than desks and blotting paper.

Mary bent down from the steps.

'Would you mind handing me some of the stars now? Yes. Well, if you don't mind, Mr Slater, I should be grateful. There! The red ones look pretty on the green, don't they?'

She came down and withdrew a few paces into the room to inspect her work. As she stood, with her head a little on one side and her hands full of scarlet thread and tinsel, Lily and Gerty from the Glebe Farm eagerly studied her brown coat and round cap with its soft fur hoping to gain a hint for their next fashionable experiments.

Mary made her judgment critically.

'I like that so far,' she said, moving forward. 'But I think there are just a few things too many on the left. Supposing we finish the actual decorations first and then see what room we have for the toys. And then—'

She broke off as a door on her right opened and the school-master entered the room.

He was a harmless looking man of thirty-nine or forty, with a straggling brown moustache and stooping shoulders, but his pince-nez hid restless, hostile eyes and his thin nostrils dilated whenever he became annoyed, which was almost always, because the world seemed a contrary place for those born without a talent for success.

Directly he came in, the atmosphere of bustling cheerfulness deserted the room.

Mary turned to him with strained affability.

'Well, Mr Coast, don't you think we're doing rather well?'

She knew he disliked her. She knew he remembered that day three years ago, when she had seen him strike Ronnie Peel in a fit of exasperation and had turned upon him with an outburst of righteous indignation. And then the testimonial. He had been told about that of course by one of those kind friends who prove their loyalty by revealing other people's nastiness.

But she was acutely troubled because somebody disliked her. Even if she was not exactly fond of Coast, that was no reason why Coast should not like her.

'I bought these blue balls in Hardrascliffe,' she said, holding out a box. 'Don't you think they're rather pretty, Mr Coast? We broke such a lot last year, and this is a nice big tree.'

'Very kind I'm sure, Mrs Robson, but we had already bought some new ornaments with the Christmas Tree Fund.'

'Oh I know, but there's no harm in having a few left over. Is there, Mr Slater?' When Mary felt opposition from one quarter, she always tried to strengthen her position by approval from another.

'Well, really they are very pretty – very nice – yes – quite. Ha, Mr Coast, ha?'

'It was very nice I'm sure, Ernie,' interposed Mrs Coast tremulously. 'They'll do beautifully. I'm sure I was wondering how we were going to get all those top branches covered. I do hate a tree to look bare.'

'Yes, it's shocking, isn't it?' sniggered Miss Taylor, then sank into a depressed silence.

Mary tried again.

'Are you having a good concert this year, Mr Coast?'

'About the same as usual, Mrs Robson.'

The schoolmaster frowned with disapproval upon the trumpets tied to the lower branches of the tree.

Again there was silence.

Miss Taylor felt that something must be done about it.

'Lucy Morrison is doing a lovely skirt dance,' she ventured. 'And the sixth standard sketch is fine. It is called "The Bells of Christmas," and the girls wear fancy costume.'

'That will be nice. Did you make the dresses, Mrs Coast? I know how clever you are at that sort of thing.'

The schoolmaster's wife lifted a timid head and hastily denied the presumption of ever having been clever at anything. But she had helped with the costumes certainly, though Ernie had told her what to do.

'Mrs Robson' – the schoolmaster passed his tongue over dry lips – 'there's a little matter I should like to talk to you about, if you could spare the time.'

'Certainly, Mr Coast. What is it?'

Mary was at the top of the steps now, fixing the Christmas fairy to the highest spire of the tree.

'I should prefer to speak to you in private, if I might trespass for a few minutes on your valuable time.'

Mary shrugged her shoulders with resignation.

'Are you in any hurry?' she asked airily.

Not for worlds would she have confessed that the prospect of an interview alone with Coast scared her, that the possibility of his rudeness was dreadful to her.

'Oh, no. Any time that suits you will do for me, Mrs Robson.'

'Will it do when we've finished the tree?'

'Of course, Mrs Robson. Naturally it would be impossible to finish the decorations without your kind advice.'

'Hand me up another trumpet then, Miss Taylor, will you please?'

Mary continued to decorate the tree, whistling a little tune below her breath. All the time she was conscious of the schoolmaster's brooding eyes, watching her from below.

They finished the tree.

Mary was putting on her fur and gloves when Coast again approached her.

'Ah, Mrs Robson, you are ready I see. Perhaps if you would step into my house we could settle that little affair more comfortably.'

Comfortably! As if it were possible to settle any little affair with Coast 'comfortably'! And certainly his house would not add to the comfort of the settling.

Mary, following Coast across the asphalt playground, wondered for the hundredth time at the weird phantasy of the too enterprising Victorian architect, who, fired by the inspiration of the Albert Memorial, had become a devotee of Gothic ornateness. She regarded its painted gables, twisted chimneys and sunless windows gloomily and decided that she was in for an unpleasant half-hour.

Mr Coast's sitting-room was as unfriendly as his manner. Even the cuckoo clock, swinging its one wooden leg, and crouching against the wall like a hobgoblin, proclaimed twelve o'clock with a forbidding voice. Mary sat down and prepared for the worst.

The room was no kinder to Coast than it was to Mary. He shifted his weight from one foot to the order and sought for inspiration.

He was acutely miserable. Mrs Robson, quietly sitting with folded hands inspecting the woolwork mats, the wax flowers under their glass cover, and the 'Everlastings' in the mantelpiece vase, seemed completely mistress of the situation.

Coast hated his room. Everything seemed to have been there a long time, but nothing was at rest. He knew it was all in execrable taste. Mrs Robson would think he didn't know any

39

better than that. She would not guess that the furniture was bequeathed by Coast's predecessor, and he, with his mind fixed upon rapid promotion, had not thought it worth while to alter things.

He sought for an appropriate beginning and found none. During the previous days he had rehearsed this interview, casting himself for the triumphant role of vanquisher of the tyrant and picturing lovingly Mrs Robson's final confusion. Now he could think of nothing to say.

'Well?' Mary from her chair raised calm, indifferent eyes to her host, where he stood by the mantelpiece frowning and biting his moustache. 'I thought you had something to tell me.'

Coast passed a trembling hand across his mouth.

'Mr Robson probably told you of my proposal about the paddock.'

If only he could find something safe to look at, he was sure he would be all right. His eyes travelled along the mantelpiece and the chiffonier to the bookcase. There in a row below faded novels and school readers were his books.

'My husband did say something to me, but I forgot.'

'He probably told you that the County Council had made a very handsome offer for its purchase.'

'They made the offer to me. The field is mine.'

Mrs Robson was looking at the books too now. Her glance had followed his. She saw a fat grey volume called *Capital* by Karl Marx and a paper backed volume called *Essays on Socialism* by Bentley Box, and a flaming orange cover, with scarlet letters announcing *The Salvation of Society* by some one whose name was too small to be legible.

'I understand,' said Coast, 'that you have refused to sell.'

'My husband wants the field for sheep washing. It's the only paddock we have with running water. I believe you want the County Council to buy it to make a field for the children to play in. I don't think it would be at all suitable.'

Even as she spoke she repictured the paddock, fenced high with hawthorn, and the stream that in summer dried to a thin thread. There John had found her one summer evening shortly after her father's death and had asked her to marry him. Well, her acceptance had been a matter of convenience rather than passion, and no courtship could have been more decorous. But in the shadowy sweetness of that evening she had dreamed of a romance she did not know, and the field was fragrant with memory. Even now she could feel the damp air on her face and smell the delicate scent of hawthorn and wet earth, and hear the tearing sound of cows feeding in the long grass.

'It is very suitable, Mrs Robson. It opens straight on the playground, right under the supervision of the school house and it's a nice level ground.'

'I dare say. But you would find the stream a great inconvenience.'

'Not at all, it could be fenced off.'

'Why, it nearly cuts the field in half.'

'Not quite, I think, if you observe it closely. I see you hardly know the field,' he added with patronizing gentleness. 'Perhaps if you came down and looked—'

'My good man!' cried Mary, losing patience. 'If you think I don't know my own land!'

She broke off with a short laugh.

'Not at all, Mrs Robson, not at all. I was merely suggesting that you might reconsider the possibility of selling. The County

Council have offered to buy this field in connection with the school. They rarely enough make generous suggestions of this kind. The field is admirably situated and I am sure we could meet you about the price.'

'It is nothing to do with the price.' Mary spoke quietly, a little ashamed of her last outburst. 'They offered very rightly to buy the land at its market value. We suggested that they might rent it from us, but my husband and I do not wish to sell.'

Coast turned away from her, but in the looking-glass above the mantelpiece he could see her smiling, determined mouth, and the complacent repose of her clasped hands.

'They don't want to rent it,' he said, wrestling with his increasing irritation, 'they want to buy the land and make their own improvements. Walls, and levelling and so on.'

'Then why don't they try for the field in the village that young Armstrong rents from the Setons of Edenthorpe?'

'It's too big and not so handy. And being in the village they'd ask more for it. It might come in for building cottages. Your field is obviously the one, Mrs Robson. You must see that you are doing a great injustice to the village if you won't sell.'

'There is no question of injustice,' said Mary, rising and straightening her fur. 'I shall always be willing to lend it for the children's games, when we are not needing it for the sheep or young horses. But I will not sell.'

'Yes, Mrs Robson.' Coast's voice trembled with anger. 'I know that you are always willing to lend your land or your presence or your pony-cart. It costs you nothing and you get a good deal of credit for it from a certain class of people. But when you are asked to part with something that means a small sacrifice, but which will be of great service to the village, then it's a different matter altogether, isn't it?'

'I think you forget yourself, Mr Coast. You will not find that your incivility makes me any more ready to sell. I don't think it is any use staying and arguing with you any longer, especially as you can't control your temper.'

She swept out of the room.

As she crossed the passage, she caught sight of Mrs Coast's frightened face, hovering like a ghost near the kitchen door. But she ignored its mute appeal and closed the front door behind her with exaggerated care.

Outside she walked with hurried steps along the path by the churchyard. Outraged virtue is a comfortable feeling. Coast had no right to speak to her like that. As if she wasn't ready to do anything for Anderby! Why, now that the Wold Farm was safe she had no stronger interest left in life than her care for the village. He could not help knowing how much she cared. It was common talk how she sat up all night when old Mrs Watts had bronchitis, and how she drove every sick child in to hospital . . .

It was dinner-time now. She would be late and that was the schoolmaster's fault. She almost wished she had let John sign that testimonial and so get rid of the man. There would have been room in Leeds for him to lose himself. You could never get away from anyone in Anderby.

All the way down the path she assured herself that Coast was an awful man and that she was suffering from her difficult act of justice three years ago.

As she turned into the village street she began to feel uncomfortable. Was it, after all, so very important that she should keep the field? She who always laughed at sentiment,

43

what did she hope to gain by it? A secret garden of romance? Or rather a convenient paddock where there were good mushrooms and running water? If ever she had loved John, it would have been different. She would have had a right to be sentimental. Still – she liked to pretend that once she had welcomed her lover like other women. The dream was so elusive that, without the field, it might vanish altogether.

And, anyway, Coast has no right to speak to her like that.

She wrapped herself in satisfaction, as in a soft, warm cloak.

The garden gate closed behind her with a clang.

She would not sell.

5

THE TREES OF THE VALLEY

It was a dreary winter. All day in the garden shrubbery Mary could hear the drop, drop of water from the trees. Christmas came and went in a sorrowful vapour of drifting rain.

Mary hated it all. She hated the long drives in to market down a fog muffled road. She hated the cold clammy feeling of curtains and sheets in the farm-house. She hated the loosened tile that allowed a slow yellow stain to creep across the ceiling of the best bedroom. Besides, she had a persistent cold in her head. It was all very trying.

She lay awake in bed in the chill half-light, awaiting for the church clock to strike seven. The curtains, drawn almost to the centre of the window, flapped and swayed, while the strip of luminous grey that must be the sky outside contracted and expanded with their wanton motion.

Below the bedclothes at her side she could see John's humped outline. That fringe of soft darkness against the pillow was his beard. The sheet rose and fell with his even breathing.

The heaviness of his sleep annoyed Mary intensely. She might toss and turn and ruckle up the bedclothes as she would, on sleepless nights when the harvest was bad, or there was a case of anthrax at Littledale, but the only sign of responsibility John ever gave was an occasional snore.

After all, it was her farm. Why should he worry?

Last night she had slept badly, dreaming that John hit her because she would not put a new cake of soap on his wash-stand. Just now she wished her dream were true. Life with John would be so much more tolerable if he would only just some-times assert his personality. Strike her? Why, he'd go for days without soap rather than make the effort of asking her for it, and as for helping himself – why, he'd sooner get drunk at the *Flying Fox* though the soap box was only in the wardrobe by their bed.

She clasped her hands round her bent knees and looked down at him. The Robson relatives said she bullied him. They did not realize that John's total inability ever to disagree with anyone about anything transformed even an attitude of con-sideration to one of tyranny. If Mary always knew exactly what men she wanted to keep after Martinmas, and what date she wanted the pig to be killed, must she refrain from expressing her desires because John's agreement was assured? What was one to do with a man who said, 'Well, honey, you know best,' whenever one asked his opinion on any subject from chicken food to Fire Insurance?

The mountain of clothes beside her stirred and heaved. John raised his head from the pillow, then sighed himself to sleep again.

Mary could just see his profile now in the dim light. Really, he was quite good-looking. People always called him 'a good-looking man.' And he was very patient and kind and unselfish – and had all the irritating negative virtues of the oppressed.

Oh, but one wanted some one young and swift and romantic! Some one who would laugh and quarrel and argue and make friends again. Some one who might occasionally utter an unanticipated remark.

The door opened and Violet came in with a can of hot water.

'Good morning, Violet; what's the time?'

'Quarter to seven, m'm. Shall I light the candle, and do you want the wall oven on this morning?'

'Yes, please. I'm going to bake for the Wesleyan tea.'

John was waking up. He rolled over drowsily and stuck his head above the clothes, blinking at Mary with blue sleepy eyes.

His customary formula greeted her:

'What's the time, honey?'

Mary believed he had made the same inquiry every morning of their married life ... Ten years and five weeks ... Three hundred and sixty-five days in a year ...

'Quarter to seven and a cold morning.'

'Oh. All right, is it time we were stirring?'

'I think so. Violet has brought the water.'

That was what they always said – the same things every morning. And there were so many remarks he might make. He might, for instance, tell her she looked rather nice, sitting there with her two heavy plaits falling across her shoulders, and the strong cream column of her throat rising above the frills of her flannel nightgown. It was a pretty throat, not reddened by exposure like Ursula's; because Mary nearly always wore high collars.

47

He might tell her she was pretty. That would give colour and excitement to the whole day. Perhaps if she said something pleasant to him he might be induced to return the compliment.

She watched him rear himself slowly from the bed, his great shoulders straining at the pyjama jacket. Clumsily his bare feet groped for his slippers on the floor.

'Eh, John, you great thing!' She laughed up at him softly. 'What a giant you are! No wonder they call you "Big John of Littledale"!'

He had found his slippers, and gathered round his body the dressing-gown from the foot of the bed. Without comment he turned and slouched across the room.

Mary felt as though he had slammed the door in her face. 'Fool!' she cried to herself. 'Fool! Wasn't I asking for it?'

Two hours later she stood in the red tiled kitchen busy with her flour dredgers and baking boards and great jars of sugar and currants. She liked the warm buttery smell of baking and the mastery of familiar instruments and quick confident movements over tins and oven and wooden spoons. She enjoyed the blast of warm air that struck her cheeks when she opened the oven door, and the greetings of men who passed the kitchen window on their way from one stackyard to another.

When Violet came from the 'front way' to make an eleven o'clock cup of tea, Mary was in a thoroughly good humour, her early-morning depression forgotten.

'I don't think,' she said, rubbing the flour off her hands, 'that you ever told me if you found your aunt better, when you went to see her in Hardrascliffe on Saturday.'

'I didn't go. Please, m'm, are you ready for me to mash the tea?'

'Yes please – the brown pot. Why didn't you go?'

'I went to the pictures with Percy Deane.'

'With Percy Deane? Why, what's happened to Fred Stephens?'

Violet flung the tea into the cups with more generosity than discretion. Mary's table suffered a little during the process.

'Oh. I'm off with Fred. Will you have a bit of cheese-cake, m'm?'

'Violet, why are you off with Fred? He's an awfully nice boy. I can't say I ever did think much of Percy. He drinks too much and he's not a steady worker. I'm sure he's not the man for you. Now Fred—'

'Oh, I'm sick of Fred. He's so rough in his talk.'

Mary leaned back against the table and sipped her tea, conscious that, in spite of her easy patronage, she was bitterly jealous of Violet, of her youth and unconscious egoism. She was jealous of the suitors who rang their bicycle bells in the road on Saturday evenings as they waited, posy in cap, to ride with Violet to Hardrascliffe.

'What do you mean by that?' she asked.

'Oh, you know. When we go to the pictures and there isn't much room, Fred just says "Shuve up, lass," right loud so as every one can hear we're common folk like; while Perce, he always says polite "Will you be so kind as to pass a little further up the seat, please?" I have myself to think of.'

Violet tossed an independent head.

'But that's so silly,' said Mary with common sense, 'if you really like Fred best. He's devoted to you. You used to tell me you liked him last autumn.'

'Well, I've learnt a thing or two since then. Anyway, I'd

much rather walk out with a tailor's assistant than a common labourer.'

'But it matters so much more whether you love him. It does really. It's not a bit of use marrying some one just because it seems a sensible thing to do.' Mary's earnestness was quite remarkable.

'Oh – love!' sneered Violet.

And there was an end of it.

But all the time she was changing her clothes and driving into Market Burton with her husband, Mary was haunted by Violet's final exclamation. Possibly she was wrong. Her obstinacy about the water-paddock in the village, her advice to Violet, her wistfulness in the morning, were all part of a sentimental legend, invented by people to hide the emptiness of their lives. 'Oh – love!'

Well, anyway, there was the farm and the village, and plenty of useful and important things to do. Really at her age, it was time she stopped being so stupid. John was a good husband, and at least he never said 'Shuve up, lass!' There were compensations even in marrying an older cousin.

Her destination that afternoon was the drawing-room of Petunia Villa, whither Uncle Dickie and Aunt Jane had retired after their farming days were over. Anne and Louisa lived with them, and on Wednesday afternoons, while the men attended the Cattle Market, all the ladies of the family congregated there among the woolwork and antimacassars.

Mary had brought her sewing and sat a little apart, listening to her sisters-in-law run through their conversational repertoire – servants, ailments, the Medical Mission's sale of work. Among her husband's relatives she had gained an unmerited reputation for silence. But she was aware that every remark she made in Market Burton was repeated and criticized from house to house, and passed on continually, with the brief prelude, 'Mary Robson says so and so,' and the probable qualification, 'Isn't she *queer?*'

Janet Holmes was concluding a long narrative.

' . . . And so I said, "Mr Jefferson, I've bought silk from your establishment for five and thirty years; but, after this, never again!" And I walked out of the shop.'

There followed a murmur of approbation from the sisters-in-law. Then the conversation, having for so long dwindled into a monologue, ceased entirely, while a new topic was sought. Mary, who had formed a habit of trying to give people what they wanted, provided one for them.

'Did you know that Toby had bought a new car?' she asked.

They fell upon it with avidity.

'He'd better by half have kept the money to pay his doctor's bills. Molly tells me they weren't paid for last time, and now, with the new one coming, I'm sure I don't know how he'll manage.' Sarah Bannister poked her knitting-needles sharply into the sock.

'Really? Another? Really? I didn't know,' murmured Anne.

'You never do,' Louisa commented severely. 'Will he drive it himself, Mary?'

For a moment Mary wondered whether the inquiry related to the prospective infant or the car; but Sarah answered for her.

'He'll drive it himself for a couple o' months, and then he'll have a nasty accident one of these fine days and smash the whole concern, and start a new craze. That's what he'll do.'

'I thought carpentering was the last fad?' Louisa transferred a pin from her mouth to the hem of the shirt she was stitching.

'He tried carpentering until their maid fell over his new-fangled draught screen at the head of the stairs and broke her leg. Then he really had to stop turning his drawing-room into a joiner's shop. Louisa, hand me that other ball of wool, please.' Mrs Bannister made a practice of exacting occasional small services from her sisters, to impress upon them her seniority.

'If we don't take care,' remarked Louisa, 'we shall find the Tobys will be another lot of poor relations.' Being dependent herself, she naturally objected to anyone else occupying a similar position.

'There's one thing I will say for Toby' – Sarah so rarely said things in favour of her relatives that the company looked up attentively – 'I don't think he ever would be a poor relation.'

'I'm sure he'll ruin himself one day,' sighed Aunt Jane.

'Being a poor relation has nothing to do with how much money you've got. It's just a state of mind.'

'What an idea, Sarah! You do say some th'ngs! I'm sure it all comes of his being a solicitor. My husband always said lawyers were no good.' Janet Holmes shook a melancholy head.

'Solicitor? I wouldn't mind his being a solicitor,' snapped Sarah. 'It's when he's a carpenter and chicken farmer and amateur photographer that I've no patience with him. He'll be standing for Parliament one day just to try something new, you see if he doesn't. I've no patience with a man who makes a profession of his hobbies.'

'I don't mind so long as he makes a hobby of his profession,' laughed Mary. 'John and I have put most of our affairs into his hands.'

'Oh. Indeed. Have you? Well, it's your own fault then if you come to grief. Did *you* advise John to go to Toby?'

'I did,' said Mary. 'He's our cousin. I'm sure I don't know who else there is.'

'I advised John to do nothing of the kind.'

Mary raised her eyebrows. This, from Sarah, was a confession of defeat. If Mary had advised John to do one thing when Sarah had asked him to do something else, and he had followed Mary's guidance, then it was strange that Sarah should acknowledge it. Sarah was strange, though ... Always had been rather clever and certainly odd. 'Odd' for Market Burton meant any digression from the straight and narrow path of conventionality. You never knew what Sarah would say next.

Callers drifted in. At Market Burton a lady's social success could be measured by the number of teas she attended on Wednesday afternoons. Nearly all the ladies of Market Burton were the wives of retired farmers.

Mary continued to sew and to be depressed by the newcomers. Their hats were depressing; their shoes were depressing; their similarity was the most depressing of all. This was what life in Market Burton did to you. Once these people had risen early and worked hard, and wrestled with the soil that gave them livelihood, as she rose and worked and wrestled. Now, if they moved at all from their chairs by the fire-side, they rose and turned round and round, through the garden-bound streets and chattering parlours of the valley town and then sat down again. It almost seemed as though the rolling hills and open country had proved too much for them. Each generation was born, brought up amongst the scattered farms, worked for a while, and reared a new generation to follow after them, then slipped back into the sheltered valley to wither and die.

Snatches of their conversation drifted towards her across the room – maids, their sisters, the price of butter.

Mary shivered. They were as lifeless as the uprooted trees, carried from the wold side and laid in the back garden of the farm, awaiting destruction for firewood. Their talk was as meaningless as the rustle of dry leaves on brittle twigs.

Mrs Holmes gasped her way across the room, and sat down beside Mary.

'Yes, you know,' she began without further prelude, 'I've just come back from Harrogate, and it hasn't done me a bit of good. Ethel, my cook you know, has given notice, and my nerves are all to pieces. You don't know a nice girl, do you? You're so lucky with maids, I know – always keep them. Then, of course, having a village like that to choose from ...'

In the other corner Anne and Mrs Toby, who had just arrived, were discussing the price of wool for socks. Aunt Jane's head was nodding in the armchair near the fire. Only Sarah sat alert and grim. 'I won't grow like them. I won't!' thought Mary. 'I won't ever leave the farm and come here to grow all withered and dry. I won't even stay alive like Sarah, and hate everything that alters because I can't grow along with it.'

She hardly listened to Janet's tale of woe.

Then there was a sudden rustle and clatter and Ursula Robson entered the room. She came in as usual unannounced, and Mary wondered if anyone could be more unlike the ladies round the fire. From her scarlet toque to her high-heeled shoes, she looked about as appropriate in that Victorian gathering as Dodo in a Cranford parlour.

'Yes, I've just dropped in for a moment,' she announced, greeting her relatives with breathless energy. Ursula had cultivated a manner that might convey to her acquaintances something of the reckless pace of that society to which she aspired. 'Foster would go down to the market – such a bore when I wanted to get home in time to dinner. The Lesters were coming in afterwards to play bridge.'

She peeled a long *suede* glove from her slim arm, rolled it into a ball and tossed it on to the sofa before she sat down by Mary and asked cheerfully:

'Well, and how's John?'

Mary with amused interest followed Sarah's disapproving glance across the room to Ursula's ankles. When Mrs Foster Robson sat down the sheath-like skirt below her fur coat slid almost up to her knees. Ursula, looking up too, caught Sarah's critical glance. With an impish gesture she thrust forward a little both her disgraceful legs and turned to Mary vivaciously.

'You haven't answered my question. How's John?' she asked.

'John's all right. I won't ask after Foster as I met him in the market.'

'Then if you saw him in the market you saw the most disreputable hat in the East Riding. Mary, what do you do to your husband when he will dress himself up as an "old clo" man? I've hidden that hat. I've danced on it. I've even put it in the rubbish bin, but up it comes again and goes to market on Wednesdays, as though he'd just bought it from Henry Heath's. What am I to do?'

'I should burn it,' suggested Mary calmly.

Ursula at least was alive. She was not in any way a tree of the valley. It was a relief to know that there still were some people with vitality left.

Louisa's soft voice cooed disapproval:

'Wouldn't that be rather wasteful?'

'Wasteful? Good Lord, if you could see it you wouldn't talk about waste! Aunt Jane, you ought to be used to dealing with this sort of thing. What do you do with Dickie when he's obstinate?'

'Dickie!' Mary looked up with apprehension to see if the roof would fall on such astounding levity. But Ursula fully realized the extent of her privilege. She knew the awe-struck pride with which her relatives watched her prowess on the golf links. Her airy impertinences and elusive skirts were forgiven because Anne and Louisa loved to impress strangers with 'Mrs Foster Robson, the Golf Champion.' And even Mrs Tilly would talk confusedly of mashies and niblicks, though she had never been on the links in her life.

'Foster's going to Scotland for a fortnight next week,' she announced suddenly.

'You'll go too, I suppose?' Mary asked.

'No. I don't feel up to knocking about much just now.'

Mary flashed a discerning glance at her cousin's face.

Ursula smiled, a subtle, triumphant smile. A dimple, never long in hiding, flickered on her rounded cheek.

'Oh, Ursula!' cried Mary softly. 'You don't mean?'

Ursula nodded, still smiling.

The sisters were all discussing an approaching sale of work, and the two women on the sofa seemed isolated. They spoke quietly. 'Do the others know?'

'Not yet. I'll feel such a fool telling them. They always make such an ungodly fuss about these kind of things, and because I've been South for so long they forget there's any such possibility.'

'When?'

'April.'

'Well, anyhow *you* are doing your duty.' Mary laughed a little, but her fingers, tightly holding the linen she sewed, were trembling. She felt a little breathless, as though she had just found in the possession of another something she had sought a long time. Then the instinct that made her respond to an expressed need came to her aid.

'Look here, Ursula, if you feel rather bored at the idea of being alone when Foster goes away, why not come to Anderby for a fortnight? We haven't had any visitors – anyway, young ones – for ages.'

'Do you mean that? I'd love it. It's so dull when I can't play golf. Are you sure I shan't be a nuisance?'

'Of course you won't. I'd love to have you.'

She would. Because Ursula was young. Anything better than this dreary monotony of middle age – when one was only twenty-eight.

'Righto. I'll come. And, Mary, I wonder if you'd tell the others after I've gone. I should feel such an ass and they're bound to know soon.'

'Of course I will.'

Ursula nodded and smiled and left her, to pay her compliments to Aunt Jane.

Mary sat and watched her. Why, she wondered, had she asked her to stay? Why had she promised to tell the family that Ursula, and not she, was going to have a baby? Why did one

57

ever tell those faded women anything? Her news would stir them lightly, as a breeze stirs withered leaves to a rustling chatter, but that would subside too, and they would forget until the next breeze blew.

Besides, why Ursula's news, when she wanted so much to give them tidings of her own? Ursula had all the luck. It wasn't as if she cared for Mary. She only looked upon her as someone useful, and staid, and a little dull.

Mary pulled herself together. After all she had her work. She had Anderby. Her needle flew in and out of her material as she nursed this thought. All that one really wanted was that things should stay as they were. What did it matter if Ursula had a private income and clothes from London and an exasperating air of importance?

She could have a thousand babies for all Mary cared! One day she would retire too, and grow old, and come to wither among the trees of the valley.

Mary never would. Never, never!

Aunt Jane beckoned her.

'Come and talk to me, love. I haven't seen you for long enough.'

Mary crossed the room and sat down by the big arm-chair. Aunt Jane sat, her bird-like head on one side, waiting for Mary to tell her something. She always sat like this, waiting for people to tell her something. It was her one interest in life, though she always forgot what they told her.

Mary knew she was waiting, but there seemed to be nothing to say. Ursula was still in the room, so she must not yet talk about the baby, but besides that she could think of nothing but dried leaves rattling on rotten twigs in a valley garden.

58

'Well, love?' prompted Aunt Jane.

'Have you been cutting down any trees lately?' asked Mary wildly.

Her sisters-in-law looked up in mild surprise, but Aunt Jane only shook her head.

'No, love,' she replied. 'You see since we gave up farming we haven't had any wood of our own.'

6

THE PERFECT GUEST

Ursula stood in front of the looking-glass inspecting the angle of her hat. It was a new hat. She had put it on to impress Mary. Mary dressed rather like the worthier type of village school teacher. She wore flannel blouses with high collars. It was time some one took her in hand. 'There's something about looking after a parish that makes a woman forget to powder her nose,' thought Ursula.

Ursula had come to Anderby on a mission of mercy. She was going to brighten Mary up. Mary had been shut away too long with that extraordinarily dull husband of hers. She thought that the only thing a married woman could do, if she had any time left over from looking after her own household, was to look after some one else's. Well, Ursula was going to show her that there were lots of other things to do. The perfect guest was one who contributed something to the life of her hostess. Ursula was going to teach Mary how to dress, and play bridge, and behave like a girl of twenty-eight instead of a woman of forty. And yet she would be tender and gentle, with the tenderness of expectant motherhood – fashionable yet considerate, thoughtful yet spontaneous.

Ursula found continual pleasure in the contemplation of her own spontaneity.

Mary re-entered the drawing-room, carrying a tea-tray. Now was the time, thought Ursula, to lay her fur coat carelessly on the sofa, and reveal the soft grey draperies of her satin dress. What a mercy she looked so much nicer than most women in these circumstances. It just showed there was no real need to let yourself go.

But Mary did not seem to notice the dress.

'We're having a cup of tea now,' she explained, arranging the tray on the table, 'because I expect you would like one after your drive, and I have to go out down the village on an errand.'

'When? Now?'

Then she would not be present while Ursula spread on the antiquated dressing-table the elaborate paraphernalia of her toilette – bottles, scent, powder, manicure instruments. She would not be instructed by the display of Ursula's fairy-like *lingerie*. She would miss part of her education.

'I'm sorry if it seems rude, but it's rather important. I dare say you will be glad of a rest, though.'

'It's something that's worrying you, Mary. What?'

'Worrying me? Why, whatever makes you think I'm worrying?'

'My dear, you're hardly an expert at disguising your feelings. Do you mind if I have a cigarette? Now then, come along! Confession is good for the soul.'

Mary must be worried if she was too preoccupied to notice the fur coat.

'I'm only going to see the schoolmaster about a boy John wants to come and work on the farm this spring. The schoolmaster says he hasn't reached the sixth standard yet, and doesn't want him to leave school.'

'What are you going to do, then?'

'I'm going to Coast to tell him that the boy is thirteen and has put in his attendances. If he hasn't got to the sixth standard now, he never will. He's keen on sheep and hates lessons. On the farm he'll be getting experience as well as making money. It's absurd to keep him sitting at a desk chalking coloured flowers!'

'Oh, you talk to the schoolmaster like that, do you? But isn't there something about education acts and things? I don't know much about it. It's not my line, but the kid seems pretty young.'

Ursula was not at all interested in lads and education acts. She wanted to talk about her own interesting condition or Mary's style of hairdressing. But she had made up her mind to be patient, and patient she would be.

'Mr Woodcock,' continued Mary with heat, 'says in the *Yorkshire Chronicle* that the people who make education acts are legislating for the normal majority. It is the business of local knowledge to determine the exceptions.'

'My dear Mary, you talk like a Member of Parliament. Are you really interested in these things?'

'Rural education? Yes, of course.'

'Why "of course"? I'm not. I never put my nose inside Middlethorpe. I don't know if there's a village school or not except when the beastly bell rings in the morning – and yet Foster seems to do pretty well on the farm.'

'It's not entirely a question of money though, is it?'

Mary looked at Ursula with grave, wide eyes.

'Isn't it? Philanthropy, then, and all that sort of thing, I suppose. Does your schoolmaster enjoy it when you snatch his lambs away from him? Does he, Mary?'

She laughed.

'No. I don't believe he does. But that's not the point.'

'I don't really see that there is a point to it at all.'

Ursula lit one cigarette from another and threw the dead end into the grate. She did not like smoking a lot just now, but really, with Mary—

'Well, some one's got to do it,' said Mary.

'Why? Do what?'

'Oh, see that nurses are provided and that the girls get situations and – oh, I don't know. Besides, I like it.'

'Of course.' Ursula smiled pityingly. 'I suppose when you have so few other ties—'

Mary flushed.

Ursula continued:

'You look tired. I'm sure you do too much. I shall speak to John about it. Why don't you go in for golf?'

'Golf? I shouldn't be any good at that I'm afraid. Besides Hardrascliffe links are so far away. I haven't time.'

'Time? Of course you have time. As much time as anyone. As me, for instance.'

Mary shook her head slowly, and began to gather up the tea-things.

'You'll excuse me going away now, won't you? I shan't be long. You'll just have nice time to unpack comfortably and I expect John will be in any moment now.'

63

She left the room.

Ursula curled herself comfortably on the sofa and putting another cushion behind her head, prepared to enjoy a grievance. Really it was rather casual of Mary to go and leave her just after her arrival. She did not seem to realize her good fortune in having her cousin there at all. 'She's hopelessly limited and narrow-minded. Poor Mary! Anybody so thoroughly pleased with herself must be disillusioned one day. She'll come a cropper soon,' prophesied Ursula.

She was too tired to go upstairs and dress. Besides, what was the use, when John and Mary never changed for high tea?

Her head sank back among the cushions.

'Oh, that you, Ursula? How are you?'

John stood before her holding out a polite but rather grimy hand. His beard was grizzled with frost. His farming boots distributed little pools of melting ice on the carpet. Leather breeches encased his great legs.

Ursula sat up and patted her perfectly-ordered hair.

'Good gracious! I must have been dozing. How are you, John? I'm perfectly fit, thanks.'

'Where's Mary?'

'She's gone off up the village somewhere. I say, John, you ought to keep an eye on that wife of yours. She works much too hard.'

John tugged at his beard and smiled lazily down at Ursula.

'Oh, I can't stop her. If she wants to do anything she will. What's she up to now?'

'She's off to tell the schoolmaster some home-truths about a lad or something. She says you want him on the farm and he's under age.'

'Jack Greenwood? I don't want him. That's her idea. How long has she been gone?'

'Oh, I don't know. Ages. Do sit down and talk to me.'

John looked apologetically at his boots. Near Ursula's fragile daintiness he felt more than ever conscious of his bulk and clumsiness.

'Where's Foster?' he asked.

'He's away in Scotland buying stock. He's crazy about crossing something or other with Highland Cattle. *I* don't know.' Ursula seemed preoccupied. Her brow was ruffled with thought. 'John, does Mary always rule things in the village in this high-handed way?'

'What? I dun' know. That's her business. I never interfere.'

'But don't you see she's wearing herself out? Making an old woman of herself while she ought to be still a girl? Besides, after all, you're the farmer, aren't you? Of course,' with a sigh, 'I know she's magnificent.'

'Oh – ay.'

'But it must make it a little uncomfortable for every one if she will set the village by the ears.'

John sat silent for a minute. Ursula lay and watched him, her sharp brown eyes quietly searching his ruminative face. There was something about John that reminded her of an ox – large, docile, fated. 'Well, it's nowt to do with me,' he said at last. 'I'd better go and clear away some of this mess. So long.'

He left her.

Well, it was evident that nothing could be done with John. She would have to concentrate on Mary. The determination to reform her cousin-in-law's existence pursued her throughout the evening. It would be an entertaining game, the sole relief of a rather monotonous visit to otherwise boring people.

Next morning she was awakened by Mary, standing over her bed with the breakfast tray. One irritating thing about Mary was that she always seemed to be carrying trays somewhere.

'Good heavens! What's the time?'

'Half-past eight. John wanted breakfast at a quarter past seven this morning. He had to go to Littledale early.'

'Well, it's awfully ripping of you, but you know you shouldn't spoil me.'

'It's not a question of spoiling,' returned Mary serenely. 'I couldn't let you get up so early, especially as I don't suppose you feel quite at your best in the mornings just now.'

How like Mary to emphasize the unromantic aspect of a really rather romantic thing! Ursula surveyed the tray which Mary arranged in a businesslike fashion by her side. Mary's manner always reminded Ursula vaguely of a hospital nurse. She made you feel as if you weren't a person at all, but only an object of her philanthropy.

Ursula decided that the time had come to assert her personality. 'Oh, Mary, I'm so sorry, but do you mind if I don't eat this bacon? I never take it now, nothing but an egg or a scrap of fish. No, no! Don't take it away. I might perhaps try to manage it.'

'Oh, for goodness' sake don't eat it if it would upset you. I ought to have asked last night. It was silly of me. You really should have told me. And perhaps you'd rather have tea instead of coffee?'

'Oh, no. Don't bother. I couldn't think of troubling you. I'll manage with coffee this morning. It mayn't make me ill.' Ursula smiled brightly.

'Oh, does it make you sick? I'll bring some tea in a minute.'

Mary vanished from the room and Ursula lay and wondered whether it was worth while getting out of bed to brush her hair before Mary returned. Just like Mary to come in and find her asleep with dishevelled hair and her face still covered with the cream she had put on before retiring. It was not at all in keeping with the effect she had intended to produce. But perhaps Mary hadn't noticed much. Ursula climbed out of bed, wincing as her toes touched the cold carpet. There were always such appalling draughts in these old houses. A rug against the door would be a good thing. She mentally recorded the suggestion.

A deft fingering of her dark hair and the addition of a rosy satin wrap transformed Ursula. She snuggled back among the pillows as Mary came in bearing a teapot, an egg-cup, a hot water-bottle and a shawl.

'There now,' she said. 'That's better, isn't it? Now put this shawl round your shoulders. It's cold this morning, isn't it?'

'Thanks awfully. No I don't want the shawl, thanks. I have my wrap. It was sweet of you to think of it, though.'

'Would you care to come out a little later?'

'I'd love to. I'm longing to see this wonderful village of yours.' She shivered a little.

'Are you cold? Do have the shawl.'

'No, thanks, but perhaps if you don't mind shutting the door.'

'Well, then, I'll come for the tray presently. Don't hurry down. Have you a book? I left a few on the table. Have you everything you want?'

'Yes, rather. Thanks awfully. And what about a bath? Do I just ring when I'm ready or what? I could go along myself of course, only I don't want to give any trouble. Perhaps Violet—'

'Violet's busy this morning. I'm sorry we haven't got a bathroom yet. I'll bring some cans up to your room.'

'Not a bathroom? Poor things! Why, if I don't have my bath every morning I feel perfectly filthy. And bathing in one's room is such a chillsome business, isn't it?'

'I'm afraid it is really. But you shall have a fire. I'll light one now.' She lit the fire and went out, leaving Ursula alone with the tray.

Ursula waited quarter of an hour for Mary in the hall, and while she waited, she reluctantly yielded to an increasing sense of irritation. She had come to Anderby prepared to be very nice to Mary – and here was Mary trying to patronize her all the time. All that breakfast in bed, and fire and bath business had subtly transferred Ursula from the position of a friend to that of a dependent. 'Perfection of service lies in the appearance of rendering none,' quoted Ursula to herself, and decided she was badly used.

And when Mary at last appeared in the hall, she came forward with an apology which implied no shame but was merely a statement of courtesy.

'I'm sorry I kept you waiting, but the butcher's cart came round and then Mrs Walker brought me her nursing subscription.'

'Oh, don't worry about me. I've been as right as a trivet – only waiting about half an hour. Where are we going?'

'Well, if you don't mind I want to go up to the churchyard. Old Jacob Jordan died a day or two ago. They're burying him to-morrow and I sent a man up to line the grave with ever-green. The old people haven't much of a garden, and they do appreciate those little attentions.'

'Do you go and decorate the grave yourself?'

'No, I only want to see how it's getting on. Here, let me open the gate. You'll spoil your gloves.'

But Ursula was already tugging at the iron bars, and with-drew her hand, grimacing at the stripe of moisture across the doeskin gauntlet. She felt that it would have been becoming in Mary to show some sign of concern. But Mary only said quietly:

'You should have let me do it.'

Ursula walked on for a little way in silence. Then she asked:

'Will you go to the funeral to-morrow?'

'Yes. If you'll excuse me for that time. It won't take long.'

'Do you go to all their funerals?'

'The people in the village? Yes, mostly.'

'Mary, how *can* you?'

'Why shouldn't I? I don't mind.'

'Funerals are so beastly depressing. If you go to a lot you'll get morbid and queer.'

'I shan't. I quite enjoy them.'

'Enjoy them? Good Lord, that just shows how fearfully bad they are for you. Enjoying a funeral! I never heard of anything so grizzly.'

'It's not a bit grizzly really. If you lived about here, you'd understand. People enjoy them nearly as much as weddings and a lot more than christenings.'

'Oh, I see.' Ursula cracked a frozen puddle with the point of her walking-stick. 'A christening may be a farce and a wedding a fiasco, but you know where you are with a funeral.'

'Yes, I suppose so,' said Mary calmly.

They had turned from the village street into a path that led up the hill to the church. Ursula took up her tale.

'All the same, I think it's perfectly beastly, making a kind of beanfeast because somebody is going to be shut up in the earth. Do you know, if you don't mind I think I'd rather not go into the churchyard just now – an open grave, it always gives me the shudders. I can wait outside.'

'Why, of course. How silly of me not to have thought about it. It doesn't matter. I can go another time. Let's turn down here.'

'Here' meant past the School House.

'What a hideous place!' said Ursula.

'Oh, I don't know.' Mary resented anyone else who criticized her village. 'Why, there's the schoolmaster.'

'Is he one of your adorers?' Ursula asked, looking with amusement at the lean, black coated figure carrying a pile of books from one building to another.

Mary flushed.

'Not exactly,' she said, but as Mr Coast approached she smiled at him graciously. 'Good morning,' she called. 'A blustery morning, isn't it? How's Mrs Coast?'

She was not going to let Ursula see that there was any fly in her ointment of patronage.

But Coast regarded her coldly without a sign of recognition. From her he turned to Ursula, in her fur coat and rakish hat. His scornful eyes swept across them and he turned away.

Ursula suppressed a giggle of triumph. This was the worship offered by Mary's beloved villagers. The family should hear of this. 'What a rude man!' she remarked airily.

'I expect the sun was in his eyes,' said Mary.

Ursula decided it would be tactful to change the conversation. Poor Mary! She looked like a lion tamer when Leo won't sit up and do his tricks!

'You know, Mary,' she began with pretty diffidence, running her walking-stick along the path, 'you're such a dear. I'd hate to see you spoiled, and living this sort of life must be rather dangerous – likely to get you into a groove.'

'What sort of a groove?' asked Mary.

'Well, all this village work and so on. And sticking so closely to your house and everything, as if you were one of your own aunts.'

Mary held herself well in hand.

'I thought I had explained all that before,' she said patiently. 'You see we've had to economize a lot because of the mortgage. We only started even having a maid last year, though we could have two easily in that house. And I do a lot of the garden myself, though it's really too big for me to manage. You know the mortgage had to be paid.'

'That old mortgage seems to have been the bane of your life, Mary. Thank goodness it's paid now and you can forget it. You ought to play bridge and dance. Can you dance? You look as if you could. You move rippingly!' Ursula hummed a few bars from a popular waltz. 'And then – I know it sounds awful cheek on my part, but couldn't you do something about your clothes?'

'My clothes?'

'Yes. You know, of course, I understand it's been awfully difficult for you. And we all think you've been perfectly splendid, the way you've toiled and pinched to pay those beastly debts, but now they're all done with couldn't you go to some one

71

rather more enterprising for your coats and skirts? Of course I get mine in town, but I dare say you wouldn't want to go so far. Still, there's York and Hull and Scarborough. Oh, lots of places where there must be a decent tailor.'

'I dare say. I can't afford it though. We're not millionaires yet. John must get some capital laid by.'

'Still, I don't see why you shouldn't do things, especially as you haven't any children to keep you at home. Now *I'm* quite prepared to settle down for a bit after April but you really might be a bit more normal. Of course, it's been bad luck, having to save such a lot and all that, but it's all over now. You mustn't get in a groove.'

Mary smiled, a queer, twisted smile.

So that was what they thought of the thing that had dictated the whole course of her life, forced her into marriage with a man old enough to be her father, and left her, now that youth was passing, deprived of every interest except her village work. Something that was all over, and might be comfortably forgotten ... Though, without it, she might be going to have a child as well as Ursula ...

'Of course I dare say I've no right to say anything, Mary. You know it's only because you're such a dear really ...'

Middle-aged. That was what Ursula said she was. Well, she often felt it. She supposed it must be with thinking about the same thing for so long. Monomania is an efficient destroyer of youth.

Well, if she was in a groove, there was no escape from it. Not by the easy way of tennis parties and bridge which Ursula suggested. She had placed herself irretrievably in the ranks of the older generation. If youth meant the adventuring towards an uncertain choice of life, then, when the choice was made, youth ended. Ten years ago Mary had made her choice. Henceforward she was captive in a 'groove,' and must descend in it steadily until the end of life, with no digressions that might lead her to the hill-tops of success or the valleys of humiliation.

She opened the gate for Ursula and passed behind her up the wintry garden.

Never mind! She would make it all worth while.

Anderby was going to be the most prosperous, popular, well cared for village in the East Riding before she had done with it. She'd show them.

She went along the passage with shining eyes and began to prepare dinner.

In spite of herself the elasticity of her youth had momentarily triumphed.

John followed her and stood in the doorway watching her with his slow smile.

She always knew when he had something to tell her. It was so irritating of him just to stand there without speaking. She thrust her tins into the oven and closed the door carefully before she looked up.

'Well?' she asked.

'Honey, I've just seen that chap Coast.'

'Oh, have you? And what has he to say for himself?'

'He says that if you take young Greenwood away from school he'll report you to the Inspector and you'll have to answer for your action in Court.'

John chuckled.

Mary tossed the oven cloth aside contemptuously. In the fine exaltation of her mood she could afford to laugh at Coast.

'Let him,' she said. 'I'd love to see him try to have me up before my betters. Think of old Sir Charles Seton's face when he saw me in the dock! He told Mr Slater, when I was put on the Nursing Committee, that I was an estimable woman.'

'Well, I wouldn't do anything rash if I were you.'

'No, I'm sure you'd never do anything rash if you were anyone. Never mind. Go along and wash your hands. There's Yorkshire pudding for dinner, and it won't stand waiting.'

7

THE SALVATION OF SOCIETY

After Ursula's departure Mary doubled her parochial activities. She visited the wives of all John's married labourers; she ministered continually to the invalids and old age pensioners; she organized a dance in the School Room in aid of the Village Institute, and a whist drive in aid of the local hospital. She was going to make Anderby the most prosperous, popular, well-cared-for village in the East Riding.

The village regarded her efforts with mingled awe and irritation. Mrs Robson was wonderful. Her generosity, her persistence, her catholicity of interest, all were wonderful. At the same time they were a little embarrassing.

'You've no sooner got your shirt in t' wash but she's after you to see if you want a new one,' sighed Ted Wilson.

But even he agreed that she was wonderful.

One day she stood in a bookshop in Hardrascliffe, tired out by a week of perpetual activity. She was looking for a birthday present for John. Lately his silence had become so wearisome that she welcomed any opportunity of rousing his admiration or dislike, if only to evoke a remark. Now he might talk about a book. He seemed to enjoy reading about agriculture and even sometimes read her passages from the *Farmer's Weekly*.

Mary herself hadn't much use for books. Once they had been well enough, but now she was too busy to be bothered with them. There were quite a lot in the house that had once belonged to her mother, but none of these would be likely to move John to the companionship of criticism.

She stood indifferently turning over the volumes offered her by Mr Forsitt the bookseller. They all looked a little dull, she thought.

'Haven't you anything more modern than these?' she asked. 'I want something with a sort of kick in it. No, not a story. He doesn't like novels. Something about farming.'

'Ah.' Mr Forsitt pressed the tips of his fingers together and meditated. Then he suddenly ducked his head and scurried off to the corner table. 'I have it,' he cried. 'The very book for you, Mrs Robson.' He returned flourishing a volume in a bright orange cover. 'Here we are! *The Salvation of Society* by David Rossitur. Essays. Just out.'

Mary took the book from him, and gazed at the vermilion letters across the wrapper. *The Salvation of Society*. Somehow the title was familiar, though she could not remember where she had last seen it. A queer title. Rather high-flown perhaps.

She opened the book and looked at the chapter headings: 'The Generation at the Cross Roads,' 'Revolution and Beyond,' 'The Reincarnation of Bestiality,' 'The Agricultural Calvary,' 'The Tyranny of Possession' . . .

No. It was not a Methodist production. What then?

'Yes, Mrs Robson. I think I may safely say I recommend that to you if you want something exciting. I have not read it myself. Not quite in my line perhaps. A little rash, I gather. A volume of essays by a young gentleman recently expelled from Cambridge – or was it Oxford?'

'Yes?'

'Quite young, I gather. Oh, quite young. A mere boy, Mr Locking tells me. The Reverend Mr Locking. He has advanced views. Very. The parishioners at St. Paul's and St. Giles's hardly seem to like him. But there, he buys a good many books from us. Then there was Mr Coast. He bought a copy – the schoolmaster from your part of the world I believe, Mrs Robson.'

Coast! That was it. Mary knew now that she had seen the book during that preposterous interview, when Coast had dared to condemn her for lack of generosity. It would be rather entertaining to discover what sort of literature appealed to him.

'Will it do for a birthday present for my husband?' she asked, smiling. Mr Forsitt was an old friend and Mary retained a childish habit of taking tradesmen into her confidence, which many of her relations thought most unbecoming.

'Oh, quite suitable, I think. Very interesting to a farmer, I dare say. Let me wrap it up for you. Seven *and* sixpence. And the next thing?'

She went home with the flamboyant cover discreetly veiled in brown paper. She quite intended to amuse herself with it that night before she handed it over to John. But when she reached Anderby Violet had toothache and the groceries weren't unpacked, and books were all very well, but one had other things to see about.

On Sunday she forgot all about it. On Monday and Tuesday

she was busy washing and ironing. On Wednesday she drove with John to Market Burton. On Thursday she always churned.

That was a busy day. She turned and turned before the butter came, and, even when the churning was done, there were golden slabs to be wrapped in grease-proof paper ready for the carrier to convey them into Hardrascliffe. Mary felt tired as she washed her hands. Nothing exciting ever happened. There had not even been a satisfactory lot of butter.

Outside the starlings were chattering in the naked trees. The mild evening air – it was warm for February – might blow away that jaded feeling. She mentally reviewed her list of pensioners and invalids.

Mrs Watts! The name flashed across her mind. She had not visited her for several weeks.

Mrs Watts, being completely crippled by rheumatism, lived in a high-backed chair in the kitchen of her small cottage, attended by Louie, her half-witted niece. But from her chair the old lady could acquire in one day more intimate and extensive knowledge of village gossip than Mary could collect in a week.

So to Mrs Watts she went.

Mrs Watts received her boisterously. For a cripple she possessed remarkable vocal and mental energy.

'Come in, Mrs Robson,' she shouted. 'Come in! Now wherever have you been all t' time? I haven't set eyes on you since back end o' Christmas. Has Mrs Foster gone yet? When's baby coming, eh?'

'Oh, of course,' laughed Mary. 'I quite see it's no use my ever telling you anything. I don't know why I come here. You always know all my news before it's happened. The baby's coming in April if all goes well.'

She drew off her gloves, laid a small packet of tea on the mantelpiece and sat down to enjoy herself. She had a whole hour before tea. One could learn a lot from Mrs Watts in an hour.

'Well, and how are you?'

'I'se about middlin'. I haven't caught sight o' t' edge o' Peter's robe yet, and they say you've got to see that before you come t' gowlden gates.'

'Well, I'm glad of that.'

'Ay. I think you are. There's nowt goes well in t' village but I think we are glad on't. I don't know what some on us would do without you.'

'Oh, you'd do well enough.'

Lately a sneaking fear had found its way to Mary's mind that the village could do without her. It was comforting to be reassured.

'Nay now, would we? Just look at Mrs Foster. What good d'ye think comes of her in her parts o' t' Wold? My nephew works for Burrages out Middlethorpe way, and I hear all goings on there. Why she didn't send so much as a jelly to Middlethorpe cricket club dance!'

'Well, she has other interests.'

Mary was guiltily conscious that she found criticism of Ursula pleasant.

'Yes, she had a lot of interest in your chair covers, hadn't she?'

'Now what on earth did you hear about them?'

The old woman chuckled and, bending forward, patted Mary's hand with stiff fingers.

'Now don't you take on about that. Your Violet told her cousin, Mrs Jellaby, what lives down in Spring Cottages. And she came in here a bit back for a talk and told me how young Mrs Foster had been staying up at Anderby, and how she'd been wanting you to get oyster satin cushions with black borders. "Ah've no notion what oyster satin covers is like," ah says, "but t' my mind, it sounds a bit messy."'

'Violet has no business to repeat things she hears in the house.'

'Why, bless you, don't you know a lass will tell owt tiv' her friends whether she's in service or not? Ye can't stop it, Mrs Robson. Ye might as well get butter out of a dog's throat as a bit of gossip back from a lass who's once heard tell on't.'

'I suppose so. But it's rather hard on me, isn't it, if I can't even keep my chair covers to myself?'

Mary smiled half whimsically, unable to be as annoyed as her dignity demanded.

'Now then don't you go fashin' yourself about your chair covers. If Violet says owt, it's never but what it's to your credit. I'm sure lass or lady, there's none better respected on whole o' t' woldside, seek where you like.'

'Don't be silly. There are lots better. What I do, I do for pleasure.'

'Ay, but it's a kind o' pleasure that takes it out of you more than you let on. What's happened to roses that used to be in your cheeks, eh? You've been fretting yourself because Mr Coast wouldn't let you have Jack Greenwood for shepherd lad, ay. Mrs Greenwood told me all about yon business. And how ye'd got him away now and all. "Of all fond fools," ah said, "yon schoolmaster chap takes a lot o' beating." As I said to Mrs Greenwood, "Eddication's all very well," ah says, "but it doesn't teach you to drive a waggon let alone a plough!"'

Mary sighed. So every one knew about Jack Greenwood too. Every one knew about everything. The fierce light that beats upon a throne is only a candle's flicker beside the searching glare of village criticism. It consoled her, though, to think that publicity could only further reveal her love for Anderby. And it was pleasant to sit in the dancing firelight, while the dusk crept up the orchard outside, and listen to Mrs Watts telling her how wonderful she was.

Mrs Watts knew that Mary found it pleasant. Mrs Robson, she considered, was a very fine young woman, but as she talked a thousand past acts of kindness, of gratuitous attention, of charitable patronage rose before her. Somehow by her crude flattery she seemed paying a little of her debt back to the mistress of the Wold Farm, and holding over her, if only for a moment, that suzerainty which belongs to people who can give us what we need.

An hour later, when Mary opened the front door and entered her lamplit hall, she recalled with a faint sensation of disgust her calm acceptance of the old woman's praise. But after all if people liked her why shouldn't they say so? And if they spoke why shouldn't she listen? 'It isn't as if it was likely to turn my head,' she thought as she drew the curtains across the dining-room windows. 'I'm not a little fool to be taken in by that sort of thing.'

She really thought she wasn't.

At the same time she was glad that John had to attend a vestry meeting that evening, for she had suddenly remembered the orange-covered book. Mr David Rossitur's acid comments on capitalist farmers were likely to prove an effective antidote to the cloying sweetness of Mrs Watts's adulation.

She produced the book from a drawer and sat down in John's arm-chair before the fire.

At first, she read with knit brows; then her eyes opened wide; then she sat up straight in the arm-chair, her lips parted in a half-amused, half-incredulous smile. It really was an outrageous book! Mary was unacquainted with any political or social theories more violent than those expounded in the columns of the *Yorkshire Chronicle*. The only excuse for this tirade against capitalism, patronage and 'the dependence of the proletariat upon the self-interested solicitude of a bourgeois minority,' lay in the youth of its author. Of course he must be a mere boy – a student at Oxford, according to the preface. And they were always very young, Mary was sure. A footnote explained that the writer had spent one summer vacation on a walking tour, investigating the conditions in which agricultural labourers of the South Country lived and worked. It added that he hoped to continue his researches in the North at an early date, for the conclusions he had reached after his Southern pilgrimage had convinced him that the only hope for England lay in social revolution. Anything less drastic – the extension of trades unionism, or the political ascendancy of the Labour Party – was merely a sop thrown to the proletarian Cerberus.

'He's very fond of that word "proletarian"' thought Mary. She was not absolutely certain what it meant.

There followed a scornful rejection of the passive optimism of the Constitutionalists. Darwin was denounced as a traitor to the cause of progress. 'Society,' declared Mr Rossitur, 'is perishing from senile decay, awaiting the fabled miracle of evolution.' Reform could only follow destruction: destruction of empty loyalties, destruction of cowardly compromise, of a tyranny based on material advantage and sentimentalism that masked rapacity.

Quotations abounded. In his zeal to carry conviction the author rarely expressed an opinion without the support of some famous authority, as if his own cheques would not hold good unless backed by a great financier.

It was all bewildering, and ridiculous and intriguing. Certainly Mary had never encountered anything of the kind before. She became entangled in a labyrinth of obscure reasoning. She was belaboured by pages of savage rhetoric. She stumbled over unfamiliar phrases that recurred here with unremitting urgency – 'Living Wage,' 'Standard of comfort,' 'Private capitalists.' Quite half of it was wholly beyond her comprehension.

'Perhaps I'm tired,' she thought. 'I shall be able to take it in better to-morrow.'

When John returned from the meeting, she rose regretfully and hid the book in the sideboard drawer.

Of course, it was all nonsense; but what amusing nonsense! And somehow, for all its extravagance, it was really rather refreshing. Some grace of youth and burning sincerity relieved its ugliest violence and crudest rhetoric. She wished she could talk to the author. It really was amazing that anyone clever enough to go to Oxford should know so little about farms. Mary would like to explain exactly why one had to look after people who weren't capable of looking after themselves and why one paid labourers' wages instead of every one sharing the profits. It was all so self-evident when one knew anything at all about agriculture. Of course Mr Rossitur didn't. He was only a boy, whose tempestuousness was too childish to be dangerous, and whose idealism was too unselfconscious to be sentimental. Quite a dear, Mary thought, but terribly ignorant of what things were really like.

'I wonder whatever John will think,' she mused as she undressed that night. The prospect of John's inevitable comment was highly entertaining.

Mary had only two days to wait before his birthday, when she handed him her present after the usual ceremonial kiss. My word, at least here was something to make him talk! All day she looked forward eagerly to his reception of the social theories of David Rossitur.

After tea she produced her sewing and, handing John his pipe and the book, sat down to await his verdict.

For three hours she sat silently sewing. The black hands of the clock crawled forward. The room was silent except when, every few minutes, John's hand flicked over another page. It was a quarter past ten.

A coal, crashing suddenly from the grate to the hearth, aroused John. He looked at the clock and put down his book.

'Bedtime I think, missus,' he said.

Mary began to fold her work. Now was the time when he must speak. He must really. Even if he had very little to say about most things, at least he must have some sort of an opinion about this.

John was poking the largest lumps of coal out of the fire. It was his favourite habit of economy.

Mary could bear it in silence no longer.

'Well, John,' she remarked as casually as she could, 'what do you think of it? How far have you got?'

'Page 121,' said John and, knocking the ashes out of his pipe against the fender, he went upstairs to bed.

Next morning Mary walked up to Littledale to see the foreman's latest baby. Coming home through the fields she recovered for the first time from her husband's rebuff of the previous night.

Really John's stupidity mattered very little on a morning like this. She wanted to race with the wind, to jump, to shout, to sing.

The freshly turned ploughland gleamed purple in the sunlight. A faintly pink haze caressed the stubble.

What did anything matter?

It was good land. What nonsense that writer person talked all about handing over property to the State to be run by syndicates of working men. As though just anyone could farm who thought it would be rather nice to walk about and watch the crops grow! Why, a hundred years ago this height of the wold had been covered by gorse and short-cropped turf. The sixty-acre and its neighbouring fields were still known as the 'Sheep Walk.' To produce this fertile soil her grandfather and her father and John had marled and manured and watched and waited as though nothing else in the world was of any importance. Even in her own day hundreds of tons of burnt chalk must have been scattered on the hill-side to make those turnips swell so gallantly.

Mr Rossitur, if you please, thought the land was easy to own. Mary wanted to tell him that to care for it as she cared one had to give up everything – even the chance of ever hearing anyone say something more intelligent than 'Page 121!'

From the other side of the hedge rose a sharp cry, half pain, half terror.

Mary looked at the thick interlacing of hawthorn, but could see nothing. Then came voices – a man's hoarse and angry, a boy's shrill with fear.

She began to run along the uneven road.

The hedge was broken by a strip of fence across the stump of a tree. Beyond, near a 'pie' of turnips, stood a half-filled cart. Near it, crouching in the road, knelt the boy, Jack Greenwood, whom Mary had prematurely wrested from the Council School. Bending over him, with a short whip in his hand, stood Waite, the beast man.

'Stop that! What are you doing, Waite?' called Mary. She climbed the fence with greater speed than elegance, slipping a little on the damp wood.

The man looked up, with surly defiance.

'I warn't doing nowt, Mrs Robson. This lad's an idler. He needs a bit o' stick now and then to keep him up ti'd mark.'

'Come here, Jack,' commanded Mary.

The boy rose and limped towards her sobbing, not at all unwilling to make capital out of his misfortunes. A furrow of pink, washed clean by tears, ran down his muddy face. He held one hand across his bleeding ear.

'What has he been doing, Waite?'

'He's an idle, good-for-nowt. Back end o' ten o'clock I sent him up to get the cart forked up wi' swedes, and as he never corned and never corned, I had t' come up mysen and see what's wrong, and here he was, with nowt to say, and nowt done.'

'Did you ask him why?'

'Ay. That I did and all.' Waite plucked a turnip from the pie with his long handled fork and flung it into the cart.

Mary was quietly examining the boy's injuries. His shoulder was bruised and his ear inflamed, but her opportune arrival had prevented further damage.

For a little while she did not speak. Her mind was again with Mr David Rossitur, and his plea for the independence of the labouring class, and for a wider recognition of the innate dignity of human nature. Then she spoke slowly, almost as though addressing herself alone.

'Oh. So you sent a boy up to do work you are supposed to do yourself, and expect him to manage a horse, and to fork turnips into a cart he is too small to reach and, because he couldn't do it, you came and beat him, did you? And thought that no one would see? You know we don't beat boys at Anderby. Jack has only just started to work. I wonder what sort of opinion he has of farm life.'

Waite continued to throw turnips into the cart. They fell from his fork with dull little thuds, punctuating Mary's speech.

'I didn't know Jack was going to work for you,' she continued. 'It isn't the first time you've done this sort of thing, you know. I can't let you go on working together because you obviously don't know how to treat a boy. And even if I take Jack away, you'll be up to the same tricks with some one else, sooner or later. So I'm afraid you'll have to go. I'm sorry – but I don't know what else to do. You shall have a week's wages, but I can't allow this sort of thing here, don't you see? Jack, come along with me and I'll give you something for your ear. No, don't cry, because you're not much hurt really, you know. I'm ashamed of you, Waite, and I hope you're ashamed of yourself. I shall tell Foreman and my husband of the step I have taken. You can consider yourself dismissed.'

The man continued phlegmatically to throw turnips into the cart, his body swaying loosely from the hips as he stooped and lifted. He might never have heard Mary's voice, but as she went down the road she sighed, conscious that she had made another enemy. First Coast, now Waite ...

The government of a kingdom was not always easy. Mary hated to be disliked. She loved to imagine herself the idolized champion of the poor and suffering, the serene mistress of bountiful acres, where the season was always harvest and the labourers worthy of their hire. Coast and Waite were somehow out of the picture.

Then she heard the squelch of Jack's boots on the road behind her. At least, in dismissing Waite, she had fulfilled her role as champion of the oppressed. She saw herself for a moment as she hoped Jack saw her, calm mistress of his destiny snatching him from peril, and she smiled again at the vision.

Then she wondered how John would take it when she told him she had dismissed the beast man. But even this, she decided, did not matter, and so went down to Anderby.

8

THE STRANGER AT THE CROSS-ROADS

Mary drove home from Hardrascliffe along a dark, wind-swept road. She had been busy all the afternoon helping Ursula to establish herself in the nursing-home where she was to await the arrival of her child.

Ursula was not on easy person to help. She had actually made Mary feel an interloper in the nursing-home she had visited all her life, by that air of offhand familiarity with which she took possession of the whole staff. She had aroused all sorts of uncomfortable desires which Mary had thought were hidden deep beneath a weight of busy complacency.

Mary had believed she was cured of that disease. After all anyone could nurse a baby. Very few people had the privilege of nursing a whole village. Mary's tenderness benefited nearly three hundred people. Ursula's could only benefit one ridiculous thing that was not even quite a person. And, if John was a little dull, Mary was sure that Foster would have driven her crazy in three days let alone three years. The way in which he danced attendance on Ursula was perfectly sickening. Carnations at 6d. each in her bedroom indeed!

All the same, Mary knew she was not cured.

The cart turned in to the last street of the town. The air grew colder and more unfriendly. Between blackened chimney stacks Mary could see tattered wisps of cloud driven across a smouldering sky. In a minute the storm would break. Still, she was glad she was driving into the storm, not lying between some one else's sheets in a strange room, watched over by a lynx-eyed nurse, all starch and propriety. A doctor, too, dropping in at all hours to stare at her cheerfully and declare, 'We're coming along nicely, aren't we?'

Having a baby was all very well, but it seemed to afford other people an excuse for conspiring against one's dignity.

With a rattle of hail stones on the splash board and harness, the storm swept down upon her. She bent her head and drove forward. Really for March this was outrageous!

She wondered if she had remembered all her shopping: the flannel for Mrs Burton's little boy, the currants and matches and mincing machine.

Ursula had *crêpe de Chine* night dresses and the basinet in the corner was covered with lace and pink ribbon. Dreadful extravagance! Foster would be ruined before he knew where he was.

She touched the pony with her whip. He sprang forward eager for the stable. Then he hesitated and dropped into a stumbling limp. Mary put down the whip, drew up to the side of the road, and threw the rug across her seat.

It was very dark now and Starlight was restless. She climbed carefully out of the cart, speaking aloud in a comforting voice:

'It's all right, old man, it's all right.'

Her attempts at conciliation were not very effective. Starlight stood, scraping the ground with his hoof. Mary felt her way cautiously along the shaft and bent to pick up the pony's foreleg. She could not see, and her groping fingers unexpectedly encountering his knee made him start violently.

Well, there was no help for it. She would have to get a light. That was a nuisance. She went back and reached one of the cart lamps. It clattered as she drew it from its socket, and again the pony jerked forward. She only just caught the reins in time.

It was all rather complicated – like one of those puzzles, Mary decided, where one had to take the geese across the stream without leaving the ducks behind with the fox. There were newly-strewn flints on the road, one of which was obviously in Starlight's hoof; but the wind whirled against her and nearly extinguished the light, and if she put it down she could not see Starlight's foot – besides, he was irritated by pain and would not stand still.

There really seemed to be no way out of the dilemma. She stood, holding the reins, and watching the steam rising from the pony's back in the glow of candlelight. If she were Mrs Watts, she supposed she would pray about it. Prayer always seemed a rather cowardly shifting of responsibility on to other people, but what was one to do?

'Is anything wrong? Can I help?' A voice spoke out of the darkness.

She started violently, having heard no footsteps. Below her

usual appearance of composure, she had always retained a childish terror of the dark.

Starlight was startled too and looked round with a rattle of harness. Mary handed the lamp to a pair of hands that reached for it into the light, and turned to pacify the pony.

'Poor old man! Poor old Starlight! Was the pain bad then?' She turned ungratefully upon the new-comer. 'Whatever made you come up so quietly like that, frightening the pony?'

'I'm sorry. I expect the storm stopped you from hearing me. I thought something was wrong. I'll go away if you like.'

'No. Hold the lantern, please. There's a stone in the pony's foot I think.' Mary spoke haughtily. She was ashamed of her display of nervous irritation, and shame always made her haughty.

The lantern held by the stranger cast a delta of golden light on the stony road and the pony's hoof, which Mary raised to her knee. There, safely embedded behind the iron shoe, lay an ugly-looking flint.

'Have you a knife?' asked Mary.

Her hands were trembling, because the pony's breath came short and nervously. Every minute she expected him to start forward, and her imagination depicted her prostrate figure trampled below his hoofs.

'I've got a knife, but it isn't much good. One blade's broken. I might try, though, if you'll let me. You'll get so muddy.'

'I won't,' lied Mary stoutly. One knee was in a puddle, and she felt very wet, but she hated being seen at a disadvantage, and thought that her dignity could only be maintained by independence. 'Give me the knife, please.'

He passed it to her in silence, and she fumbled with frozen fingers at the blade.

'Can't you undo it for me?' she complained querulously.

The stranger unfastened the blade and stood silently holding the lamp. Mary struggled with the flint, but her usually capable hands were incapacitated by cold. The lamplight danced and glimmered across the snow. Cold trickles of melting sleet insinuated themselves between her collar and her neck. The flint did not move.

The stranger spoke again, very meekly:

'Won't you let me try?'

Mary stiffened herself for a refusal. Then he added plaintively: 'After all, it's my knife, and you're breaking the only whole blade.'

It was a young voice, certainly cultured, and possibly might have been attractive, had its owner not been suffering from an obvious cold.

'All right.' Her assent was ungracious. 'You can come if you like.'

She rose stiffly to her feet and took the lantern. The stranger knelt in her place. She could see slim shoulders below a mackintosh and the back of a bent head covered with red hair.

The shoulders worked for a moment. Then a triumphant 'Got it!' announced the success of masculine superiority. Unfortunately at that moment Starlight also 'Got it.' His foot being at last released he sprang forward, ungratefully knocking his benefactor to the ground.

Mary seized the pony's head. The stranger rolled adroitly towards the middle of the road and there was a small confusion.

Mary cried 'Are you hurt?'

The stranger said 'Damn!' calmly and without prejudice.

Starlight backed slowly towards the hedge.

Then things became more peaceable.

The stranger rose rubbing his shoulder and announcing strangely:

'There are no bones broken, but the patient must be kept quiet.' It was then that Mary first suspected him of not being quite sane.

Mary, who had managed in the confusion to retain her hold of the lantern, said:

'Oh, I'm so sorry. It's such a shame. And I was being so horrid to you, because you startled me, and really I was longing for some one to come.'

Together they drew Starlight cautiously away from the hedge and replaced the lamp in its socket.

'Where are you going?' asked Mary. She had time now to notice that they stood near the crossroads where the road to Anderby dissects that between Cattlesby and Beaverthorpe.

The stranger was brushing mud and water from his trousers.

'Well,' he remarked ingenuously, 'do you know, I'm not at all sure?'

'But where do you *want* to go?' repeated Mary. No one could possibly go wandering about just anywhere on a night like this – not if they were in their senses.

'I don't think I want to go anywhere.'

His voice was suddenly small and pathetic. 'In fact, I'm sorry, but I think I'm going to be sick.'

He was.

Compunction seized upon Mary.

'Oh, I'm so awfully sorry! Are you hurt badly?'

She thought the pony must have struck him in some vital

94

part of his anatomy. A desperate sense of helplessness assailed her. Supposing the man died here by the roadside, and she miles away from a doctor, unable to lift him into the high cart, unwilling to leave him alone in the dark. On the other hand he might only have had too much to drink.

'I'm all right now.' The stranger's voice was shaky but more cheerful. To Mary's relief he walked across the road quite firmly and stood by the cart. 'I wasn't really much hurt, only sort of winded and very much surprised. I know it's bad manners. I'm sorry.'

He actually laughed, but his teeth were chattering, and he held tightly to the shaft as though he were not sure of his balance.

Crises made Mary practical. 'Can you get into the cart?' she asked. Without further comment he climbed up and sat down in her seat. 'That's my seat. Please move to the other side. And take care, the pony always starts forward directly I get in.'

She scrambled up and they drove forward in silence. It was very dark.

'Are you all right?'

'Quite, thanks. Only a little shaken, not hurt at all. I shouldn't have let go like that so soon, I always go and spoil things at the end.'

'Do you? Oh, I know that feeling so well! I do it too. And it's so much worse than if you'd been stupid all the time, isn't it? Because you forget all the times you've been clever and only forget what happened at the end.'

Mary couldn't think why she said that. She did not usually talk in that sort of way. She did not usually feel so excited, as though something wonderful was going to happen. And yet it was nothing to give a stranger a lift on a stormy night. She pulled herself together.

'Look here, do you really want to go this way?'

'Where are we going?'

'Towards Anderby.'

'What a pretty name! Yes, let's go there.'

As though it were a matter of free choice, made on the impulse of the moment because of a nice name!

Mary turned towards him with frowning brows. The drink theory recurred to her. She wished it was not quite so dark. Or he might be suffering from concussion of the brain. It did make people queer.

She stopped the cart and began to turn the pony towards Hardrascliffe. She must find the doctor.

'What are you doing?'

'I'm turning the cart. We've come the wrong way.'

'This is the way we were going before. We're going to Anderby.'

'Yes, but we want to go to Hardrascliffe.'

She must humour him.

'We don't want to go to Hardrascliffe. You were wanting to go to Anderby. So was I, though I didn't know it. How far is it?'

'Three miles, but—'

'Please go on. Is it on my account you want to turn back? Because if it is, please don't. I'm quite all right. I suppose there's an inn or something there where I can stay the night. And I'm quite well. Only muddy. I had this cold before I fell,' he added apologetically.

'But, really' – Mary was only half reassured – 'where were you going? You must have been going somewhere.'

'I really don't know where I was going. I suppose I was lost. But now I'm going to Anderby. Once I've made up my mind to do things I always do them. And really, in a wet March, one village is much the same as another.'

'But what are you *doing*?'

'Oh, didn't I explain? I'm on a walking tour.'

'What on earth are you doing going for a walking tour in March with a cold in your head?'

'I didn't start with the cold. It came. It's my job.'

'The cold?' Mary was completely mystified.

'No. The tour. The cold's my necessary infirmity. All great men have them. Look at Julius Caesar with his epilepsy and Pepys with his stone – I beg your pardon. That's not quite polite, is it? Look at St. Paul then, and the thorn in his flesh, and me with my colds.'

'But how are walking tours your job?' Mary clung resolutely to the point to save herself from complete insanity.

'Because I'm a sort of a journalist on a holiday. I got headaches in Manchester, reporting and writing silly articles and things in the very plainest street you ever saw, so my chief, who is a very decent fellow, suggested that I should walk about in Yorkshire a bit, collecting materials about the life of the agricultural labourer, and lots of juicy statistics about capitalist farmers that will make them sit up and see the iniquity of their ways. Do you know anything about them?'

'Capitalist farmers?'

A little while ago Mary thought she knew very little. Mr David Rossitur had enlightened her. She added smilingly, 'I think I know a good deal. You see, I am one.'

The stranger threw back his head with a laugh. It was that

laugh which betrayed at once both his youth and his sanity. Nothing so gallant and infectious could have come from a diseased mind. His laugh seemed to shake the years from Mary and set her again in the company of youth.

'My sworn enemy!' he cried. 'Don't you think you'd better set me down? I warn you, you are bringing a traitor into your camp. I am a rabid socialist of the dangerous and most disreputable type.'

'You are nothing so romantic,' retorted Mary. 'You are quite a young boy with a bad cold who has just been sick in the middle of the road, and you are coming home with me. Evidently you are quite unfit to be wandering about the wolds by yourself. I don't care whether you're a socialist or not. If you're rabid, it just shows that you're not capable of looking after yourself.'

'I'm not a boy. I'm twenty-four, and I take myself and my politics very seriously. It's the prerogative of mediocrity. And I'm out to smash your rotten social system into little bits.' Then he sneezed three times. 'And I warn you that I will never break bread in the house of a declared enemy of society.'

'I never asked you to,' Mary replied. Her pulses were beating furiously. A queer excitement caught her by the throat. She forced herself to be very matter-of-fact. 'I think you will be very silly to smash anything. It's so wasteful. I think socialism and all that very silly. So does my husband.'

For the life of her, Mary could not think why she had dragged John into it.

'I read a book,' she continued, 'about a month ago. A very silly book called *The Salvation of Society* by David Rossitur. He thought he was so clever and modern because he prophesied that England was going to the dogs. My sister-in-law, Sarah, came to exactly the same conclusion long ago, though she hasn't been to college.'

Mary spoke with heat. She felt annoyed because she could not talk more cleverly, though it was silly to be excited about a book, when the boy beside her, socialist or no socialist, was cold and wet and needing a hot drink.

'I'm glad you didn't like the book. It shows your sound judgment. I think it's rotten. Pessimism is the refuge of the unimaginative. I've outgrown all those destructive ambitions long ago, though when I wrote it—'

'When you – what?'

'When I wrote it I thought it was rather clever.'

'But – what do you mean? You're not the author, are you?'

She turned towards him, but the darkness came between them, an impenetrable curtain.

'I'm afraid I am. My name's David Rossitur.' His teeth were chattering with cold. 'But of course I see now that co-operation, fostered from above simply with the idea of ultimate revolution, can never result in constructive reform. Now my idea is . . . '

In the darkness Mary could dimly discern a hand waved with passionate gesticulation. She chuckled softly. David Rossitur suddenly checked himself.

'Of course, now you know who I am, you probably won't want me in your cart.' He spoke with dignity.

Mary laughed. 'I'm delighted that you're David Rossitur. It's very exciting, sitting in the same cart as a real live author, and still more exciting to think that you can take him home and put him to bed with eucalyptus and hot whisky, just to show

99

what a very ordinary person he is. Now you can't be dignified when you're inhaling Friars' Balsam.'

'I've not been very dignified at all,' sighed David. 'And really you must put me down at the village inn. I know what these colds are. I shall be sneezing all over your house for days if once you let me in. Please tell me where I can find the inn or something.'

'You're coming home with me,' said Mary firmly.

The church clock was striking nine as they drove up the avenue. The light of a lantern swung fitfully towards them across the stack-yard.

'That you, shepherd?' called Mary. 'Is everything all right?'

A tall figure loomed out of the darkness and the swinging lantern stopped beside the cart.

'We've just landed a lovely little pair o' twins, Miss Mary. Prime little beauties. Black as a parson's cask.'

It was a moment before David decided he meant 'cassock.'

'Good,' said Mary, and turned to grope for parcels on the floor of the cart. 'You see,' she explained to David, her head under the seat, 'it's lambing time, and I get all the black ones. Isn't it a night, shepherd? You'd better come in for a drop of whisky, I think. Now then' – she re-emerged, her hands full – 'is that everything? Mr Rossitur, will you please look and see if the mincing-machine is below your seat, and I think you're sitting on the cheese. Now, Shepherd, what about the shelter in the horse pasture? Did you get it up this afternoon?'

'Ay. Maister Robson lent a hand and all.'

David climbed out of the cart and stood silently in the rain while Mary handed over the pony to a groom, who appeared from the darkness, and recounted to him in detail the tale of the flints. David felt very cold and sore and stiff. Also he was holding a mincing-machine, a Stilton cheese, four pounds of sugar, and the roll of cotton wool for Mrs Watts. Still it was all very entertaining and the lady of the farm seemed unusually kind and companionable.

The lady of the farm summoned him, and following her and the shepherd, he stumbled across a spacious yard and up a step into another enclosure of inky darkness. A door rattled in front of him, and a flood of orange light streamed across the snow. Standing in the doorway, he saw a tall broad shouldered young woman, wrapped in a dark coat. Her cheeks were whipped to crimson by the sleet, her wide eyes shone; her lips were parted in a welcoming smile.

'Come in,' said Mary.

He followed her into the brick-tiled kitchen and stood there silently dripping, his arms full of parcels. Violet from her station by the fire-place regarded him open mouthed. Mary gave hurried instructions about sheets on the North room bed, and hot whisky and something to eat at once.

'May I put these down on the table?' asked David, ruefully regarding the mincing-machine, cheese, sugar and cotton wool. 'Then I can take off my cap like a gentleman.'

'It's off already,' remarked Mary, taking the parcels from him. 'I suppose you lost it on the road. Give me those.'

She saw him plainly now as he stood with little rivulets of water running off him on to the floor. His clothes clung to a slim, drenched figure that was not so tall as Mary's. Thin wrists above nervous, delicate hands protruded from a jacket whose sleeves were too short. David was small, but his neck, wrists and ankles always seemed to be straining out of his clothes, so eager were they to get on with this tremendous task of reforming the world. His face was a pallid grey tinged with purple, because he was very cold and still felt rather sick and more than a little tired. His eyes were grey too, not very large, but amazingly alive for all their weariness, and his thin lips had a humorous twist, half gay and half pathetic, that went straight to Mary's heart.

At present he was the colour of mud all over except his hair. The only peculiarity which David could ever share with Samson was that the secret of his personality lay in his hair, for David's was wild and wiry, the colour of very old wet bricks. It started up everywhere over his head, declaring brazenly to the world its owner's intention of going everywhere and seeing everything and smashing up heaven and earth in an hour to build new ones next day.

Before Mary had completed her inspection, heavy footsteps clumped along the passage, and David saw a tall bearded man standing by the doorway. He was not very like Mary, but David decided he must be her father.

'Oh, John,' said Mary, 'this is Mr David Rossitur. And he is very wet. Can I have some of your clothes for him? Mr Rossitur, this is my husband.'

An hour later David, who had completely abandoned all former notions of correct behaviour in a strange house, lay back against the pillows of an enormous bed in a candlelit room, while Mary sat beside him and rubbed his chest with Elliman's Embrocation. It was the biggest bed he had ever seen, and John's pyjamas in which he was enveloped were the biggest pyjamas he had ever seen. But the meal of hot whisky and tea and fish and cheese cakes, which he had just eaten, was the queerest he had ever tasted, the interview between the shepherd and his mistress the strangest he had ever heard, so nothing, he felt, could really surprise him now.

He surrendered himself with resignation to the firm hand of Mary.

'You're going to have a shocking cold, Mr Rossitur,' she remarked severely. 'I simply can't imagine why anyone in their senses allowed you to wander loose in the country at this time of year. Where do you live when you're not losing yourself in Yorkshire?'

David, speaking as distinctly as he could while Mary's energetic hand paraded between his collar bones, replied that he did not exactly live anywhere. He'd given up his digs in Manchester because the landlady underpaid her maid and he refused to countenance sweated labour. A fine comment on the same refusal was lost in a shudder as a cold stream of embrocation trickled gleefully down his arm-pit.

'Keep still. It isn't cold really. I warmed the bottle. You don't look as if you came from Manchester. People there are usually rather sensible. *Don't* wriggle so!'

'You're tickling. Although I'm very grateful for all your trouble, I cannot help observing that you are tickling. At least, the embrocation is. I've only lived a year in Manchester. I lived in Hampshire until I quarrelled with my father and cut myself off with a shilling. Then Manchester seemed as good a place as any to – atishoo! Tishoo!'

'Quite so. I understand perfectly. When you have quite finished, I'll put this flannel on your chest.'

David, now completely tamed, bared his bosom for the sacrifice. Mary regarded it critically.

'I'm sure they don't feed you properly at Manchester.'

'I always was thin as a child. It's nothing to do with the amount I eat. You can't have such a beautiful disposition as I've got, and not expect some counterbalancing disadvantages.'

Tears gathered in David's eyes but they were only the result of a copious inhalation of embrocation. He fumbled for the pocket of John's pyjamas, where a handkerchief once had lain. 'I had a handkerchief, I know. But it is a strange habit of my handkerchief common to nearly all my possessions, that it vanishes when I most need it.'

He was wondering what Harcourt would think, if he could see him now – Harcourt, the president of the Union at Oxford, who wrote to him once a fortnight to implore his immediate resumption to a brilliant university career, abandoned for the purgatory of third-rate journalism. The phraseology is Harcourt's.

'Oh, I'm glad you have a beautiful disposition,' remarked Mary, passing him her handkerchief. I know you won't go off with my teaspoons then. I never trust socialists as a rule.'

She corked the bottle decisively, and wiped her hands on a towel. She was enveloped in a large white apron, and her hair, as usual when it had been wet, curled in soft brown tendrils round her flushed face. She knew that she looked rather pretty, but she announced sternly:

'Now the candles and matches are here, and you're not to get up in the morning till I've been to take your temperature. I expect you'll go to sleep now because you've had so much whisky and stuff you must be a little sleepy. You don't feel sick again, do you?'

'Oh, no, thanks.'

'That's all right then. Good night.'

'Good night. Oh, I say, Mrs Robson, I've never said thank you yet. I expect you'll think me awfully queer, but I do think you're a brick. I've been a perfect nuisance. I wouldn't have let you do all this only it's so nice to be made a fuss of.'

Mary smiled down upon him. She seemed all rosy cheeks and white apron, and candlelight.

She told him that there was a glass of water by his side in case he was thirsty in the night, and that if he felt ill John's room and hers was only along the passage.

A sudden desire had seized her to kiss this absurd, fragile boy whose mocking, wistful eyes watched her from the pillows. Only he might mistake her strictly maternal intentions, not realizing, like many young things, how very young he was.

She took up her candle and left him. In the other room John lay solidly on the shadowed bed, large and tranquil and very very different.

She did not stoop to kiss him, though that would have been perfectly proper.

Meanwhile David lay staring into the darkness. He was very tired and stiff, and his throat felt as though some one were rubbing it with hot sand paper. John's large pyjamas were wrinkled below his bruised shoulder.

Thoughts streamed through his brain like sheep through the gap in a hedge. A week had passed since he left Manchester and he had written nothing. Why did the shepherd persistently wink one eye? Was it because 'in modern agriculture the increased productiveness and quantity of the labour set in motion are bought at the cost of laying waste and consuming by disease labour-power itself?' Why, that was Marx! How silly. Good old Marx. He told the truth if no one else did.

Only what was the use of trying to fight injustice if one always caught colds in one's head and was sick after a few days' tramping? Colds, sore throats – well, that was what a thousand labourers, underpaid and underfed, must be feeling ... feeling, ... that dull ache all down one's side ... feeling ...

Mary Robson, a large, rather comely woman, standing in the doorway with a flood of orange light behind her ... her hands, rosily transparent in front of the candle flame ... the smell of embrocation ... 'consuming by disease labour-power itself.' ... 'Mr Rossitur, this is my husband.' ... Queens – kings ... queens with smiling faces in orange candlelight ...

Because he had a cold, David snored a little in his sleep.

9

THE ENEMIES OF SOCIETY

'That's all very well, but when you've said everything you know the fact remains that you're not a farmer and never will be. You seem to have spent your time at a large country-house where you were as far removed from the agricultural classes as though you were in the moon, and at Oxford where as far as I can make out you pretend to know something about everything without having learnt it. And you've read a few books by Germans and cranks, none of whom have done more than look into a farm from across the hedge from the high-road. And now you come to Anderby, and pretend you know more about farming than John and me, who've done it all our lives, and our fathers before us for hundreds of years! Just hold the end of this sheet, will you?'

Mary was turning linen sheets 'sides to middle' and arguing with David about the nationalization of land. David took the end of the sheet solemnly while her scissors slipped along the middle.

'It all depends what you call knowledge,' he said. 'You only know what your villagers are. I know what they might be. Perfect knowledge recognizes capacity as well as achievement. That's why I know more about it than you do.'

Clip! Mary's scissors cut through the hem near David's fingers.

'What next?' he asked patiently. It was difficult to portray his pet theories with becoming dignity when at any moment Mary might fill his arms with yards of linen, or send him on to his knees after a strayed cotton reel.

'Next you put the two pieces together like this – no, not that end, the other, and then I sew them up the middle. You see, Mr Rossitur, my point is that Anderby has been pretty much the same for four hundred years, and I don't see how talk is going to alter it. When it comes to that, I don't see it wants altering. That idea of small holdings you were talking about may do all right in some places, but, believe me, it's absurd on farms where you grow wheat and rear sheep.'

She took a pin from the sheet and placed it between her teeth, then removed it to give greater emphasis to her statement.

'It's so *stupid* to unsettle something that's quite happy as it is just because of a silly theory.'

'But they're not happy here, and it isn't silly.'

'Of course you don't think so – just put some more coal on the fire please – I've heard all that before. You've got heaps of statistics, but you confessed yourself just now they were nearly all drawn up in the last century. Don't you see how behind the times you are? Because fifty years ago the labourers were underpaid, it doesn't mean they're not all right to-day. Just you wait till your cold's quite better, and you can have a look at my people in Anderby.'

'It's not I who am behind the times, Mrs Robson, it's you,' he responded hotly. 'You've just acknowledged the evils of a benevolent despotism, and now you deny that your rule is a despotism because it's benevolent. Why, what hope is there for social stability when the happiness of men is a matter of phil-anthropy, not of right? If you and Mr Robson were rotters, Anderby wouldn't be fit to live in.'

Mary bent over her sewing-machine, and the wheel span with amazing rapidity. David regarded her across the table. She was maddening, with her amused complacency, her indifference to all his arguments. And yet kind, and intelligent too in a way, and not without a sense of social responsibility. Clearly a con-vert worth making. He started again.

'You think you're a queen because you govern this village and your subjects seem to like you. The only real kings and queens are those who stand above their generation and rule cir-cumstance.'

Mary looked up and smiled indulgently.

'Do sit down,' she said. 'You'll get another temperature with so much talking.'

'It's no argument, Mrs Robson, either to send me after a cotton reel or to tell me I've got a cold. The one is on the table. The other is on my chest. You are shirking issues, and only rob-bing me of my dignity without gaining any yourself!'

'But it's a great advantage to me to rob you of your dignity. Look at you! A full blown author, who has published a book, though you do say a lot of silly things in it. And who has been to college, though you don't seem to have been taught much sense there! If I do try to bring you to my level a bit, by making you mend the fire – and, by the way, you've held that shovel in your hands for quite five minutes – surely you can't complain, you, who so hotly uphold the cause of equality.'

'You are cruel,' groaned David. His mock-heroic voice was rendered doubly effective by the cold in his throat, and Mary looked up to laugh. But he suddenly sat down, his elbows on the table, and his chin resting on his hands. 'Honestly though,' he added seriously, 'can't you see a little bit what I'm driving at, or am I unutterably stupid and boring? Or am I just rude? I don't want to be just rude, because you've been kinder to me than I could possibly have imagined.'

'What you call kindness,' remarked Mary, with an airy gesture of her scissors, 'was merely a piece of propaganda on behalf of my fellow-capitalists. What I'm really worried about is that you will insist on going to-morrow. You're not fit to, you know. You had a temperature till last night.'

'But I can't stay here. I've taken up three of your days already, and though I may consider you waste your time, trying to pauperize a village, and might spend it far more profitably restoring to health a friend of society like myself, I can't exactly expect you to look at it that way, can I?'

'Oh, do be serious for a minute. You know that you're not any trouble here. John regards you as a harmless lunatic who would be quite a pleasant fellow if he didn't pretend to know something of agricultural conditions. And I find you very useful in folding sheets for me – to say nothing of keeping my wits about me. You are a very strenuous conversationalist.'

'All right. I will be serious.' He seated himself on the table. It was always impossible for him to remain in the same attitude for two consecutive minutes. 'I can't stay here because I mean to blow up this house, and this farm and, if necessary, this village. I think that you and Mr Robson are charming as people, but iniquitous as an institution; and, if I stay here any longer, I shall like you both so much that I shan't be able to hate you. As it is, every time you are nice to me, I have to recite little pieces of Marx to myself to convince me what an abomination you really are.'

Mary's eyes twinkled.

'Oh, do recite some now,' she begged.

'Oh, but you're not being particularly nice to me. Look how hard you've been making me work! I'm sure I've sides-to-mid-dled enough sheets to stock the East Riding.'

'Well then, stop working, and have a cigarette – oh, I forgot, you don't smoke. Well, then, sit down and be at peace – and have some toffee.'

They had made the toffee last night, after Mary discovered that David had abjured smoking on principle, and adored sweet things. She had declared it to be an essential item of the treatment for colds, and had shown him how to mix sugar and treacle and vinegar over the dining-room fire.

David passed her the tin, placed a large lump of toffee in the side of his mouth, and lay back luxuriously in John's arm-chair. Presently he began to chant:

'Nowhere does the antagonistic character of capitalist production assert itself more brutally than in the progress of English agriculture and the retrogression of the English agricultural labourer . . . '

There were voices in the hall, and a knock at the door. Violet entered the room. Mary saw, to her horror, a smudge down one side of Violet's nose, and her cap awry above her left ear. She announced spasmodically:

'Mr and Mrs Bannister, m'm!'

Sarah, in her bugled bonnet and calling cloak, sailed into the room.

'My God!' murmured David, under his breath.

Mary rose. She would have been more capable of dealing with the situation had her mouth not been full of toffee, but her composure was heroic.

'This is nice of you!' she said. 'Good afternoon, Tom. Come along in, Cousin Sarah. You'll excuse the room being rather upset. I'm mending sheets. Mr Rossitur – Mrs Bannister, Mr Bannister.'

'Is John in?' asked Sarah, going briskly to the point.

'No, he's up the fields. He won't be long, though. I'm sorry.'

'Oh, I'm sorry too. I particularly wished to see him.' Sarah had bowed stiffly to David, and paid him no further attention.

'He ought to be in about five, but he's gone to Littledale to see how the new barley is doing – the sort that Burdass brought over from Siberia.'

'Quite.'

'But you'll wait and have tea, won't you?'

'That depends how late it is.'

Then they were all silent. It was dreadful, Mary thought. Sarah, refusing to remove her cloak or bonnet, sat erect on one of the more uncompromising leather-covered chairs. Tom hovered, ill at ease, in the background. The only tranquil person was David, who stood silently polite, but, Mary guessed, secretly entertained, on the hearth-rug. Once he cast a look of whimsical inquiry at his hostess.

'Did you put your trap up?' asked Mary.

'Yes, thank you. There was no groom in the yard, so Tom had to unyoke by himself.'

'Oh. I'm sorry. You see, we only have one man to do the stable and the garden, and he happens to be in the garden this afternoon.'

She tried to sound indifferent; but she was wracked with anxiety. Sarah was obviously annoyed about something. John might not be home for ever so long. Then, worst of all, the Bannisters were the last people whom she wished to encounter David Rossitur. They would disapprove of him dreadfully.

'Which way did you come?' she asked.

'We came from Hardrascliffe. I have been to see Ursula.'

'Oh, any news?'

Sarah cast a decorous eye at David.

'None,' she remarked discreetly.

Mary smiled. David already knew all about Ursula. For a stranger whom she had only known three days, he must have heard a good many queer things, she thought.

'I think it was most inconsiderate of Ursula to go into a Hardrascliffe nursing home. It is a very long drive there.'

'Perhaps she did not realize that so many of her relations would go to call on her.'

'She knew we would do our duty. She had no right to make it so uncomfortable.'

She may have thought she had a right to make it impossible, thought Mary. Here for once she agreed with Ursula. She tried to change the conversation. There were two topics she especially wished to avoid – Ursula and socialism. She tried to escape from one without encountering the other. If only

113

she had had time to warn David not to air his views in company!

'Were the roads very bad?' she asked.

Sarah ignored her efforts.

'Naturally,' she continued, determined to air her grievance, 'she must realize that we take an interest in the only child in that generation of Robsons.'

'Of course.'

'And naturally she realizes that we are glad for her to take every precaution.'

Mary resigned herself to the inevitable. At least this could hurt no one but herself.

'It will be a comfort to know that Middlethorpe at least won't pass in to the hands of strangers when Foster dies,' continued Sarah.

Mary flushed. It wasn't fair, she thought, for Sarah to reproach her for something that was not her fault. It wasn't fair to remind her of one of the things she was always trying to forget.

'Aren't you a little premature?' she asked. 'The child isn't born yet.'

Tom who stood awkwardly looking out of the window coughed. David smiled his twisted smile.

Sarah drew herself up. 'It will be,' she said. 'Ursula's not the girl to fail us in this kind of thing.'

'No, I suppose not. I hear you've been having your house painted, Tom.'

Sarah frowned. The house belonged to her, and she belonged to a people that treats ownership seriously.

'We intended to paint,' she replied for her husband. 'It is the year for painting. In fact when last we had it done I said to Tom, in 1913 we will have it done all over.'

'But aren't you going to, then?'

Mary looked from Tom to Sarah. Painting was a safe topic. It afforded no possible opening for David. If David started to tell Sarah what he thought about capitalist farmers, it would be terrible. Strangely enough, she was thinking, 'It will be terrible for Mr Rossitur. He's never met anyone like Sarah before, I'm sure.' She wanted to protect him from the rigidity of her sister-in-law's defiance to progress. She played for time.

'Why aren't you painting?'

'There are some things, Mary, which I never thought I should have to put up with. And one of them is the insolence of local work people. A Billings has painted houses for Robsons round Market Burton since my grandfather's days, and never but what there was straight dealing all round.'

'Oh dear, have you been having trouble?' From the corner of her eye she could see that David had cocked his head at the mention of 'work people,' as a terrier pricks his ears when you mention rats.

'Trouble? I don't have trouble when there is any impertinence from my dependents, Mary. I dismiss them.'

'Yes, but what happened?'

'They had begun last Tuesday to scrape the paint off the front porch. We were to have three coats of that good dark green. What I cannot stand are those vulgar fawns and reds that people seem so fond of now. We have always had green on the front door since I was a child.'

'Did Billings want to paint you red, then?'

She was conscious of a sudden convulsive movement from

David, temporarily overcome by the idea of anyone painting Mrs Bannister red.

'Well. I'll say nothing of that, though at the time we may have had words.' Sarah was eyeing David up and down, slowly and deliberately, a habit of hers when encountering strangers in a relative's drawing-room. If she had possessed a *lorgnette*, Mary was sure she would have used it now. 'I say nothing of the colour, but when I wanted them to stay for five minutes longer in the evening to finish off round the bell – you know what a mess it makes if you leave it overnight round the bell – would they stay? They said, if you please and by your leave, that their union wouldn't let them work overtime. Their union indeed! A pretty pass we're coming to if we have to be told what's right by a union! At my own front door too!'

Unions! Heavens, David's favourite opening! Three days had taught Mary the danger signals. She rushed into the breach.

'Oh, yes, how trying! Now, Cousin Sarah, wouldn't you like' – she was about to add – 'to take your cloak off,' but David forestalled her.

Turning from the fire-place towards Sarah he regarded her with his most charming smile, and running one thin hand through his hair – a favourite gesture, he began, with dangerous calm:

'But, Mrs Bannister, don't you think there is something to be said for the unions?'

'Now, young man, if you've anything to say for the unions you'd better say it. You may be very clever. I'm sure I don't know. All you young folk to-day think you know everything. I heard tell you were a socialist or something at Hardrascliffe to-day—'

'So that's why she called,' thought Mary. 'Ursula told her, and she wanted to see what he was like.'

'And you may have written books, and met a lot of people and done a deal of talking, but when you come up against Sarah Jane Bannister you'll find yourself in a very different situation.'

Well, of course, that settled it. There was no longer any hope of leading Sarah gently away to remove her bonnet. An appealing glance at David met with no response. Mary knew she might as well ask the wind to stop blowing as ask David to stop talking once Sarah had practically defied him to do his worst, her slow stare sweeping him from his red head to his shabbily shod feet.

'At least he's a gentleman,' thought Mary. 'Thank Heaven she can't help seeing that!'

And David spoke. For ten minutes not even Sarah was able to utter a word. Standing on the hearth-rug as though it were a public platform, his thin arms jerking with electric energy, he addressed them. At first he argued quietly enough about the disadvantages of capitalism, the need for co-operation among the lower classes, the slow growth of organized resistance. Slowly his passion rose. 'You can say what you like,' he cried. 'You can shut yourself up in snug little houses locked up against cold and change and misery, and you can say to yourselves "No change will come. We and our fathers have seen the world as it is. Only fools meant it to be, or think it can be any different. We, the middle class, the half-cultured, half-emancipated, half-refined middle class, with our safe bank balance, and vested interests and comfortable prosperity, we are the salt of the earth. We are in power – we are happy. Fools and extremists may rage and storm outside our gates. We are safe, fortified by the solidarity

of human conservatism, battening on the fruits of human folly."
But I tell you that your gates are shut, not to shield you from
the change, but to blind your eyes to it, till it is too late to see.
The nineteenth century has gone, and though you and your
class, unfortunately for England, have survived it, you can't
carry your century with you to the grave.'

Sarah blinked at him with wide, indignant eyes.

'You stand for an ideal that is, thank Heaven, outworn. The
new generation knocks at your door – a generation of men,
independent, not patronized, enjoying their own rights, not the
philanthropy of their exploiters, respecting themselves, not
their so-called superiors. You can't stop them, but they may stop
you. You can't shut them out, but they may shut you in.' He
swept his hand round with a dramatic gesture, that brought it
into unpremeditated contact with one of Mary's china jugs on
the mantelpiece. A tragedy was narrowly averted. 'I tell you
that you are locking yourselves up in a house of circumstance
which has been condemned as unsafe at the tribunal of
progress. You've got to move, and if you can't see that, there are
those waiting who will thrust realization upon you when it's too
late to find a remedy.'

He paused, out of breath, looking at Sarah with pleading
eyes. He really was sorry for her, as he was sorry for every one
who could not see his point of view. He wanted to help her, to
counteract by his eloquence opinions that were the deposit of
generations. He was still young enough to believe habit to be
amenable to reason.

Mary, horror-stricken, bent forward.

'Oh, Mr Rossitur,' she begged below her breath, 'do stop,
please.'

Sarah saw the action, though she could not hear the words. She rose with dignity.

'Thank you, Mary,' she said, 'for this most unusual form of entertainment. If John is not coming back soon, I think I'll be getting home. Come, Tom.'

Mary stood up, her hands full of linen sheets, her wide eyes troubled.

David saw that his conduct had in some way been disastrous. He came forward.

'Mrs Bannister, I'm awfully sorry. I shouldn't have ranted at you like that. It was awfully bad manners. I had no right – only it's my chief thought night and day and it makes me forget myself. If you'd rather not stay in the same room as me after what I've said, I'll go. Mrs Robson only took me in out of kind-ness because I had a cold—'

'It's quite unnecessary to apologize, young man. I assure you it makes no difference to me what you say or whether you stay or go. I'm sure my sister-in-law chooses her guests without ref-erence to the feelings of her relations, and far be it from me to drive anyone away.' She turned to Mary. 'I only wanted to give John a message from Tobias Robson.'

'Well, won't I do? Or won't you stay? John's sure not to be long.'

'Thank you. I really do not think I shall wait. I meant to get home before it came quite dark.' Seeing David's miserable face she added, 'Don't flatter yourself that I'm leaving on your account, young man. Let me tell you I've read all that sort of stuff before in the papers my maids leave about over Sunday. And, mark my words, you and your like nearly always end in prison and a lot of fuss over nothing.'

During the drive home Tom tried to pacify her.

'I'm sure it was rare nonsense that young fellow talked. But they don't mean half what they say, those chaps. It just comes out with a gush and there's no stopping it – like our old pump when the washer's gone.'

Sarah snorted. 'It's pretty clear that Anderby Wold's no place for John. When Ursula told me today that Mary had gone and picked up a sort of socialist tramp on the road I can't say I was surprised. Mary would do anything. I always knew she'd make a fool of herself one day. What he says to me is neither here nor there, though of all the impertinence I'm sure I never heard such. But what I say is, mark my words, if Mary takes up with folk like that, before long there'll be trouble at Anderby Wold and John will be the one to suffer!'

Meanwhile in the dining-room at Anderby David, scarlet with mortification, was standing among piles of linen.

'Oh, I can't tell you how sorry I am. Please forgive me! I can't think why I did it. It was insufferable. I—'

But Mary, who had lived for ten years with one of those ninety and nine just persons who had no need for repentance, found it sweet to forgive.

'Please don't be upset. It didn't matter. I'm sure it must do Sarah good to have a mental shaking up now and then.'

David was running his hands through his hair and changing colour from grey to scarlet.

'You've been ripping to me – ripping. And I've been nothing but a nuisance. I've upset this house for three days and now I go and am rude to your guests. And I'm not going to stop at that either,' he groaned. 'I've got to go out now into the village and tell your labourers that they're ill-treated when they're not, and unsettle things that are quite happy as they are. And there's no knowing where it'll all end.'

There wasn't. David did not know. Mary did not know. They looked at each other across the table, then David sat down and buried his face in his hands, half laughing, half miserable.

It really was funny. The whole thing was funny. Mrs Bannister's frigid face and the nodding osprey in her bonnet, and her nervous little husband clucking like a distracted hen in the background. And David, he was funny too, swooping down out of the darkness upon Mrs Robson, and cramming his social ideas into Sarah Bannister's inhospitable brain, or lack of brain – anyone so hopelessly enslaved to tradition must lack brain. He could see again his lean arms swaying and the tuft of hair rising with enthusiasm from his forehead.

It was always rather a trial to David that he could not help seeing how funny he had been when it was too late to alter things.

'You're not going to be sick again, are you?' asked Mary anxiously.

'No, I don't think so. I'm not feeling ill now. Only penitent. I'm not even surprised. I never am where I've done anything outrageous because I'm always doing it. I talked rather like that one night at Oxford when my father came as the "distinguished visitor" to the Union. He's a Tory M.P. you know. And after that we had a scene.' David's eyes twinkled at the recollection, though he found it sobering too, for he was as fond of his father as he could be of anyone so alien to his ideal of life. 'And he said that if this was what I was learning at Oxford I should be better away from it. And he'd only pay my fees if I'd promise to stop propagating scurrilous politics. And of course I couldn't, and there we were – and here I am. I can't think why I'm talk-ing like this about myself. You must be sick of the sight and sound of me.'

'I'm not. You're very young. You can't help it.'

'So you see I must leave you and to-night. I'd clear out of the village if I could, only it's the very centre of this part of the wolds and I've got to start somewhere – and even if I didn't some one else would.'

'It's all right, Mr Rossitur. You can't help it. You're made like that. After all I suppose it's far better to be carried away by your ideas than to have no ideas at all.'

It was just then that John came in. He was in a hearty mood.

'Going, Rossitur? Now why ever?'

Preaching socialism was a fool's job. He'd far better give it up and take on with something else. Of course if he felt he had to do it, there was an end on't, but he wouldn't get much change out of Anderby. He'd a deal better stay there and amuse Mary, who must be dull sometimes. She was looking better already since he had come.

But David went.

Mary, drawing the curtains that night, thought of David and wondered if they had aired his sheets at the *Flying Fox*. His cold wasn't nearly well.

Poor boy! He cared so intensely for such silly things. Life was never kind to people who cared as much as that.

If it was land they cared for, it denied them heirs; if it was ideas, it proved them false.

Of course some people never wanted anything very much. Like John. She could never imagine John eating out his heart in longing for the unattainable. He was safe enough, securely fenced in behind his limitations. But David – David who believed in such stupid things that were bound to let him down one day, David who was such a child, who needed so much some one who could help him when the inevitable hour of disappointment came – what was one to do for him?

If John had been like David she would have watched and protected him. If John had been like David ... If David had been John ...

She snapped the fastener down decisively.

There were some things that it was wiser not to think about.

10

THE PROPHET AND THE MOON

At six o'clock the following evening all Anderby was having tea. From fifty chimneys in the valley rose columns of white smoke. In the Hinds' house at the Wold Farm, the foreman was carving a huge beef pie while Ezra Dawson buried his face in a mug of steaming tea. Mike O'Flynn, paying tribute to his military training, washed himself with indiscreet enthusiasm over the kitchen sink. Jack Greenwood, whose agricultural career had brightened somewhat after Waite's dismissal, sat by his mother's table stuffing his mouth with cold bacon while for the seventh time that evening he explained how he had 'mothered up' in the horse pasture.

In the Wold Farm John and Mary faced each other across cold ham and boiled eggs. Both of them disliked cold ham and boiled eggs, but Mary had driven to Market Burton that afternoon and had found no time to prepare a hot meal. Besides for the last three days they had fared sumptuously on chickens and scrambled eggs in honour of a guest.

One of the few people in Anderby who was not having tea sat in the 'smoke-room' of the *Flying Fox* and wished himself back at Oxford – or even Manchester.

David's omission of tea resulted from a disquieting interview he had had that morning with his account book, after which he had been convinced that only by the strictest economy could he afford to spend another fortnight on an unremunerative tour of research and propaganda. He had lunched at twelve o'clock on bread and cheese and beer. He would presently sup on similar wholesome fare. Tea was a superfluous luxury, easily foregone by one who was determined to live as the labourers lived. All the same, the scent of frying sausages and bacon from Mrs Todd's kitchen across the passage was irritatingly savoury. Against his will, David found himself recalling memories of brekkers in Harcourt's rooms at the House, of dinners at the paternal table in Hampshire, even of beefsteaks eaten in the congenial company of Merryweather, the journalist, and Moore, the lecturer on economics, in a chop-house near the Manchester offices of the *Northern Clarion*.

This was not at all what he had intended to think about. Really, he must pull himself together and forget his physical demands for a little. Unfortunately, there was nothing particularly pleasant to distract his attention. The smoke-room of the *Flying Fox* was not a beautiful place. David had decided, when he first saw it, that romantic novelists describing the picturesque interiors of wayside taverns could never have dreamed of such a room.

It was hateful. David hated the bilious green of its painted walls. He hated the wooden table, covered with brown oilcloth. He hated the unfriendly outline of the high-backed settle, and the china spitoons, and the smoking lamp. Most of all, he hated the smoke-grimed placard that hung against the wall, and announced to all comers that Bass's Beer could be obtained on the premises. Why Bass? Why not Symond's Ale – no, he was Soups – or – David failed to recall other brewers of renown.

The only comfortable thing in the room was the fire, leaping and crackling like a live creature. David bent towards it, warming his hands.

'Praised by my Lord for our Brother Fire, through whom showest us light in the darkness, and he is bright and pleasant, and very mighty and strong,' he quoted softly. David at that time cherished an ardent admiration for St. Francis of Assisi as poet and communist, though, being a conscientious agnostic, he felt bound to regret the saint's theology.

The door opened, and Mrs Todd entered bearing a bucket of coal-dust and damp slack.

'Oh, you here still, Mr Rossitur,' she remarked with suggestive irony. She disliked strange young men, who announced their intention of occupying the cheap back room for several nights, and who bought nothing more costly than bread and cheese and hung about as though they had eaten roast beef and Yorkshire's. Besides, he might have evil designs on Victoria, her buxom daughter. Mrs Todd, being a person of small imagination, had divided mankind into two classes, those who had designs on Victoria, those who had designs on Beer. Last night she had come to the regrettable conclusion that David had no true appreciation of Beer.

'Yes, I'm still here, and probably will stay for a little if I'm not in the way.'

Mrs Todd by way of reply swung her bucket over the fire,

smothering flames and glowing cinders in a torrent of black coal-dust.

'Oh, Mrs Todd!' groaned David, lamenting the extinction of his brother Fire. 'Must you?'

Mrs Todd regarded him slowly and with dignity. 'I don't say nothing about gentlemen coming and sitting all hours in the smoking room, and paying no more for their beer – *when* they gets it which is not as often as might be considering how good – than if they drank it at the bar. What I say is that this fire has to last until closing time, and there being others what comes at proper times and stays as is right and fitting, and goes away again to return when wanted, there being no call to keep a fire at all when they're not due till 7.30 if that, and mebbe later.'

Having delivered this lucid exposition of economy, fore-thought and natural preference for regular customers, she departed. David fell on his knees before the hearth and tried with a rusty poker to rescue the fire from its smothering burden. His efforts only resulted in an avalanche of fire coal, that fell, rattling through the bars of the grate, on to the stone below. A few angry bursts of flame sputtered and hissed before they died away.

He smiled ruefully. It was all very well to start out from Manchester with a mission of prophecy, all afire to challenge the indifference of agricultural labourers to their own interests; but it was quite another matter to kneel, tealess and with a sore throat, before a choked fire in a hideous room, feeling utterly alien and unwanted.

He heard steps in the passage outside. Some one was enter-ing the bar. In a moment, he might be faced by the magnificent opportunity of confronting the downtrodden and exploited.

Surely now he should be elated and indomitable, ready with pregnant arguments to assault the calculating caution of Yorkshire stolidity!

'I'm not a genuine enthusiast really,' he groaned to himself. 'I want to go back to the Wold Farm, and sit in front of Mrs Robson's fire, and drink hot whisky and eat roast chicken and tea-cakes swimming in butter! I don't want to talk to labourers about their souls.'

This was a perilous state of affairs. He rose and glanced round the room. After all, its very ugliness bore witness to the tyranny of capitalism – capitalism that robbed the hired labourer of all approaches to beauty; that set him to manufacture, by the thousand, lamps of such detestable design; that drove him, his day's work done, to sit on chairs so unbeautiful, in a room decorated solely by the advertisement for the watery wares of a capitalist creature called Bass. And even the one decorative part of the advertisement, the scarlet triangle, had been obliterated by smoke and dust! That was more the sort of thing.

With sudden resolution, he crossed the room, snatched the placard from its nail and stuffed it, crumpled and torn, between the bars of the grate. Then he felt better.

The footsteps he had heard before resounded again down the passage. Some one rattled the latch of the door, and Waite, followed by Ted Wilson, entered the room. Waite looked ill and worried. Since his dismissal from the Wold Farm, he had obtained no further work. His fourth child had appeared prematurely in an unwelcoming world, and his wife's tongue was more bitter than ever. Just now he was in no amiable frame of mind. He flung himself down on the settle and glowered at the smoking fire.

David, watching the smouldering fragments of the placard, wondered whether he could examine the new-comers without discourtesy.

Here were two choice specimens of the exploited proletariat. Waite, red-bearded, stocky, unclean, Wilson, lean and saturnine. Neither appeared to be in love with life. Both were shabby and disconsolate. There was excellent virgin soil in which to sow the seeds of progress. David was perfectly well aware of that. Now was the time to prophesy, but the prophet was dumb. David, fidgeting with the poker, mentally suggested and rejected a dozen introductory remarks. He found himself unable to think of anything more intelligent than the grease spots on Waite's coat. There were five grease spots – five and a half, if you counted the little one near his collar.

Nobody spoke.

Victoria Todd bounced into the room, planked down on the table two glasses of ale, and retired.

David began to make bets with himself, which of the two would speak first. If only some one would start to talk, he was sure he could go on. He had hoped that his unexpected appearance might arouse comment, not having yet learned the indifference to strangers of a Yorkshire labourer. He tried to reason with himself. These men were the very ones for whom he had left Oxford and Hampshire, and all the quite desirable advantages of capitalist luxury. It was absurd, now that he was here, to find no opening for conversation, simply because the red haired man had five and a half grease spots on his coat.

Wilson raised his glass, and deliberately blew off the froth. Light as a feather, a flake floated on to David's coat sleeve, and rested there.

'Now isn't that too bad?' inquired David of the world in general. 'I haven't got any beer. I haven't any money to get any beer; yet here the beer comes to me, and sits on my coat sleeve, jeering at me.'

Wilson turned slowly, and regarded him as though he were a lion in a travelling menagerie. Then enlightenment dawned across his face.

'Travelling?' he asked laconically. Commercial travellers sometimes stopped at Anderby on their way from Market Burton to Hardrascliffe.

David nodded. 'Yes, in a way. And precious cold it is too at this time of the year. And then, Mrs Todd is such an economical housekeeper that she won't even let the fires burn.'

'Mean old cat,' murmured Wilson sympathetically. He felt conversational after a day's solitary gardening. 'Had any luck lately?'

'Not much, but I hope to have some soon.'

'Hope's a fond thing. It fills no bellies. We had a fellow travelling round selling laces and the like to my missus t' other day. "Done much business lately?" I says. "Ay," says he. "I sold two yards o' ribbon to a girl at Cattlesby back o' Thursday, and now I'm going to sell your missus these here cards o' buttons." "Is that all?" ah says. "All?" says he. "How much do you want? That makes 9d. and 2½d. profit. And I spent 5/- since I sold the ribbon and that only means 4/8½! loss in three days. Ain't that a lot o' business?" says he. Hope's a fond thing.'

'He seems to have had a pretty rough time,' said David.

'Rough time? Ay, poor chap. He tried travelling in shoes next, but that weren't no good.'

'Does that help?'

'What?'

'Travelling in shoes? Why not boots. Had his worn out?'

Wilson looked on him pityingly. 'He sold the shoes. Leastwise tried to. Drowned hisself last week. Poor chap. You new to these parts?'

'Yes. I came from Manchester.'

If only there was something to say that would arrest their attention – or if only the inn was full! David was aware that his methods were best adapted for addressing large audiences. Here he felt stifled and stupid.

'Ay – hope!' sneered Waite irrelevantly. He was gazing into the sulky fire with brooding eyes.

'You down on your luck too?' asked David.

'Luck, d'you call it? Pretty sort o' luck I say when you're turned out o' your job at worst time o' year, without a month's notice and your missus with another little 'un coming. That's luck, isn't it? It's luck when t' master sends 'is missus up t' farm to spy on you. It's luck when you don't go down and lick her boots like other fond fools, and she turns on you and tells a pack o' lies and get you chucked out. That's all luck, ain't it?'

'Is that what happened to you?' David asked quietly.

'Happened? Oh, no. These things don't happen. This is a fine land this is, and we're all free labourers. There's a lot of brotherly love about this, an' psalm singing and the rest on't. And they come round at Christmas w' puddings and bits o' beef till it fair sickens you. What we wants is justice. We don't ask no bloody charity.'

'Who was it turned you out?'

David looked gravely towards him. They sat on opposite sides of the fire-place; Waite on the settle, one hand on the empty mug, staring suspiciously at David to see if any guile lay behind his intent questioning. David sitting forward in his chair, his lean hands clasped round his knees, his grey eyes dancing now with excitement, sympathy and indignation, his lips a little parted, his bright hair flaming in the lamplight.

Waite spat into the hearth.

'Who done it? Ay, who does owt in this village? Who turned Schoolmaster out o' his better job, and keeps him here kicking his heels up o' top o' Church Hill? Who pays starvation wages, and then takes coals an' Christmas cake round to stop our mouths so that we shan't grumble? Who goes about preaching and lying and telling tales to our wives, and making men fairly sick with her bits o' sermons an' patronizing ways? You ask Wilson here if Willerbys weren't going to pay him three pound a year more till they heard tell what Robsons give'd their men, so they'd go no higher?'

'Ay,' Wilson spoke with his usual deliberation. 'It's all right for Robson's lads, an' it's all right fer Robsons noo, but one o' these fine days Missus'll sicken of playing providence an' then Anderby will know a bit o' which way its hens were laying.'

'Robsons?' asked David. 'Not the Robsons at the Wold Farm?'

An hour later, Mike O'Flynn and Ezra Dawson opened the door of the smoking room at the *Flying Fox*. There were about a dozen habitues of the tavern gathered round a generous fire; but tonight they no longer wore that air of independent exclusiveness which most Yorkshire men assume while drinking, just to show that they need no support from their fellows in their progress through life or through a pint of Guinness's stout.

Instead every face was turned in one direction, and the smoking lamps illuminated varying expressions of incredulity, bewilderment or vacuous attention. At one side of the fireplace, opposite the high backed settle, stood one of the thinnest people the shepherd had ever seen, his arms waving in grotesque gesticulations, his hair standing from his head in a fiery halo, a torrent of words pouring from his impassioned lips.

'Wages!' he cried. 'The wages of sin is death and the wages of labour, of lifelong labour honestly given and painfully wraught out by the sweat of the labourer – that, too, is death! Death to social competence – when a man labours from daybreak to nightfall for a miserable pittance, which stands in no proportion to the service he has rendered – Death to initiative and enterprise! When it's no use ever trying to do anything better than it was done yesterday, because the only person who will profit is the capitalist. Death to progress! Since how should men progress, who have become machines, bodies and hands – not brains. Those were dead long ago.

'They say in the Bible which some of you may have read when you were at Sunday School, "Ye are gods." I say "You are beasts," animals who rise to labour for another man, who sell your souls and bodies, and all the fine things of which your growing manhood once was capable for eighteen shillings a week, and a dole of beef at Christmas. To labour till your backs ache and your hands stiffen and your brains decay, until when the day's work is done you are fit for nothing but to feed grossly like beasts round a sordid table and to swill down beer in a public house before you roll to your dens and fall into a sodden sleep. Beasts, beasts, beasts!' he cried. 'And you were born to be gods!'

Half of David's audience had no idea of his meaning, but

they realized that he was very angry and on their behalf. He was telling them in this strange way that it was a poor thing to work on a farm – which some of them had thought for long enough – and that the farmers were their enemies, and that something – they weren't quite sure what – had to happen before this distressing state of things could end.

But Elias Waite leaned forward from the settle hearing at last the true interpretation of many of his own half-formed ideas. His face was flushed by excitement; his hands twisted; a new look of hope and understanding lit his brooding eyes.

David had paused. He felt no longer like a cold, hungry boy, listening with apprehension to footsteps along the passage. He felt inspired – a prophet – upborne on the waves of his own eloquence. The idea that he might possibly be talking nonsense never seemed to occur to him, or, if it had entered his head, he must have waved it away with an airy 'Never mind. It doesn't matter whether this is sense or not. We've got going.'

Ezra approached Wilson, who sat near the door, and tapped him on the shoulder.

'Who's yon lad?' he asked.

'A sort o' preaching chap,' murmured Wilson, his eyes still fixed upon David. 'Ay, but he's a rare speaker.'

Victoria Todd shouldered her way through the crowd, and handed the shepherd his mug of ale. Mike O'Flynn deftly intercepted it and drank it heartily, winking meanwhile at Ezra. The shepherd merely smiled indulgently, knowing Mike would pay for the next, and, anyway, it was no good crossing O'Flynn after he had tasted his second glass.

From the group about the fire came a voice, half jeering, half in earnest:

'Ay, young fellow. It's all very well for you to call us beasts, but who's to start righting matters? We can't do nowt. If we asks more wages, we'll only lose our jobs and stand waiting long enough next Martinmas for hiring.'

'Whose going to right it? Why you, and you and you—! The power lies with you, and you alone. Why can't you get up now, and demand high wages? Why do you behave like frightened children instead of standing up for yourselves like men? Because each of you stands alone, and fights alone. There's no co-operation among you.'

Abandoning his rhetoric, David began to speak more slowly and calmly, of the possibility of forming an agricultural union, of the progress towards self-government already made in industry, and of the suggested centres for labour organization.

Opposite him a square uncurtained window glowed, faintly luminous, like a pale jewel in the painted wall. A round moon rode across the window pane, followed by a trail of tattered clouds, smoke white on a clear sky of delicate blue. David, glancing up, saw it and stood fascinated by the contrast between the room, reeking with tobacco and oil, the red glow of firelight on faces and clothes and knotted hands, the oppressive clamour of that little company, and the cold perfection of the moon. It mocked him, that remote beauty. It made him suddenly aware of the emptiness of his rhetoric and of the hopelessness of his task, but he responded gallantly to the challenge of its indifference. He turned again to his audience, who were becoming restive now, bored by the duller description of practical details after the excitement of denunciation.

'Of course there will be difficulties,' he added, smiling as though these would be welcomed rather than dreaded. 'But since I came north I've discovered that nothing is impossible to a Yorkshire man except shooting a fox or riding over seeds.'

'There's another thing I'll be telling you is impossible!' said Mike O'Flynn from his seat near the door.

'And what's that?' David inquired confidently. He was showing a brave face to the cynical moon, that still sneered from the window upon the folly of human aspirations.

'And that's for an interfering stranger like yourself to be blarneying us into thinking we could be better off than we are. And sure it isn't Mike O'Flynn you'll be telling is an animal, without feeling the weight of his fist!'

'Oh. This is interesting. You are satisfied with your condition then?'

'Satisfied, bedad! I'd like to know of anyone who isn't if he works for Robsons of Anderby Wold.'

David gave a slight ironical bow. 'Gentlemen,' he said, 'allow me to introduce to you an agricultural labourer without a grievance! May I congratulate you, sir, on your contented disposition, no less than on your unique blindness of the truth of your situation?'

It was a mistake. Mike had reached that border line between sobriety and intoxication, when the sense of personal dignity is most vulnerable. He became deeply incensed.

'And may I congratulate you, sir, on the boldness of your impertinence in talking against them who have done most in the world for us, and never a farthing's worth of harm to yourself?'

'I think you misunderstand me. The farmers have, in many cases, done their best according to their own ideas, for their labourers, but misplaced philanthropy does more harm than indifference. If ever you had read the works of a certain gentleman called Aristotle – which from your exclusive attention to the particular, when I am discussing the general, I gather you have not – you would have learnt that "There comes a time when from a false good arises a true evil."'

'I'll thank you not to mention your particulars and generals when talking with Mike O'Flynn. I've neither read the works of that gentleman you spake of nor do I want to. But what I do say is that if ye's got anything to say against farmers and their wives, the same including Mrs Robson, God bless her, you'll just step outside the house and repeat it to me slow and careful like before I knock it back down your dhirty throat. For when I had pneumonia and like to die I was with a pain in my chest like a hot iron and seeing the gowlden gates—'

Dawson placed a restraining hand on Mike's shoulder.

'Coom now, Mike, we've heard all that before. Sure enough there's one way yon young chap has you fair beat – at least 'e stops when 'e's finished.'

David had finished. His enthusiasm had burnt itself out, and he felt subdued and exhausted. After a few concluding remarks and a suggestion that he would be at the *Flying Fox* next evening, he left the inn.

The village crouched grey and ghostly in the moonlight under the circling hills. Beyond the road a frosty meadow gleamed like water frozen to white tranquillity. The cottages clustered together for company beside the ribbon of street. David stood at a turn in the road, between the *Flying Fox* and the Wold Farm. The air was cold, and he shivered a little, after the heat of the smoke-room. Always, when he had allowed himself to be carried away by his emotions in public, he suffered afterwards from depressing reaction. The worst of it was, he was never quite sure exactly what he might or might not have said. He could only remember hearing how the Robsons had treated that poor fellow, Waite, and then becoming violently excited. As the room filled, he had talked faster and faster and more and more wildly. He was as certain now as he had frequently been before that he had made a fool of himself, yet how, and why and to what extent he did not know. Only that Irishman, the discharged soldier, Mrs Robson's protégé – perhaps one ought not to have been quite so ruthless. But then, as if he needed to be told that the Robsons had never done him any harm when all the time he was feeling such an unspeakable cad for criticizing, not them, no, not them, but the class to which they belonged, among the people whom Mrs Robson believed to be adoring subjects.

'Well, Mr Rossitur,' called a clear voice, 'it seems as if something meant us to meet on the road at night. How are you getting on, and how's your cold?'

Mary had emerged from the path which led to her garden through the smaller pasture. She was carrying a basket on her arm and in the moonlight looked taller than ever.

David stood stupidly silent, staring from Mary to the moon and back again to Mary. This was the woman who paid starvation wages and pauperized a whole village to satisfy her nauseated conscience. That was the moon which told him that he had just made a fool of himself and probably a cad and, anyway, it wasn't worth while forgetting that one was supposed to be a gentleman.

'Good gracious, Mr Rossitur, you don't mean to say you've gone and lost your voice as well? Though I'm not surprised, sleeping at that inn where I'm sure they never air the sheets and standing about without a coat on.'

'I – beg your pardon. Good evening. My cold really is better. Thank you very much – Yes, I must go – in a hurry—'

'In a hurry to be standing moonstruck again? You'd better by half go up and talk to John a bit and have a glass of hot lemonade. He's all by himself. I've got to go and see Mrs Watts. She's rather ill to-night. But I shan't be long away and John would like the company. You go right on in. You look half starved. It's a real frost to-night.'

'I'm all right. Really. It's awfully good of you, but I mustn't really.'

He felt for his hat, remembered that he had lost it, bowed awkwardly, and hurried off down the road.

This was awful. Why on earth had he ever gone to the house, or even let them be kind to him? What would Mrs Robson say if she knew how he had been talking at the inn? Really, it had not been necessary to say quite so much perhaps. Yet when he once started, the Lord only knew where he would stop.

He stumbled forward under the moon – the round white moon that had watched him through the window of the inn. It stared at him, unblinkingly, from a clear sky.

David stopped short and suddenly shook his fist at it.

'You may stare as hard as you like,' he stormed. 'Looking so wise, smiling in such a superior way! I know I'm an ass, but I know too that it's a good deal more sensible to make a fool of yourself over the right thing, than to be a model of decorum over the wrong ones. Mrs Robson's as kind and sensible as anyone could be, but she's wrong, wrong, wrong, and you know it. And I'm right – though I some times wish to Heaven I weren't. So there!'

Then, because he was very tired and hungry, David went back to eat his bread and cheese at the inn. It was 'after hours,' so he missed his beer.

Mary, returning along the silent street from Mrs Watts's cottage, was asking herself, miserably, 'Why did he snub me? What's the matter? Why did he go away like that?'

Back in the Wold Farm, she scolded Violet with quite unnecessary rancour, because the coffee was cold.

11

A DEFINTION OF FELICITY

April came and brought to Ursula a fine pink boy, whose body, bundled in rolls of shawl, squirmed deliciously in Mary's arms as she cuddled him in a sunny room of the Hardrascliffe nursing home. Ursula lay on a sofa near the window regarding her offspring with amused satisfaction. Her pale blue gown and lacy cap, and the light rug across her knees mingled so admirably daintiness with discretion, that Mary thought she looked more like an advertisement for somebody's invalid wine than a woman who had recently emerged from the disturbing crisis of motherhood.

The baby roused from a light doze and turned, whimpering a little, in Mary's arms.

'Poor little Thomas! You've woken him up, Mary. I'm sure you're not holding him right. Give him to me. You're crushing his feet or something.'

Mary had been gazing dreamily through the window at the circling flight of gulls above the sunlit garden.

'He's all right,' she said, rocking Thomas softly with practised hands. 'But take him if you like. Hush, little love! Diddums, diddums! Did your old aunt then squeeze your little tootsies?'

She crooned over the bundle, smiling tenderly.

Ursula fidgeted on the sofa.

'There, there, hush-aby, sweet lamb, hush-aby!' cooed Mary. Thomas nestled comfortably against her.

'Oh, Mary, I wish you wouldn't talk that silly baby talk. It's such nonsense – brings them up to bad habits. I don't intend the kid to hear anything but good English. I read in a book that the misnaming of common objects definitely retards a child's mental development. Fancy calling feet "tootsies" and dogs "bow-wows" when the real words are so much easier.'

Mary smiled a little.

'Oh, it's all very well to smile. You're so old-fashioned, Mary. Come along to mother, sweetheart. He has been held by a stranger quite long enough, Mary. The new system is that children should be brought up to lie in their cots and not be dandled about all day like handbags. They must hate it. Put him in the cot, will you?'

Mary laid the protesting Thomas in a nest of bows and muslin, and stood waiting for Ursula to gather him up and comfort the wails which greeted his deprivation of protecting arms. But Ursula lay back serenely.

Before the arrival of her son, she had declared that all babies bored her to sobs, but recently, having consumed vast quantities of literature on the subject of their upbringing, she had learnt all about them that was to be known. Mary, who had only nursed several dozens of Anderby infants through croup and colic and teething, and cuddled them in unenlightened arms, felt terribly behind the times. She hated to hear children cry.

'Don't you ever want to cuddle him though, and say silly things? I thought all mothers would.'

'Well, of course I consider Thomas's good before my own pleasure.' Thomas from his cradle, objected loudly to his mother's altruism, but Ursula only put out a cool, white hand and touched his shawl. 'He must be trained. He will soon learn.'

The training was still in progress, when half an hour later Mrs Toby arrived in a state of fluttering jubilation, to congratulate Ursula on her triumphant achievement.

'Well, my dear, this is nice! How lovely! How quite sweet he is! Dear, dear! I must say you look quite well. Better than I did, after my first. Toby drove me over from Market Burton, and I'm sure I wanted to come, though he does go so fast round the corners, and we always break down on Casserby Hill. But I thought I must slip up for a minute and see how you are and the dear child. Why, he's smiling! Dear little man!'

An appropriate tear stole down Mrs Toby's cheek. She had four children of her own, whose existence had been to her a perpetual source of distressful agitation, but she still regarded the advent of other people's babies as a matter for tearful congratulation.

She hovered over the cot, blinking and smiling, and absent-mindedly dropping one or two little parcels on the floor. Mary decided that those strange, clucking noises she made with her tongue were intended for the edification of Thomas, who ungratefully declined to be amused.

Ursula was politely attentive to the privileged absurdities of a mother of four.

'I thought I might just bring along a few of Lucy's flannels, and the cot cover I bought for Gladys. When you've had four like I have, you'll know how these little things come in handy. And I just slipped one or two other little things into a parcel. Dear me, where is it?'

'How nice of you! That's ripping!'

Mary observed Ursula's occasional lapses from pure English with malicious relish. They compensated a little for her feeling of exclusion from the experience of the two mothers. She was not used to being out of it and disliked the sensation. Even little Mrs Toby seemed to assume an air of faint patronage towards her uninitiation.

'Toby's talking to your husband, Mary,' she said. 'I left them together in the market. I thought I'd just slip along and see how Ursula and the precious child were.'

Mrs Toby's deference towards life was so great that she never presumed to make an unqualified statement. She would never go shopping, or visit Ursula: but only 'just slipped round the corner to buy a few things' and 'slipped along to the nursing house.' 'Life must be a very slippery affair for her,' thought Mary, with uncharacteristic spitefulness. Usually she was rather sorry for Mrs Toby. To-day, seeing her permitted as an experienced mother to hold Thomas for the unprecedented period of five minutes, she felt inclined to be spiteful. Lately, she had noticed several occasions on which she felt inclined to be spiteful.

'There, there! Hush then, little man!' murmured Mrs Toby.

Ursula, bowing before a fourfold experience, offered no reproof.

'How's Toby?' she asked instead.

'Well, I'm sure I don't know. I really get a little worried sometimes, my dear. I do indeed. He works so hard, poor dear.' Mrs Toby shook her head, and her dangling veil became entangled with Thomas's safety-pins.

'Is he really busy?' asked Mary with relief. 'Then his practice is going well? I suppose he has a lot to do just now when so much property is being sold.'

The solicitor's wife pushed back her veil. 'Well, it's not exactly the practice. For I'm sure, I don't really know. Poor Toby is so busy with other things. He doesn't seem to get much time. All this last month he has been getting a paper ready for the East Yorkshire Archaeological Society. It takes such a lot of time. It's about the churches of the wold villages or something, and I'm sure he has to go out nearly every day to look at something or other.'

Ursula felt that Mary had blundered on to an unwelcome topic. Tactfully she changed the subject.

'How is your socialist friend, Mary? The one who stood up and defied Cousin Sarah in your dining-room? It must have been a glorious scene! Foster heard about it from Tom Bannister.'

'Oh, he's gone,' said Mary casually. 'I only took him in for a night or two because he had a bad cold, and it was such horrid weather.'

'He sounded an awfully violent young man. You do seem to pick up some queer characters, Mary. I gathered from what you told me after you first met him that he was rather odd. What was he really like?'

'Oh – I don't know. Young, you know, and rather excitable!'

'Where has he gone to?'

'He's travelling about the wolds somewhere, speaking on socialism; but I really don't know.'

'Oh, yes, you do! Look at her blushing, Mrs Toby! Come on, Mary. Tell us the horrid truth!'

'There's nothing to tell. I met him, as I told you, before driving back from Hardrascliffe. Starlight knocked him down and I took him home for three days, as he was quite ill. Then he went to stay at the inn and talked a lot of nonsense to the villagers, but I don't think they understood. He stayed about a week, and took up with the schoolmaster a good deal. He's a most objectionable man, that Coast. But I only saw Mr Rossitur twice in the street after he left us, and hardly spoke to him then.'

Mary hoped that she sounded off-hand and uninterested. She kept her angry, miserable eyes steadfastly on the cradle, so that they should not betray her.

After that encounter in the moonlit road outside the *Flying Fox*, she had only seen David once. She had met him in the village climbing towards the School House – going to visit that wretched Coast, she supposed.

An overwhelming impulse had conquered her pride and driven her to invite him to tea. But David had turned away abruptly. 'Very sorry, indeed, Mrs Robson. It's awfully good of you to ask me. But I've promised to go up and see your schoolmaster – a most interesting person, full of ideas. He's part of my job, you see, so I mustn't disappoint him.'

'Part of his job' indeed! This was the second time he had snubbed her. Very well, then, let him mind his job. Mary would mind hers. She tossed her head.

'Well, I'm sure I don't know what the world's coming to,'

chirruped Mrs Toby. 'Sarah Bannister was only saying yesterday that the wolds soon won't be fit for any farmers to live on. They've got a labourer's union down at Holderness, and I'm sure I don't know what will happen if we start strikes and things on the farms. The coal strikes last year were bad enough.'

'Oh, Sarah Bannister's always thinking we're all going straight to the dogs,' said Ursula. 'When she goes to heaven she'll always be expecting Lucifer to make another war among the angels.'

Mary rose and went to the window.

She wished she had not come. She wished that John would arrive to take her home to Anderby. She wished that she had never left home. It wasn't worth while being irritated by Ursula's superiority and Mrs Toby's silliness when she couldn't even have the compensation of cuddling Thomas.

She wanted just then to cuddle Thomas very much indeed.

'Why, here's Toby coming along the path,' she announced, welcoming a distraction. 'He looks full of news.'

'I don't really know whether I'm fit to receive a man,' murmured Ursula, patting the curls below her cap. 'Mary, be a dear and hand me that mirror and the powder. Your husband's so particular,' she added archly to Mrs Toby.

Mary brought the powder-box and silver mirror. She didn't see why she should wait on Ursula just because Ursula had a baby.

'Heavens! why didn't some one tell me that my nose was like a looking-glass? How could you let me go on looking such a fright?' Ursula's busy hand dabbed at her already well powdered face.

It was obvious, thought Mary, that she was delighted with

the contrast between her daintiness and her visitors' dishevelment. Mary had driven to Hardrascliffe between scattering showers of April rain. Her hair was blown just anyhow, and there was a hole in her driving gloves.

Toby entered with a boisterous flourish. He liked Ursula tremendously. She was a good sort. Had more go in her than the rest of the family. She knew a thing or two. Not a conceited frump like Mary.

'They said that I might come in for a minute if I was very good. Well, Ursula, how are you? And how's the nipper? By Jove, the very image of his father. By the way, I saw Foster in the town. Never met a man so set up in my life! Well, Mary, I've been talking to your man in the market – you come baby worshipping? By Jove, Ursula, wait till you've got four! Then you'll say something!'

He winked at her delightedly, caught Thomas from his wife's reluctant arms, and held him at arm's length for inspection.

'Oh, by the way,' he exclaimed suddenly, almost dropping Thomas back on to Ursula's sofa, 'I've got something for you, Mary. Have you seen this week's *Northern Clarion*? By Jove, your little friend's been at it all right. There's a stinger there, a regular stinger. He's got you farmers pretty well on toast. He's going to make things hum a bit.'

'What little friend?' asked Mary indifferently.

Her heart was in her mouth. She hardly dare open her lips lest Toby should see it.

'That socialist chap who set Sarah by the ears. We've all heard about that little business, Mary. You can't hide your light under a bushel in the East Riding. I met a chap at the Archaeological Society who told me to read this. He'd met your young fellow – what's his name? Rossitur? up beyond Foxhaven way, ranting round like a Salvation Army soul-snatcher. Great little fellow, what? You read this.'

He handed Mary the crumpled leaves of a newspaper.

The black letters danced madly on the printed page. Mary folded it, laughing rather breathlessly.

'Oh, it's too long to read now. I came to look at the baby, not to read the newspaper.'

She could not face it here, in this little room, before the scrutiny of six unfriendly eyes. Toby, no doubt, thought it all a great joke; and Mrs Toby, silly little hen! Mary Robson of Anderby Wold, who had always thought herself so clever and superior – that she of all people should have harboured a raging socialist, let him insult her relations in her own dining-room, and then go away and write inflammatory articles about her and her village in the most notorious of radical papers! Her hands round the paper tightened.

Toby, highly amused by her confusion, continued his chaffing. 'By Jove, he's let you all have it! Starvation wages and coals at Christmas! "Coddlin' and short" he calls it – coddlin' your men and paying them short. Do you read your Dickens? Good joke, eh? No, … that was in the letter. There's a letter too, by a chap called Hunting. Same thing though – friend of Rossitur's.'

'Oh, is there?' Mary spoke with cold indifference.

'And there's a bit on rural education. Says the farmers won't have the children properly educated because that makes 'em discontented. All about the intrigue that goes on behind the schoolboards – children being snatched away to work in the fields before their time is up and all that. Quite a real scandal!'

'He got that from Coast,' thought Mary. She wondered how

much David had learned from Coast – how much about her and her kingdom at Anderby. How they must have laughed at her together in that hideous parlour at the School House! Her visits to Mrs Watts, the Christmas Tree, the dances she organized. Probably Coast had been immensely entertained by the story of the embrocation, and the way in which she made David fold sheets, and her naive delight in having an author to stay in the house.

Toby and his wife were bending over the cradle, Ursula lay back on her cushions smiling luxuriously at them. The atmosphere of violet powder and hot milk and drying flannel became suddenly stifling.

Mary rose, clutching the paper.

'Oh, Ursula, I've just remembered. I have to order some cheese at Maryson's. I'll go now, and if John calls please tell him to wait.'

She fled from the room. On the stairs she turned and, through the half-closed door, caught the sound of her name and David's, and then Toby's laugh.

The esplanade was deserted. The straight, shower-washed streets shone like polished metal above the dancing grey and silver of the sea. Blank, flat-chested boarding houses with lace-veiled windows lay swept and garnished, ready for the transitory influx of summer visitors. A paper bag blew forlornly along the path till it found a resting-place in the gutter at Mary's feet.

The breeze pulled at her scarf, and the newspaper in her hands flapped and struggled like a live thing. She found a seat facing the sea, and sheltered on three sides from the wind by an erection of glass and wood, built for the convenience of summer visitors. There she sat and unfolded the paper.

The *Northern Clarion* was unfamiliar to her. She missed the genial friendliness with which the *Yorkshire Chronicle* greeted her each morning. She wrestled with the fluttering pages, turning them over and over to find David's article.

His name suddenly faced her at the head of a column.

'Progress and the Wolds' by David Rossitur. There was a column and a half of little black letters, dancing and wriggling on the paper. If they only would keep still for a minute, she could read what he had to say – what he had the amazing impertinence and ingratitude to say!

She folded the paper and began to read steadily, from the head on one column to its foot, then up again and half-way down the next, and that was all. She lowered her hands, and looked across the sea.

It might have been worse. After all, he really said very little. The tone of the article was more restrained than that of his book. He had begun by drawing a picture of the agricultural conditions, in East Yorkshire – a little exaggerated in outline, of course, but less grossly distorted than she had imagined. The passage about starvation wages was rather bitter, but the reference to education might have applied to anybody – not specially to her. Perhaps Coast had never even mentioned to him the incident of Jack Greenwood.

Perhaps her anger was unjust. David had to do his work after all. Perhaps she had not taken him seriously enough because he was such a boy. He sounded serious enough here. She shifted her position on the seat and turned to Hunting's letter. This surely was 'the stinger.' Toby had confused the two writers. Hunting declared that he wished to confirm David Rossitur's theories. He denounced the Eastern Farmers in half a column of crude virulence, and finally stated his intention of following up Mr Rossitur's valuable work by the organization of a union among farm labourers.

Mary frowned.

Was this really what David meant when he spoke of the fellowship and courage necessary for reform? She turned again to the last passage in his article. It contained an appeal to the organizers of more advanced industries to have patience and sympathy with their comrades, the agriculturists. Although the evils of the countrymen were less flagrant and the sufferers less articulate, there was just the same need for encouragement. He warned them against the cowardice of complacency.

'Progress is not the movement towards a single, recognized goal. Because some of you have reached a condition of comparative prosperity, that is no reason why you should now withdraw from the race. It is cowardice to refuse to relinquish present good for the sake of future excellence. "Felicity is the continual progresse of the desire from one object to another, the attaining of the former being still, but the way to the later ... so that, in the first place, I put for a generall inclination, of mankind, a perpetuall and restlesse desire of power after power which ceaseth only after death and there shall be no contentment but proceeding."'

Mary read that, and one passage further back about kings and queens. It was addressed to the masters of hired labourers. 'You, who think you hold suzerainty over men, beware lest you find that time has robbed you of dominion. For those alone are kings and queens who sit enthroned above their generation and rule circumstance.'

He had said something like that to her, standing by the mantelpiece in the Anderby dining-room, smiling at her with wistful, half-humorous eyes. Here it seemed a direct appeal to her understanding. Did he mean her to read it and remember?

She put down the paper. A man and a girl passed the shelter linked arm in arm. The girl wore a dark hat, trimmed with bright little scarlet wings. She looked up, laughing, in the man's face. He bent towards her, and Mary could not hear what he murmured, though they passed so close that the girl's skirt brushed her knee.

Their footsteps died away along the pavement. Mary was left alone with the wheeling gulls, and the sound of the wind striking the shelter.

David had said very little, but it was enough. She knew now what he thought about her.

David and his kind, the man and girl who had just passed her, the young labourers at Anderby, Jack Greenwood and Fred Stephens, they were the heirs of the future. They wanted to go forward because 'there shall be no contentment but proceeding.'

But Mary had placed herself in the ranks of the older generation who would have time leaden-footed. She cherished no longing to proceed. 'Her restlesse and perpetuall desire for power after power' had taken her as far as she dared go.

She had John. She had Anderby.

Further progress could bring her no increase of power, only enforced abdication from the only dominion she could hold.

'Those alone are kings and queens who sit enthroned above their generation and rule circumstance.'

She stared across the sea.

A gleaming sail, far out across the bay, caught a momentary flash of sunlight, then vanished into the grey waste of water.

And she was no older than David and Fred Stephens and Ursula and Violet – only different.

The sharp clop, clop of hoofs along the Esplanade caught her attention. She turned her head. Through the glass at the back of the shelter she saw John driving towards the nursing home. She waited until he turned the corner, then rose and quickly followed.

The dog-cart was drawn up outside the gates of the nursing home. John saw her coming, and raised his hand.

'Where have you been, honey? I thought you were with Ursula?'

'I went out on the Front a bit.' She climbed wearily into the seat beside him.

Once, on the drive home, he broke the silence: 'I was talking to Toby up in the market. He was saying to me that the Diamond Assurance Company, the one we deal with for the house and farm buildings and so on – fire insurance – it's going to pot. He says we ought to transfer our policy to Mallesons'. They're clients of his – good people. What do you think?'

Mary was not listening. Her eyes were looking beyond the falling road to the grey village, in the cup-shaped hollow of the walls.

'Eh, honey?'

'Oh, yes, if you think so.'

Between the generation that was passing and the one coming forward was a great gulf fixed – Mary and John were on one side. For a moment rebellion seized her. Why could she not relinquish this – the dim hills before her, the bearded figure

154

beside her, the responsibilities that preyed upon her? Why not escape to the other side?

They were passing the cross-roads where Starlight had picked up the stone in his shoe. Mary leaned forward; one vision rose before her; her rebellion culminated in one need – David, David Rossitur.

She saw him again as she had last seen him, climbing the hill towards the School House, his lean figure bent forward, against the wind, the sun on his eager face, his red hair blowing in untidy locks across his forehead, the sleeves that were always too short for his long wrists . . .

John spoke again.

'Then you think it will be all right if I tell Toby to transfer that Insurance Policy?'

'Oh, yes. Anything you like,' answered Mary.

On the hall-table at Anderby a note awaited her. She opened it listlessly while John removed his hat and coat.

'Anything the matter?' he asked suddenly, noticing her white face. 'What's that?'

'This? Oh, nothing. Only a note from Coast to say he's afraid he can't let the boys have a holiday to go brassocking this year. He is a fool.'

'There's going to be trouble with that fellow,' muttered John. 'Brassocks will grow like anything this spring unless we get in extra boys to hoe them. You can't expect the men to get the fields cleared quick enough.'

'Oh, you're always seeing trouble ahead! You're as bad as Sarah,' snapped Mary. 'Why can't you look on the cheerful side of things for a change? Anyone would think you were an old man from the way you talk.'

John looked up, hurt and surprised. Mary's outburst was unexpected. She never said such things.

His puzzled glance curbed her irritation, the instinct to comfort being stronger than the desire to wound some one else.

'I didn't meant that,' she said quickly. 'I didn't mean that, John. I don't know what I'm saying. I've got such a headache.'

His surprise deepened to speechless bewilderment when she turned and suddenly kissed him on the forehead, then fled upstairs to her room.

John stood in the hall, silently scratching his head.

'Now what on earth did she do that for?' he inquired of the hatstand.

It ventured no reply.

12

THE FRUITFUL GROUND

'I really think you might have had more common sense, Mr Coast,' said Mary. 'It isn't as if the boys had never had a holiday for brassocking before. I really don't see that you have any right to stop a thing that has gone on for so long.'

The schoolmaster smiled.

'That's just what you all think about here, Mrs Robson. No one has a right to stop anything that's gone on for any length of time. It doesn't matter whether a thing's good or bad so long as it's old.'

'Well, it wouldn't be old if it wasn't good, would it? Some one would have stopped it long ago. The boys are all going to be labourers in a year or two. It wouldn't have done them any harm to have a day or two's holiday in the fields.'

'It wouldn't have done them any harm to play football in your field, Mrs Robson, but as they had always managed without a proper playground I suppose it was right that they should continue to do so.'

'That has nothing to do with it. And I told you last year I had made up my mind about the field.'

'Naturally in that case there's nothing more to say, is there?'

Mary looked at Mr Coast and Mr Coast looked at Mary.

She thought he would have irritated her less if his black coat had fitted him properly. Once, any sign of poverty or pathos appealed to her. Lately it had only aroused a grudging annoyance that anyone should be silly enough to add to the world's accumulation of misery.

'Of course there's nothing further to say.' Though she knew quite well it would be better if she could leave things alone, she added: 'Oh, except that it may have escaped your notice that the lock on the door of the class room cupboard, where we keep the tea-things, is broken. I can send the joiner up to mend it if you like.'

Coast turned away.

'I have already attended to the matter,' he replied.

A whist drive was in progress at the village school. Fourteen collapsible tables, with a fixed determination to fulfil their destiny by collapsing at every possible moment, filled the room where, five months ago, the Christmas Tree had stood. Fifty-six ladies and gentlemen from Anderby and the country sat around, intent and upright, clutching the fateful cards on which hung their chance of possessing a silver-plated toast-rack, a pair of gent's gloves, size 8½, or a currant loaf.

Mr Coast presided over the entertainment. At intervals that seemed all too short for perspiring players desperately pursuing the odd trick, he blew a shrill whistle, and fifty-six wooden chairs shrieked and grated along the well scrubbed boards.

Mrs Robson was not playing. Instead she stood near the

door, now talking to the schoolmaster, now vanishing into the adjoining class room to superintend the making of coffee, the arrangement of tarts and jellies, and the fair distribution of ham and chicken sandwiches that awaited the supper interval.

The vicar, arriving shortly after nine o'clock, approached the schoolmaster as the one unengrossed person in the room.

'Dear me, yes. A nice gathering you have here to-night. A very nice little gathering. I have just spoken to Mrs Robson in the passage. Very good supper there – ha? Very good indeed.'

'Excuse me,' remarked Coast dryly, and blew the whistle.

The chairs scraped. Miss Taylor, who was left for the seventh consecutive game at the corner table, sighed expansively.

'Oh, dear, isn't that just too bad now?' she lamented. 'If only Mr Armstrong had returned my lead in diamonds we should have got the odd that time. Mr Slater, isn't it just vexing that when I get to the only broken chair in the room I should be kept sitting on it seven times running? I'll be sprouting roots into it if I don't get a move on soon.'

'Clubs,' gloomily announced Mrs Armstrong, turning up the last card, and frowning at Miss Taylor.

'Well, of all the dreadful luck! When I haven't—'

'If you talked less, Miss Taylor,' suggested Coast severely, 'both you and your partner might have more chance of moving on, unless, of course, you want to get the booby prize.'

Miss Taylor flushed, and bent disconsolately over her cards.

'Never mind, Miss Taylor.' Mary had returned from the class room. 'Luck in cards isn't everything. I never saw the supper room more prettily arranged, and if you can decorate as nicely as that you deserve the toast-rack at least, even if you don't make the highest score.'

'May I beg you not to talk to the players, while the game is in progress, Mrs Robson? Strictly a matter of formality of course, but rules are rules.'

'Ha ha! we can't have our hostess called to order, can we, Miss Taylor?' laughed the vicar jocularly. 'Not before supper anyway, Mr Coast. She might go off with all the jellies – and the chocolate moulds, ha? Mustn't kill the goose that lays the golden eggs.'

'Oh, good evening, Mr Slater.' The schoolmaster might not have existed for all the attention Mary paid him. 'Have you seen how charmingly Mrs Coast and Miss Taylor have decorated the class room? Come and look.'

She led the way from the room.

Coast stood, watch in hand, waiting for the time to blow the whistle.

Through the open door he could see Mrs Robson standing beside the laden table. Her tall figure, in its plain, black gown, was outlined against the delicate green of budding branches, fastened at each end of the supper table. Paper lanterns of scarlet and blue swung from the pliant saplings like vivid flowers. Among the creams and trifles, three great bowls of daffodils lit the table with a golden glory. All this springtide elegance was Mrs Robson's device and Mrs Robson's gift to the village. The name whispered most frequently by the players, in the little bursts of conversation that heralded the union of fresh partnerships, was that of Mrs Robson. She had given the prizes; she was the foremost contributor to the supper-table; she had organized the last whist drive before the approach of summer, in aid of the children's annual holiday to the seaside. But that the real burden of responsibility lay on the shoulders of quite another person, the schoolmaster knew well. The chief sufferer from the inconvenience of disarranging the whole school, of upsetting the precarious equilibrium of Miss Taylor's temperament, of settling down, after the departure of the last card player, to tidy the room, was Mr Coast. But, of course, no one thought of him!

He did not doubt the efficiency of his handiwork, only the adequacy of its reward.

Of course with his miserable salary he couldn't send creams and trifles to grease the throats of these toadying villagers. He couldn't fatten his cows on the grass that should have been the school playground. He could only work the skin off his hands, serving an ungrateful society.

He blew the whistle with savage but ineffectual violence two whole minutes before its time.

'Oh, Mr Coast, I've just got my cards gathered together, and I had such a lovely hand!' protested Miss Taylor.

'I think that was a little too early, Mr Coast,' said Mary. 'Don't you think they can play on for the other two minutes?'

They played on.

Two hours later the last whistle had blown, the prizes had been presented, and the card players were struggling for hats and coats in the crowded lobby. The schoolroom was almost empty. Three tables, which had collapsed irretrievably, lay huddled in one corner. The scattered cards lent the scene an air of unwonted dissipation. Coast stood, frowning at the wreckage and wondering how long it would be before he could cross the asphalt yard to his own house and bed. He was tired, and the atmosphere of the crowded room had brought upon him one of his worst attacks of neuralgia.

The vicar was saying good-bye to Mrs Robson.

'Well, a most satisfactory evening. I think I can congratulate you on a really successful evening. Fifty-six multiplied by two shillings – let me see. Very good indeed, very. What should we do without her, eh, Coast?'

Coast had already done his duty to Mrs Robson. Before she presented the prizes he had praised her many virtues in a masterly speech. He had said enough.

A little hammer of hot iron seemed to be thumping at his right temple with maddening regularity.

'You look tired, Mrs Robson,' said the vicar. 'Mustn't do too much. We can't afford to have you ill, you know – can't afford it, can we, Mr Coast?'

'Oh, I'm all right,' said Mary wearily. 'I've been rather off colour the last few days. It's nothing – indigestion I expect, and the warmer weather.'

She began to gather up her coat and scarf from the chair beside her. The vicar groped clumsily for them.

'Let me help. Mr Coast, those are Mrs Robson's gloves over there I believe, if you don't mind.'

'I'm sorry. I have to clear the room. Got to hurry up.'

Really, if he had to fetch and carry for the woman!

'Oh, I'll stay and help,' suggested Mary mechanically, laying aside her coat.

'Please don't trouble. I can manage better by myself. Mrs Coast and Miss Taylor will help me.'

'Very well.'

Mrs Robson plainly did not care whether she stayed or went.

Indeed, from her listless movements it was clear and she did not much mind what happened at all.

The two men watched her go. The vicar rubbed his hands.

'Capital woman. One of the best. Splendid worker. Example to the whole parish, ha? But doesn't look well. I should say – mark you, I don't know, but I should say – she had been over-doing things.'

Coast's self-control deserted him.

'No wonder, when she can't let the wind blow without puffing it on a bit! If she minded her own business a bit more and other people's a bit less, she might look better. I believe she thinks the Almighty can't get along without a deputy providence.'

'Really, Mr Coast!' said the vicar.

It was two o'clock in the morning before Coast locked behind him the heavy door of the school and turned towards his own house. It was a moonless night, and he stumbled across the yard, scraping his shins for the hundredth time against the low parapet near the gate.

His neuralgia was worse than ever.

Mrs Coast trotting timidly behind him sighed forlornly.

'Well, that's done! But what ever shall we do about those tables? And did you hear Miss Taylor say she hadn't prepared her lessons for to-morrow yet? But what a lovely supper – only poor Mrs Robson doesn't look well, does she?'

'Oh, don't talk. Can't you see I have a headache? Where did you put the matches? Are there never any matches in this confounded house?'

'Aren't you coming upstairs, Ernie? You must be tired.'

'Oh, for God's sake leave me alone! Go to bed. And how many thousand times have I told you not to call me "Ernie"?'

'Oh, I'm sure I didn't mean anything. Only I'm sure you're tired. Would you like a cup of cocoa, Ern – Mr Coast?'

'Cocoa! Cocoa!' His voice rose to a shrill scream. The headache was closing in upon him now in a swirling horror of nausea. 'Get out. Get out for Heaven's sake!'

Mrs Coast fled.

Coast sat in the parlour, his head on his hands, his elbows on the table. He knew that there was something at the back of his memory which would console him, if only this cursed pain would stop for a moment and let him think. Ah! He rose unsteadily and went to the table in the window. On a woollen mat, in the shade of an aspidistra plant, lay a copy of the *Northern Clarion*. He spread it on the table before him. Slowly he re-read an already familiar article, repeating softly the words, as though he found consolation in them. Rossitur, of course, was a fool. He had known that after half an hour's conversation with him. Enthusiasm was all very well; but enthusiasm totally detached from common sense was about as useful as a bell without a clapper. Why, the man didn't know what he was talking about. He wanted to turn the whole world into a sort of socialistic Sunday School with every one singing 'Oh happy band of pilgrims' to the tune of the 'Red Flag.' Of flesh and blood and men with passionate and petty jealousies, with magnificent desires and sordid greeds, he knew nothing.

Still, even fools were sometimes useful.

Pictures chased each other through his mind. Mrs Robson standing more like a stuffed duchess and handing Bert Armstrong's young woman a plated toast-rack. She thought there was no one like her in the whole East Riding; Mrs Robson, sitting in that room, saying 'The Field is mine. I will not sell'; Mrs Robson walking down the village street, raising up and putting down whomsoever she would, acting deputy God.

How would she like one day to discover that she was only a cog in a worn-out economic machine? Now that chap, Hunting, talked sense. An agricultural labourer's union would soon show Mrs Robson her place in society. Hunting seemed a practical chap. No nonsense about him. Said what he meant. He'd know just how to deal with a woman like Mrs Robson.

Coast, holding one hand to his aching head, drew towards him a sheet of note-paper and dipped his pen in the inkpot. There was no ink. What on earth was the use of marrying a wife who never filled the inkpots? He wasted ten minutes groping about on shelves and cupboards before he found a sixpenny bottle behind Mrs Coast's workbasket.

It was nearly four o'clock when he finally began his letter.

'To W. Hunting, Esq.,
Organizing Secretary of the Farm Labourers' Union. Northern Branch.
'Dear Sir . . . '

Two days later David sat in a small but comfortable eating-house in Manchester. He was combining, without marked success, the complicated operations of disintegrating a particularly tough piece of steak and composing the final sentence of his article for next week's *Clarion*. There was a smudge of ink on his nose, because his fountain pen always leaked, and a similar smudge of gravy on his cuff, but he was happily absorbed and quite annoyed when some one touched his arm and summoned his attention. Looking up, he saw a dark cadaverous person, in an aggressively ready-made suit, who inquired, with a pronounced Manchester accent, whether he was Mr Rossitur who wrote for the *Clarion*.

'Er – yes, I think I am. At least, I sometimes do.'

David was not sure whether he ought to be deferential, or affable, or non-committal. He always found it hard work to differentiate between the manners one assumed when dealing with editors, fellow journalists, labour delegates and creditors. Also he was not sure whether there really was a smudge of ink on his nose.

The person went straight to the point.

'My name's Hunting. I am the Secretary of the Northern Branch of the F.L.U. You may have seen a letter I wrote to the *Clarion* a fortnight ago, as it appeared immediately below an article of yours.'

'Oh, I know. On the possibility of working up the East Riding. I thought it was splendid – at least, I liked the idea of getting a union started there. Please sit down. Have you had lunch?'

'Yes, thank you.' Hunting sat.

'Do you mind if I go on with mine? I had a rather sketchy breakfast. It's just as well that you have lunched, because this is a very hard steak. Do you know whether they ever try to unfreeze meat before they put it on the table? I think this a piece of fossilized dynosaurus. However,' with a sigh, 'it's a good exercise for the digestive organs, I suppose.' He resumed his labours.

'I hear you went for a tour round East Yorkshire this spring?'

'Oh, no, not spring. March, if you like, and the beginning of April, but nothing even remotely connected with spring, I do assure you. If you could have seen some of those roads, and felt the wind across the hills—! Not spring, Mr Hunting.'

'You went to observe the conditions among the labourers and to do a certain amount of propaganda on our behalf, I believe?'

'You seem to know a lot about me.' David looked sideways at a speck of dust floating on his beer. He was not very favourably impressed by this intimidating person, with his determination to avoid side-issues.

'I rang up your chief this morning. I want some information.' He drew from his pocket an envelope, a small black notebook and a fountain pen. 'Now then.'

David felt uncomfortably reminded of his Oxford days, when, confronted by four insatiable examiners, he had racked his brains to supply them with information that was not forthcoming.

'I received a letter yesterday from the schoolmaster of a village called Anderby in the East Riding of Yorkshire, asking me if I can offer any assistance in the way of forming a branch of the agricultural labourers' union. He says you have visited the village and that the men were interested in your statements.'

He looked rather incredulously at David, who was rolling bread balls with inefficient absorption.

'I shouldn't have thought it,' murmured David.

Hunting's glance seemed to say 'Neither should I,' but aloud he continued 'I should like to know something more about that village.'

David stopped playing with his bread and turned to Hunting. 'Well?'

'Perhaps you will be good enough to read this letter.'

'From Coast?'

He had been attending, then, in spite of the bread balls.

'Yes. That's the fellow's name. Rather intelligent. Got quite a sense of practical issues.'

Hunting's praise implied a reproach to David, whose unfinished article was blowing about the floor in scattered leaves and who was evidently without much sense of practical issues.

David read the letter.

'Well, what do you think of it? Eh?'

'I'm not sure,' said David thoughtfully, turning over the paper.

'Well, but what do you think? You know the man. Is he to be trusted? What do you think about my going up there for a bit of looking round and seeing what can be done? You've heard of my work in the Midlands?'

David nodded.

He was not sure. There was some bitter taint of egotism in Coast which he distrusted. The men at Anderby had seemed on the whole more prosperous, less prepared for change than in other places. They had on the whole not been very interested in what he said. Only Coast and Waite – neither of them quite disinterested. In a year or two . . .

'Well, well?' Hunting's sharp voice sounded impatient. 'What do you think?'

After all David had sown the seed. What right had he to declare which should be the fruitful ground? The love of humanity must be honest – must not wince at every contact with imperfection. If not he – then some one perhaps less suitable . . .

'I wish it wasn't Coast,' said David.

'Why? Isn't the man all right? What is there against him?'

Hunting's relentless little eyes flashed from David to his notebook.

'I don't like his moustache,' said David – which was true, but not the whole truth, because by this time he had decided that Hunting was one of those people to whom one cannot tell the whole truth. He was too relevant.

Hunting shrugged his shoulders.

'Is that all?' he asked with determined patience.

David reached for his hat, and hurriedly collected the fugitive leaves of his article.

'Not quite all,' he said, smiling. 'But, if you don't mind coming round the corner to my digs, I'll give you all the information I can. I think your work is needed.'

13

THE SHADOW ON THE KINGDOM

The twenty-second of June was Waggon Day and the waggons were timed to start at eight o'clock.

All night Mike and Fred Stephens had kept vigil in the saddle-room at the Wold Farm, polishing brass and leather and fastening rosettes on to the best harness. The crowning triumph of their work, two painted and beribboned paper fans to be attached to the collars of the horses, lay beside the smoking lantern. The saddle-room was littered with green and scarlet papers, brass buckles and bits of harness.

Mike knocked the ashes from his pipe and opened the door. A rush of chill fragrant air shook the flames of two candles stuck on the dusty mantelpiece.

Fred extinguished the lantern and followed him to the doorway. It was a morning of pale mists and dewy freshness.

'I think it bound to tak' up,' he remarked cheerfully. 'What about it, Mike?'

The two men collected harness and decorations and trudged

together towards the stable. From the stackyard a belated cock crew, and in the stable it was still dusk – a warm straw-scented twilight astir with the movements of chewing horses and the whispered scamperings of mice along the rafters.

Dolly and Polly, the grey pair, stood sleekly brushed awaiting the master strokes of their toilet. Soon they would lumber up the Church Hill to take their places in a team of competitors for the prize offered by Sir Charles Seton to the best decorated waggon.

'It'll be a fine day for t' bairns,' murmured Fred.

'Violet going?'

'Nay. Ah'm holdin' no truck wi' Violet now. She's too stuck up for the likes o' me.' But Fred spoke regretfully.

An hour later the waggon was jingling and rumbling through the mist. Fred, no longer overburdened by the weight of his responsibility for the decorations, turned to Mike.

'Well, Mike, what did ye think to yon fellow on t' bridge last night?'

Mike spat carefully but emphatically over the side of the waggon.

'I thought he had just one fault.'

'Eh? Ah thowt you couldn't abide him! What fault was that, then?'

'Just that he was born at all, bad cess to him! Coming down here and rantin' around as though he was a howly Father himself – telling us what we ought and ought not to do. 'Tis in the church we hear enough of being miserable sinners. I'm not wantin' any more preaching from the laity.'

'Bain't you going to join t' union then?' asked Fred, deftly turning the horses round the post office corner.

'Union? Union o' fools who get all on end if a boy from the town comes to them with an old wives' tale. What do we want wi' unions at all? Will they put a head on the beer or give Foreman's missus a lighter hand with the pastry? Will they make owd Mare Becky pass the *Flying Fox* w'out a bit o' the stick? Will they stop mud getting through your leggings in the sheep-fold on a December morning? No, no. "Mike, me boy," I says to meself, "that fellow's a fool and so are them that listens to him."'

Fred nodded. He had heard all this before.

'He didn't speak so well as Mr Rossitur,' he remarked meditatively.

The great horses strained and jolted up the hill, shouldering through the mist from the low lying road. Up above, the air was clear and tender. Knots of women and children stood about talking volubly.

Mike laughed scornfully. 'Rossitur, bedad? Now then, Fred, don't you go thinking that red headed lad was any better than the rest o' them. The gift o' the blarney he may have had, "Gentlemen," he says, "allow me to introduce you to an agricultural labourer without a grievance." By Holy Mary, if ever I catch him alone there'll be work for Constable Burton if he will stick his nose into the affairs o' we. The thrashing I gave that blathering idiot, Eli Waite, will be like tickling a girl with a feather beside it.'

Fred was used to Mike's truculent threats. Irishmen were made like that, and there was an end of it.

'There'll be just one bit of advice, I'll be giving you, me boy,' continued Mike. 'And one day you'll thank me. You've got the best mistress in the world. You know her and she knows you.

Never listen to them who know nothing but the sound of their own tongues.'

They reached the brow of the hill. Mrs Robson stood on a bank by the roadside and waved her hand as Dolly and Polly rattled by. She smiled at them too, but the smile faded when they had passed, and she stood gazing dreamily across the mist veiled valley.

Up on the hill Sir Charles Seton was judging the waggons. Soon she would have to pass along the line of horses and holiday makers bestowing praise and encouragement upon the competitors and wishing good luck to the children about to ride away for one glorious day of adventure by the sea.

It was not quite time yet, and she might have a little respite. She walked slowly away from them down the hill. It was just as well not to stay too long there in the crowd. Coast was there, and she didn't want to see him. They had not met since the whist drive and she felt sure that their next encounter would be unpleasant. Lately she had shrunk from all contact with unpleasantness.

Little bursts of laughter and shouting floated down the road. The mothers were being hoisted into the waggons, with shrill screamings and personal jokes. The children clutched string bags and hoarded pennies in hot excited fingers.

It must be lovely to be going on a holiday like that, thought Mary, with such excitement and good humour, to be engrossed all day by the joys of swing boats and pierrots, to bounce wildly on donkeys up and down the sands. It must be lovely to sit hand in hand with one's sweetheart, sucking Hardrascliffe rock, and listening to the distant music from the band on the esplanade. To feel so young and care free, so much welcomed and beloved, to enjoy warm human kisses and pleasant non-sense – not to walk alone through a village grown strangely unfamiliar, while all the time one thought hurt and hurt and hurt . . .

'Mrs Robson! Mrs Robson!'

Miss Taylor came panting down the hill.

'Aren't you coming to see the waggons? It's nearly time to start. And you'll never guess! Your Fred's got first prize for the greys. They *are* lovely!'

There was no peace then.

Mary retraced her steps and did her duty. She always did when it came to the point. There were so many people to be noticed, so many questions to be answered. Was she going in to see the tea? Wouldn't she drive down later in the day and look at them all on the sands? Would she come now at this very moment to inspect Eva Greenwood's new doll which was also going to the seaside?

But at last it was over and Mr Slater, standing by the head of the procession, raised his hand for the signal of departure.

The final ceremony followed.

Mary held her breath. This was her moment, when balm might be poured on her troubled spirit. Here in the public recognition of her suzerainty she found all the reward she asked from life.

'Three cheers for Sir Charles Seton!' called Coast from the leading waggon.

They were given heartily, but this was merely a prelude – a preliminary trial of vocal power before the real event of the morning.

The holiday makers paused, awaiting the next command.

Small boys drew in their breath ready for the next outburst of sound. Everyone looked at the schoolmaster.

'Drive on,' called Coast.

With a cracking of whips and rattling of harness the waggons moved forward.

For the first time in ten years no cheers had been given for Mr and Mrs Robson of Anderby Wold.

Mary stood and watched them pass. They looked at her curiously with vague bewilderment. She stared in front of her, smiling mechanically. Only when the last waggon had rounded the bend in the road the tension of her attitude relaxed. She walked quickly down the hill.

On her way through the village she encountered a dark figure hurrying up the street. She knew who it was. She had heard from several people that for a week or more a towns-fellow called Hunting had been organizing t' union, that the *Flying Fox* had become the centre of a strange new business in Anderby, and that Coast was the chief lieutenant of the leader of industry.

Six months ago she would have laughed at it all, declaring that such a scheme was unpractical. Or that a union was very nice and would do no one any harm, and she was sure the men might join if they liked, for it wouldn't lead to anything.

Now she regarded with sick apprehension the self-confident tilt of Hunting's hat and the purposeful energy of his stride.

She raised her head defiantly.

'Good morning, Mr Hunting,' she said.

The man bent his head curtly and passed on.

He had heard from Coast and Waite and others how this woman had tried to get round young Rossitur. He would make it quite clear there was to be none of that little game with him.

Mary continued her journey.

'This is ridiculous,' she told herself. 'I'm letting things get on my nerves. There's nothing wrong really.'

She decided to go and call on Mrs Watts. The old lady would be pleased to hear about the waggons. Besides, she was a cheery old soul.

But the old soul refused to be cheery. Mrs Watts was full of fears and fancies. She sat gazing through the windows across the sunlit orchard, seeing nothing but shadows that were not there.

'I'm sure I don't know what we're coming to,' she sighed, shaking her head. 'What with such goings on at the *Flying Fox* and preachin's on the bridge at evenings. Anderby isn't what it was, Mrs Robson.'

Mary agreed that it was not. But that did not necessarily imply the changes were undesirable.

'You can't expect to keep things always the same, you know,' she remarked brightly.

'You don't allus like things any better because they're what you expect,' said Mrs Watts.

'What "goings on" do you mean at the *Flying Fox?*' asked Mary, looking for a change of subject but thinking the time had not yet come to talk about the waggons.

'Do you mean to say ye've never heard tell o' Mike O'Flynn and Eli Waite fighting up at t' *Flying Fox?* Where ever have you been?'

'Busy lately. I've been staying at Market Burton a few days. Mr Robson's uncle – Dickie Robson – died you know, and I went to help them with the funeral.'

'O – Ay, Violet said as much. I forgot. Well, as I was saying' – Mrs Watts brightened perceptively at the prospect of relating an unspoilt bit of gossip – 'Mike an' Eli was up at *Flying Fox* a week come Tuesday it would be, and both a bit t' worse for drink, though Eli, 'e were worse nor' Mike. Irishmen can stand a lot o' drink, not but what Mike isn't a good 'un with his fists once he gets well liquored up. Well, Eli was cracking up yon Mr Rossitur what was here, and saying what a good speaker 'e was an' all. And how this here Mr Hunting was going to put what 'e'd said into practice like, and Mike, 'e flies up all at once like 'e do at times, an' says what Mr Rossitur and Hunting an' all was a pack o' fond fools and ought to be shuved in tid' pond. And Eli said som'at – I don't know – about young Rossitur and a lass – they didn't tell me who – and then – I don't know – but Eli struck t' fust blow they said – or mebbe Mike – but anyway there they were at it hand an' fist when Constable Burton came up an' stopped it all. Ee but it must 'a been a rare fight! Ye don't get many such now.' She shook a regretful head.

Mary frowned anxiously.

'Oh, dear, I wish I'd known. Mike mustn't go fighting like that. I'll have to stop him. He's very excitable and when he was ill the doctor said a little too much excitement on the top of drink might send him off his head.'

'Ay. 'E's a rare fighter, is Mike O'Flynn.'

'I know. But it isn't safe. All these agitators and people are very bad for him. Old soldiers need discipline, I think. It's very difficult.'

'Ay. There's queer goings on at Anderby.'

Mary rose to go. She was worried. 'Queer goings on.' That was just it. Nothing tangible, nothing that one could fight in the open.

She bade farewell to Mrs Watts and walked home along the sunlit road.

It would be a fine day for the children. That was something. After all, there was nothing very wrong. Things had gone on the same in the past. They would be the same again. Ardently she tried to assure herself of this. For it meant nothing to any but a feverish and over-sensitive imagination that Mike should fight with Eli Waite, that old Deane should have omitted his customary greeting to her in the street, that Coast should refuse to cheer her and John when the waggons drove away.

Waite naturally was a cross-grained man. Mike was temperamentally unable to keep the peace. Coast and she were old enemies.

It was nothing, this shadow on the kingdom, only the ghost of her own brooding thoughts and frustrated longings.

She closed the gate behind her and paused in the blossoming garden. She needed new flowers for the dining-room table and there were roses on the prim standard bushes up the path to the house. She bent above their vivid fragrance, her fingers hovering, like the heavy-laden bees, from flower to flower.

Here at least she found tranquillity and assured possession. The anxiety died from her eyes, the strained lines from the corners of her mouth. She moved slowly about the garden.

Here, as though she were really a queen, the courtier yews cast cloaks of shade before her on the golden grass. Roses, peonies, starlike daisies against the night dark hedge of yew, delphiniums catching the blue of the sky on their delicate spears, these were gentler subjects than the men and women of Anderby.

If it were only in the village that she found her trouble, she

178

might have sought comfort here. But she turned restlessly to the house and went to a desk in the drawing-room. Laying the roses on a table, she opened a drawer and took out a sheaf of newspaper cuttings, neatly dated and pinned together. Again she read them, though she knew their phrases by heart. 'Organization of agriculture.' 'The beginning of a great campaign.' 'Yorkshire caution and progress.'

'Progress.' He was always talking of progress. Mary laid the papers down and looked through her window across the gold and green of the garden, but saw neither sunlight nor shadow.

She was drawing towards her the image of a red head, gallantly poised, thin hands that swept away the difficulties of the world, and laughing youthful eyes.

The butcher's cart rattled up the drive to the back door. They needed a leg of mutton. She must tell Violet.

She rose and locked away the papers.

'At least,' she thought, 'we know what he thinks of us all.'

14

THE SHADOW ON THE WHEAT

It was the last week in July when, late on Saturday evening, John and Mary drove back together from Hardrascliffe market. As the dog-cart rounded the corner near the post office in Anderby, they saw a cluster of men on the bridge that spanned a dry watercourse winding through the village.

'More agitators,' commented John. 'That chap, Hunting, I suppose.'

It was not 'that chap Hunting,' though he was there too, leaning against the low parapet of the bridge with an air of easy patronage. On the parapet, his vivid hair dulled in the failing light, but every angle and movement of his slim figure unmistakable, stood David Rossitur haranguing a lethargic group of labourers.

Mary sat erect, her hands tightly clasped, the colour drained from her face. The cart rattled up to the bridge. One or two of the men standing in the road gave way and nodded a sheepish 'Good night.' Mary looked across them straight to David, where he stood with his figure darkly outlined against a transparent evening sky.

For a flashing minute she caught and seemed to hold his eyes. She thought he stopped speaking, but only for an instant. Then the pony sped past, trotting cheerfully up the street. Mary sat very still in the cart.

'Wasn't that the young fellow who was staying with us – Rossitur?' asked John. 'My eyes aren't so good as they might be. I can't see very well in this light.'

'Yes, I think it was.'

'What's he up to here, I wonder? With Hunting too. I don't like that chap, Mary.'

'Who – Rossitur?'

'No. I've got nothing against Rossitur. He's a bit of a clatterbrain, but he's young. He'll learn sense. I mean that man Hunting. He's civil spoken all right. And the union's all right, I suppose. They've got 'em in other places. I expect we've got to put up with it.'

'I suppose so.'

What was David doing there? thought Mary. Why had he come again? He was a journalist. Journalists didn't wander round the country-side preaching in the villages, except, of course, when they needed a rest or – a wild hope caught and held her spellbound – when a particular inclination drew them.

'I was talking to Willerby at the market this afternoon. He's not a bad chap, Mary, though he's no farmer. He says he's used to unions in the West Riding where he came from. Where the masters and the men get on all right, they don't seem to give much trouble. I suppose we were bound to get them here one day.'

John, thought Mary irritably, always spoke of trade unions as if they were a mild though regrettable disease, like mumps or chicken-pox. He had no eyes at all for their real significance. If he had read the *Northern Clarion* which now arrived every week at the Wold Farm with the library books, he would soon have lost his easy optimism.

But Mary could not bother with John that night. She never knew afterwards what replies she made to his occasional remarks, throughout the evening meal. One point in John's favour was that he never wanted to absorb her attention. It was Saturday, and Violet had cycled in to Hardrascliffe with the young man of the moment, so Mary washed up the tea-things alone in the lamplit kitchen.

So David was in Anderby. Why he had come or whence or for how long mattered little. He was here, quite near to her, and it was an illusion, then, that strange feeling she sometimes had, that she had only dreamed of his existence. Those three days when he had stayed in the house and she had talked to him and argued with him, and watched the foolish tossing of his fiery head and made him pick up cotton reels from the floor for her – all that had been real. She might even speak to him again.

The plates she had washed lay neglected in the sink. The saucepan lay unscrubbed in the cooling water.

No – she was wrong. It mattered very much why he had come. For there was one explanation of his coming which would change the whole world. Why should he not care? Those two meetings, when he had turned away so queerly and been so embarrassed, was it just possible he had been upset because she was a married woman and so beyond his grasp?

She was only twenty-eight. She was quite nice-looking. She had been kind to him. She wasn't quite a fool.

Of course it was nonsense. A dowdy farmer's wife – not even quite a lady.

Yes, but then he was so queer. People weren't like that for nothing. And then – she cared so . . .

A moth fluttered in through the window and flapped clumsily along the ceiling. The last pale line of sunset died beyond the ridge of the wold. Mary rose and shut the window.

Somewhere in the village was David.

Backwards and forwards in her mind that ceaseless questioning tossed her from hope to despair.

'Why has he come? To see me?'

'Who are you that he should want to see you?'

Up the passage she heard John kicking off his boots. He called to her from the foot of the stairs.

'You're a long time, honey. Ain't you finished yet?'

'Coming in a minute,' she replied.

The water in the basin was cold. Yellow islands of congealing grease floated on its unlovely surface. She emptied it away and turned to the kettle for more.

It was a nuisance, this thing which took possession of her thoughts and made her forget the water in the basin. No one had a right to claim so much of her time, she on whose personality rested the well-being of a whole village.

Angrily she wrung out the dish-cloth and hung it on a nail, yet, as she walked up the passage with a queer revulsion of feeling she found herself humming a tune, gay and elated as she had not been for weeks. For he was in the village. She might see him to-morrow. To-morrow anything might happen.

But afterwards in the dining-room sitting over her sewing and listening to the ticking clock and the regular breathing of John who had fallen asleep over his paper, her mood changed again. What was the use of thinking about to-morrow, when she wanted him so much to-night?

Next day after morning service she loitered outside the church on the brow of the hill talking, now to Mrs Coast, now to Mrs Armstrong. When the Willerbys asked her to drive over with John to Highwold for tea, she declined their invitation.

Miss Taylor approached her, blushing furiously and stammering that a young man from the training college had at last come up to the scratch, and would Mrs Robson care to come and see his photograph?

Mrs Robson considered. The way to Miss Taylor's lodging lay down the village street. If one wanted to meet some one staying in Anderby the likeliest place of encounter would be the street after morning service. Mrs Robson accepted the invitation.

The village street was full of shadows and strange unexpected presences. Figures emerged from garden or cottage, to set her pulses beating wildly, before she dropped to a flat level of disappointment as Jack Greenwood or old Deane appeared. Footsteps on the path behind her, that might herald his approach, died away drearily when the shepherd or Bert Armstrong overtook her hesitating progress.

The grudging ten minutes she granted to the inspection of Miss Taylor's young man were torture to her. While she was there, he might pass unseen.

When one o'clock struck sleepily from the church tower she hastened home to dinner, sick and exhausted, and closed behind her the gate that shut the garden away from the village street.

'You expecting anyone this afternoon, honey?' asked John across the cold beef.

'No. I don't think so.'

'But you said to Mrs Willerby when she asked us to go over—'

'Oh, I know. I thought then that Ursula and Foster said they were motoring over this afternoon. I remembered afterwards it was next week.'

'Decent chap, Willerby,' murmured John wistfully, but he did not suggest that they should go.

They stayed in the house and garden all the remaining hours of the long, hot day. But nobody called.

Monday morning dragged on through a cloud of steam and scolding and the scent of soap and wet linen. Mary had spent two sleepless nights. After dinner she found the stifling atmosphere of the wash-house unendurable. John had ridden over to Littledale. The clothes drooped lazily from long lines in the sunlit paddock. Mary escaped to her room and changed her dress.

Half an hour later she hurried through the stackyard and passed up the chalk road that shimmered, dazzlingly white, between its borders of sun-dried grass and ripening corn. There was no shade, but Mary never noticed the sun beating down on her head and shoulders from a cloudless sky. She hurried forward and upward, away from the village and mocking street and the garden path up which nobody came. Once she paused in her flight and pressed hot, dry fingers across her throbbing temples.

There were footsteps behind her, hurrying footsteps that stumbled along the deep ruts of the uneven road.

She was sick of footsteps and voices and torturing shadows. Again she resumed her rapid climb, shutting her ears to the sound behind her, resolutely refusing to turn her head.

A low branch of hawthorn from the hedge reached out and caught at her skirt. She wore an old-fashioned dress of green muslin with a skirt that flowed about her like a cool, soft sea. It was not made for scrambling walks across the fields. She bent to disentangle it with trembling fingers. Again the footsteps sounded behind her, drawing nearer up the road.

Impatiently she jerked her skirt free from the thorns, only to find that in her reckless movement she had caught herself again by the sleeve. She pricked her fingers, but the muslin remained twisted with devilish ingenuity among the thorns. Tears of impotent anger trembled in her eyes.

'Can I help, Mrs Robson?' asked David.

For a little while she neither spoke nor turned, but stood quite still staring at her torn sleeve and the dusty hawthorn.

'You *were* in a hurry,' panted David. 'I called at the Wold Farm about a quarter of an hour ago, and Violet said you had just gone out in your best frock – she didn't know where. Then I met Shepherd and he said you had gone along the field road towards Littledale. I've nearly had a heart attack negotiating these young mountains of chalk. What does happen to your roads in summer? I've never seen such ruts.'

Still she did not speak, but stood quietly, wrapping her handkerchief round her pricked finger, while golden hills and blue sky and green hedge danced giddily about her.

'You're not angry with me, are you?' he asked anxiously. 'You see I've really come to apologize because I'm afraid you think I've behaved rather badly. I don't know what you think about Hunting. I know you always resented anyone else interfering in your village, though why, Heaven knows, for it's really no more yours than anyone else's. He's not a bad chap really – Hunting I mean – though his clothes are appalling. And I did warn you, didn't I?'

She turned now.

'I'm not angry at all. How do you do, Mr Rositur?' she said primly, holding out her hand.

'I'm all right, especially now I know you're not angry, or rather I shall be all right when I've recovered from this obstacle race. But you – I say, Mrs Robson, you don't look a bit well.'

'It's this heat,' said Mary unsteadily. 'I was helping with the washing all the morning. It's very hot here.'

'It must be. Look here, won't you sit down a minute? Unless of course you are in a great hurry to go wherever you were going so quickly. You do look tired.'

He looked round for some shade. The sun was scorching the dusty grasses at their feet. On the other side of the road the ripening oats rose hardly waist-high above the shadowless ground.

'I was going to Littledale, but I don't think I'm in any particular hurry. It is so hot. There's some shade on the other side of the hedge.'

She led the way to a gate in the hedge. Beyond, the bank dropped abruptly two or three feet to a tangle of tall sweet grasses, between the dark hedge and solid golden wall of wheat. They closed the gate and passed up the alley of grass till they came to the shelter of Mary's hawthorn tree. There they sank down, shut away from the glaring heat in a cool green world of scent and shadow.

'Oh, it's lovely here!' David laid aside his hat and ran his fingers through his hair. 'Days like this were meant for idleness. You've no idea what bliss this is after Manchester.'

'Is it? Is Manchester very bad?'

'Oh, it's not so bad really, I suppose, only rather stuffy, and I don't much like any city except London. They're all such cheap imitations.'

He lay back luxuriously and, plucking a tall scabious flower, pressed its perfumed softness to his cheek.

'Is that why you came back?'

She had to say it.

'That and because Hunting wrote such glowing accounts of his work here. I had to come down and see whether he was as good a liar as I thought him.'

'I suppose you're staying at the *Flying Fox* again?'

She did not dare to ask 'How long are you staying?'

She sat very still, her arms clasped round her knees, her eyes staring into the tremulous life and movement of the field of wheat before her.

'No. As a matter of fact your schoolmaster, Coast, offered to put me up. I only stayed here Saturday night. You passed me, you know, on the bridge when I was talking to some men in the evening. They're not really easy to talk to – can't see beyond the immediate future. That's the worst of working among men without education. You can't have progress without imagination and you can't have imagination without a basis of knowledge. We ought to begin by reforming the schools.'

She held her glance tightly on the delicate tendrils of

convolvulus encircling the stalks of wheat, on the scarlet pimpernel among the haze of gold and green, on anything but David – David lying among the fragrant grasses, as much at ease as his strenuous vitality would ever let him be.

'Oh, we'll just have to go on doing the best we can – organizing first, educating after. It's the wrong way round of course, but it seems the only way at present. When I was in Cattlesby yesterday—'

'Oh, you were in Cattlesby yesterday?'

So that was why he had not come.

'Yes, I went there directly after breakfast and did not come back till to-day. I'm leaving to-night by the six o'clock train from Hardrascliffe.'

'I suppose you had business here to do before you left, otherwise it's surely rather out of your way.'

'It is. Horribly.' He laughed, at her or at himself. She could not tell. 'Six miles out of my way along a dusty disagreeable road, with the Hardrascliffe hills, and the springs broken in the saddle of my bicycle. What do you think of that?'

'That it must have been very important business.'

'It was. Look here, Mrs Robson, I've been thinking an awful lot about you lately.'

One quick little indrawing of breath and she sat still as a statue.

'I know I behaved rather badly last time I was at Anderby. You were splendid to me. I shall never forget it. Then I put my foot in it so badly with Mrs Bannister and I'm afraid you may have thought I was rude, hurrying away like that to the inn. But you know, I couldn't stay. It wouldn't have been right. It wouldn't really ... Of course you've got to oppose me, I suppose, and I've got to oppose you, and unless you give up all this' – he waved his hands at the fields around him – 'I don't see how we can be anything but enemies. I'm doing my best to knock down the things you think are fine but I think are an abomination—'

'An abomination?'

'Oh, you know what I mean. Please don't misunderstand me. I don't think any the less of you because I hate the things you stand for – patronage and capitalism and the old Tory school and all that sort of thing. I think you're splendid.' With his irrepressible tendency to gesture he sprang up and confronted her. 'Of course I think you're splendid. Why, I—'

Mary rose too and they stood face to face between the wheat and the hedgerow. Hot waves of perfume blew from the ripening corn across their flaming cheeks. In the hawthorn tree a thrush was singing.

'Do you really mean that?' asked Mary.

'Why, of course I do!'

'Splendid, David? How splendid? What does that mean?'

The glimmering bowl of sky closed in upon them. The golden hills crouched waiting.

'Why it means—'

Earnest, excited, longing to clear himself from the last taint of ungraciousness, David flung out his arms with an impulsive movement. One moment Mary stood waiting, wild hope and joy questioning in her eyes. Then she bent forward.

'Oh, David, David!' she whispered. 'Do you mean that?'

Somehow, she lay in his arms. Somehow, their lips met. For Mary, time stood still. Her life hung poised on one consummate happiness, that knew neither past nor future.

A slight noise in the road above her broke the spell. She moved away. They stood facing one another, David flushed and panting, Mary, white and still, while a shadow fell across the wheat, and slowly moved above them. David's eyes were on Mary's frozen face, but Mary, looking past him, saw the back of John's head and shoulders as he rode along the grass at the other side of the hedge that bordered the road from Littledale. Whether John had seen them as he approached, she did not know.

They stood motionless, until John's horse had rounded a bend in the road. Then Mary spoke:

'I think you had better go,' she whispered. 'You may miss your train.'

Silently he stooped for his hat, then stood there, hesitating, as though there was something he would say.

'Please, go,' she whispered again. 'I would rather.'

He turned and left her. The last she heard of him was the sound of his uneven footsteps on the broken road. Once, they stopped and her heart stood still as she awaited his return. Then they passed on again, and died away down the hill.

Two hours later, Mary opened again the door of the Wold Farm. The house was in confusion. Violet came to greet her with quivering lips.

'Oh, m'm,' she cried, 'do come, Mr Robson's had a stroke.'

15

BEFORE THE HARVEST

'Good evening, Bert. What is it you've come to see me about?'

Mary stood in the dining-room smiling at the embarrassed figure of Bert Armstrong, who waited, shuffling his feet along the carpet.

'Have you seen that chap Hunting, Mrs Robson?' he asked. He hated having to come to her like this – and her having such trouble with her husband an' all.

'Yes, I have, and I'm glad you came to see me about that. Won't you sit down, and smoke if you like. I wanted a talk with you.'

Bert looked round, seeking the least committal seat in the room. They all looked too large or too small. Finally he chose John's arm-chair and crouched there miserably, trying to find somewhere to put his hands and his knees.

Mrs Robson, for all her kindness, had always been an alarming sort of person, and lately people said that she had been acting very queerly. She certainly looked queer, with her dull expressionless eyes and the lines running from her nostrils to the corners of her smiling mouth. And there was a sort of restlessness about her, as though all the time she was expecting something unpleasant to happen and yet didn't care very much if it did.

'Did 'e say that if we don't give three pund ten this harvest the men are all coming out on strike?'

'Yes, he did.'

'Does 'e mean it, Mrs Robson?' the young man asked anxiously.

'I'm afraid so. These people generally mean what they say, and he has got the men pretty well in hand.'

Bert leaned forward, his clasped hands between his knees. 'It means ruination for us, Mrs Robson. There was me just getting on like. The farm well stocked up, and going to begin to put a bit on one side. If these goings on don't stop, I'll have to give up.'

'I see.'

''Taint as if I was the only one, Mrs Robson. There's others, like Andersons of Stowall, and Baines on the Glebe Farm. It's all very well for yon big farmers, like you and Willerbys at High Wold. But what shall we do? We can't pay high wages.'

'What do you want me to do?' Mary raised unsmiling eyes to Bert's crimson face.

He moved uneasily in the arm-chair, summoning his courage.

'Why, they say down in the village that you're going to give in – because of Mr Robson. Rare bad luck it is having a stroke like that just now, and they say he mustn't be excited, but if you pay what they ask, we'll have to give t' same and we can't do it – we can't. We'll have to give up. Just when we're starting.'

'Who said that I was going to give in?'

Bert blushed and looked at the floor. 'Oh, they say in t' village – of course, we know you've had a bad time – Mr Robson ill and all. And then you knew that young fellow, Mr Rossitur. And they say he was all in t' favour of unions like, and perhaps you, being clever, and seeing you understand all these new ideas—' He paused, stumbling and intimidated, the words with which he had been carefully primed before the interview oozing out of his mind like water from a sponge.

'Oh, I see,' said Mary slowly. 'They say in the village that because I am supposed to be rather better off than the rest of you, having a larger farm, I can afford to play with socialistic ideas and pose as a kind of enlightened high-brow introducing new methods into Anderby. Is that it? And that I choose my friends from among the class that spreads discontent among the labourers because it amuses me. And that I shall make the excuse that my husband isn't well to give way to the first difficulty, no matter what it may cost the rest of you. Is that it, Bert?'

'Why' – he hung his head – 'I wouldn't go so far as t' say that.'

'That's what you mean, though, isn't it? I've been busy the last ten days. I haven't been much in the village, but Hunting came to see me, here. Would you like to know what I said to him?'

She rose and went to the window and Bert saw her strong profile and tall figure outlined against the sunlit lawn and shrubbery. Very straight and confident she looked – queer, though. Bert felt he was in for it now. You never knew what Mrs Robson would do next.

She was not looking at Bert but at the roses and hollyhocks along the garden border, as her even voice continued:

'I told him that he was mistaken in thinking that co-operation and public spirit lay among the labourers alone. I told him that up till now the men had had good wages, and that until he came into the village there had been no complaints. I told him that whatever might happen in the towns, here we were friends together, masters and men, that many of the masters had been labourers themselves once, like your father, Bert, and had risen to be foremen and then bought a bit of land on their own. I told him that except on one or two of the larger farms, there was a continual struggle between the smaller men and the land they held, that every extra penny of capital was needed for manure and stock and that to increase the labourers' wages meant to starve the land, and in the end the labourers as well as the farmers lived on what the land produced. Do you understand that far?'

Bert nodded, though he felt that Mrs Robson was getting rather out of his depth. Still, she seemed to know what she meant and women – even such superior ones as Mrs Robson – will talk.

'I told him also that I was not a rich woman. Until last year my farm was mortgaged and though I might this year be able to pay the wages he asked, it would mean that I should have to spend my savings and that in the end would have to be made up from the land. But I said that even if I were as rich as the Setons of Edenthorpe my answer to him would be the same. If there was any real need to increase my labourers' wages I would do it, for we Robsons haven't farmed at Anderby for nearly four hundred years without knowing that the first condition of success is good feeling between fellow-workers. But when I saw discontent spread among ignorant villagers by men whose profession it was to spread such unrest—'

Her quiet voice hesitated a moment. Bert saw her hand make a slight involuntary movement as though she were in pain.

'When I saw demands being made simply because journalists and union organizers and paid agitators – men from Manchester – were interfering where they had no experience, when I saw that one demand would lead to another, one interference, from outside grow into an enforced separation of master from man, then I said I would fight that movement until my last penny was spent and the last sheaf of corn had gone from Anderby. Will you tell them that in the village?'

Again Bert nodded, because Mrs Robson seemed to have got well away and there was no stopping her anyhow.

'Do you think you understand? Because I'm busy with my husband and can't speak for myself. Will you tell them that if the men will strike we must let them? We can all join together and get the harvest in somehow. Dawson and Foreman and Mike O'Flynn and a few others at the Wold Farm here won't go out I know – mind you, there mayn't be a strike.'

'I doubt it.'

'I doubt it too. The men know well enough which side their bread is buttered. The agitators'll go away and forget all about it and stir up trouble somewhere else where they'll be better paid and everything will be settled down just like it was before – oh, and I've spoken to the Willerbys too, and they'll do whatever Mr Robson and I think best and I think the same thing applies to the other farmers. Now do you know what to say in the village?'

'Ay. Thank you, Mrs Robson. I'm sure I always said—'

Mary smiled again. Her intensity relaxed, and Bert sighed with relief as she suddenly became again an ordinary farmer's wife entertaining a visitor.

'Oh, that's all right then. You'll have a glass of wine and a piece of cake before you go, won't you?'

Later in consultation at the market with a group of other young farmers, Bert delivered his message.

'Nay, she'll not give way, she says. Ay, but she do talk! She's a rare woman, is Mrs Robson, but not the sort I'd like to have about t' house days and nights out. She's a bit unchancy like.'

He would have thought her yet more 'unchancy' could he have seen her outside John's bedroom, hesitating on the dark landing, clasping and unclasping her hands while her breath came in quick, gasping sobs.

During the last ten days her life had become a jagged patchwork of moments when, composed and self-confident in the presence of others, she met the increasing difficulties of the labour question, and the moments when alone she wrestled sobbing and abandoned with her doubts and fears and shames.

There were three things to be remembered directly she opened John's door. First, she must give him the doctor's message about getting up. Secondly, she must satisfy his querulous curiosity about Bert. Thirdly, she must avoid if possible all topics which might recall to his mind the scene in the wheatfield.

She pulled herself together and entered the room.

John lay still and sullen on the great bed. His beard had grown thick and straggling and his rumpled hair and restless eyes did not increase his comeliness. But he was better. It had been a slight stroke.

'The doctor says you can get up next Saturday.'

'About time too. I never saw such tomfoolery, keeping me here just before harvest for a touch of sunstroke. Who's been up to the house, honey?'

'Bert Armstrong came for a bit of advice about harvesters. He's not a bad sort of boy, John, but I think he finds the responsibility of farming a bit too much for him after his father's death.'

'Ay. It's not in the blood, you see. Old Armstrong was a good hedger and thatcher, but his son's not bred to be a farmer.'

'No. I suppose not.'

Mary moved about the room, setting straight the cushions and bottles and a vase of crimson roses. If only she knew! If only John would show whether he had seen her that afternoon – her and David. The doctor said it was a slight stroke brought about by riding in the hot fields after a heavy meal. But a shock might cause the same sort of thing. And she did not know what he had seen.

'Sarah Bannister sent you some peaches. Would you like one for lunch?'

'I might as well. Any more about that chap Hunting lately?'

'No. I don't think so. Things seem fairly quiet.'

'Rossitur still here?'

Mary clutched at the mantelpiece, where she had been replacing a fallen rose in the vase.

'Mr Rossitur? No. Why should he be? He only came for that night we saw him on the bridge, and left again on the Monday.'

'Did you ever see him to speak to?'

Was he tricking her? Trying to force her to a confession? She bent above the roses. This was too absurd. Like a scene out of a novel. And it was happening to her – Mary.

She spoke very quietly.

'Yes. He came to call on Monday afternoon.'

'Oh, the day I was taken ill. I thought you were out then.'

'I must go quietly here,' she thought. 'Then it will be all right. He may not have seen. He may never remember.'

'I was out,' she said. 'So he came up the fields to find me and apologize. He thought quite rightly that he had behaved rather badly, coming to stay with us and making an upset in the village.'

There was a sound from the bed. Mary dared not turn round. She awaited the sharp exclamation of surprise and recollections, the ensuing scene – which must be avoided at all costs because John had to be kept quiet.

The sound swelled and died.

John had yawned.

His drowsy voice came again from the bed.

'Well, I'm glad he had the decency to realize he'd behaved shabbily. But of course, whatever sort of fool he may be, he is a gentleman, Mary; I always said so.' John yawned again. 'I think I'm going to have a nap now.'

'All right. I'll bring you some tea about four.'

She left the room.

Then he did not know. Or, if he had seen, his temporary

seizure had driven all recollection from his mind. And she must go on, hourly expecting the possible return of his memory.

Of course it was absurd to make a fuss. It really was nothing – a kiss in a cornfield on a hot day. Lots of farmers' wives might have done it – only Mary was not lots of farmers' wives. She was Mary Robson of Anderby Wold and her conduct must be without blemish. And then John was not like lots of farmers. His trust in her was as absolute as his loyalty to her was unquestionable. Any small lapse from propriety became doubly a breach of confidence. And then – and then, it was not so much what she had done as what she was ready to do . . .

She passed through the quiet house. In the kitchen Violet was singing as she cleaned up after a day's baking.

Mary returned to the dining-room and closed the door. As she turned the handle she felt she was shutting herself up with a swarm of pitiless thoughts that danced round her like gnats on a summer day, leaving no respite.

David had written. Oh, yes, he had written all right. She had his letter now in her desk in the drawing-room – a most proper letter that would fully clear her character should her husband accuse her and she wished to prove her innocence. Of course he hadn't meant it for that. David had written just because he was David and couldn't leave well alone – must all the time be spoiling things by trying to make them better . . .

She knew it by heart. She knew the characteristic writing with its finely formed letters, impetuously looped, the upward sweep of the lines – even the smudge at the end where he had blotted it too hastily. He never could do anything quite perfectly.

'Dear Mrs Robson,

   'I can't imagine what you think of me.'

No, that was obvious. He never would know either.

   'I won't ask for your forgiveness, for I know I don't deserve it.'

Mary smiled bitterly. Quite true again. She never would forgive him, never – for thinking that forgiveness was necessary.

   'But I want to say that what happened in the cornfield was my own fault, but not my intention. I can't think what possessed me that I should behave so extraordinarily to you of all people whom I really respect so profoundly. It must have been the scent of the poppies or something. It all happened so suddenly. But please believe me it was quite unpremeditated. Think of it as a kind of momentary madness if you like – anything but an act of deliberate disrespect. I knew as soon as it happened how appallingly I had behaved, and how angry you must be. Of course I don't expect anything so nice could happen as your writing to say you understand and forgive me.

   'Yours very very sincerely.

      'DAVID ROSSITUR.'

Poor dears! Men always thought they did it all themselves. If they only knew. Mary smiled again.

Well, she supposed she must answer it – even after a week's delay. There was no reason why he should suffer from something which he showed clearly – so very clearly – was not his fault. She would make the excuse that her husband had been ill. There had been no time to write before.

She fetched paper and envelopes and sat down, passing her tongue thirstily over dry lips. The flowers on the table were untidy. She rose again, and picking up two petals that had fallen dropped them into the waste-paper-basket.

Then she chose a pen from the inkstand, and began:

'Dear Mr Rossitur.' Her writing was large and round with black down strokes. This was the first time that she had written to him. How hot the room was! Perhaps, with the window open ... She tried again.

'Dear Mr Rossitur,

'Thank you for your letter. I quite understand. I expect it was the hot afternoon. It seems to have affected a lot of people. John got a slight touch of sunstroke. Perhaps you had one too – I quite understand you did not mean it. I was angry at the time, but now we will forget all about it. Please don't worry any more.

'Yours sincerely,

'MARY ROBSON.'

It did not seem a very wonderful production, to have taken nearly two hours to write, but it was what she meant to say, and she could not think of a grander way in which to say it. Besides, she must reassure him some how that she was not angry. He must not suffer even a momentary humiliation for her own deliberate and shameless fault.

She blotted her letter and re-read it, repeating aloud the written words. What, after all, was the use of saying anything when there was one thing alone that she wanted to say, and could not? Quickly she tore the paper in small pieces, and let them drop into the waste-paper-basket. She walked to the window, and thence to the mantelpiece, then up and down the room that had become too small for the tireless thoughts which began to attack her in regular procession.

By the fire-place, she realized again the triumph of that moment in the cornfield, and the two hours afterwards when deliberately she had blinded herself to every consideration but the intensity of her desire for his love – when she had believed only what she wanted to believe, and forgot everything which common sense and propriety and experience recalled. Up the room again, she confronted the disaster of John's illness and the shock of her probable responsibility. Back again by the tables and chairs that she touched in passing with her fingers, she lived again through the hours of fearful expectation, awaiting the return of John's memory and the ensuing scene. Finally, by the door, she received once more that letter from David, when, as the hottest shame of all, she read that she had no cause for shame, that her fruitless waiting after church on Sunday and her flight up the fields had been the truth, and the quivering ecstasy of her stolen delight a sentimental lie.

That was what she was – a sentimental neurotic fool. Cheap, vulgar, sentimental. Those names hurt even more than calling herself disloyal, which she knew she was. Thinking herself starved for romance, and snatching at the first young man who came along, however unwilling he might be, she had known, oh, she had known all right, all along, that he could not care.

She had failed John. She had shamed David. Well, there was still the village. Hunting? There was that interview with him, and the long vista of defeat and deprivation it disclosed. But she had not lost the village. There at least lay a way to regain self respect.

That was what one must have – self respect. She couldn't bear life without it. She couldn't bear that fugitive shame that kept her starting at every sound, that burned her at every thought of David.

She looked up in surprise, for a sound of low sobbing filled the room. It could not be she who was crying. Why, she'd just made up her mind that in her work in the village lay the royal road to the only thing in life that really mattered. There was a real battle to be fought against Hunting, that would cure her of hysterical fancies.

But the choking sobs continued, for she did not care. She did not want to regain her self-respect if that meant shutting herself off from all thoughts of him. What did the village matter? What did she matter if it came to that?

'Oh, David, David,' she moaned. 'And I loved you so.'

Footsteps sounded along the passage. Violet called to her from the hall.

'Are you there, m'm?' She rose and pushed back the fallen hair from her face.

'Yes. What is it?'

'Please, m'm, is Mr Robson to have toast for his tea, and may I have the key of the dairy, because that there cat's been at the butter again?'

'Yes, you'd better make some toast. I'll get the butter.'

As she went up the passage on her way to the kitchen, Mary kicked the cat.

16

HARVEST AT ANDERBY

'Foreman would like to see you, m'm.'

Violet entered the dining-room and looked hesitatingly from John to Mary. Foreman's real request was for the master, but since his illness Mary had given her orders that all such messages should be brought to her. Violet's upbringing had been on strictly evangelical lines, in the fear of a God who loveth righteousness and hateth a lie. She found it difficult to accept Mary's creed that small fibs are a very present help in trouble.

She looked so unhappy about it that John noticed her perturbation.

'What does foreman want, d'you know?'

Violet did know. She had been talking to Fred Stephens, leaning across the kitchen window sill, and discussing in hushed tones the probability of a strike on Monday. No one talked about anything else just now in Anderby. But again she perjured her soul.

'I don't know, sir.'

John's attention drifted again to his fried bacon, and Mary followed Violet from the room.

'That was right, Violet. Remember that Mr Robson's not to be worried about these sort of things. I'm the farmer these days till the doctor says he's all right again.'

Violet sighed. There would be many confessions of falsehood to be muttered that night into her pillow before she went to bed. Life was very hard in Anderby – to say nothing about Fred Stephens who must be persuaded not to strike even if she had to throw over Percy to do it.

Mary hurried along the passage. She, too, found life rather difficult in Anderby just then – difficult, but exciting, and because exciting, then tolerable. The strike really was coming. Neither native caution nor the foreman's contempt nor the force of habit had availed against the rhetoric of Hunting. Anderby intellect had yielded to his eloquence as it would never have yielded to argument. The *Flying Fox* became the head-quarters of an active organization for industrial enlightenment. Coast as an unofficial friend of progress at last found himself a person of importance in an appreciative world. Waite was enabled to turn his ill-fortune to good account. The labourers from various farms awoke to the fact that they were victims of an unbearable tyranny – when they had time to think about it. Mrs Robson was going to have her hoped-for fight with something real.

It was all very satisfactory.

'Well, foreman, what is it now?' asked Mary.

He removed his cap and scratched his head.

'It's a bad job this, missus.'

'It's a bad job for us, but it's worse for the men. Have they any strike pay put by, foreman? They can't have. It hasn't gone on long enough.'

'Why m'm, it's like this, you see. Mr Rossitur comes down and says "You're all beasts. You've got to be men," an' rates 'em worse nor Parson on Advent Sunday. And he makes 'em all uncomfortable like a pup wi' a kettle tied t' his tail. Then comes Mr Hunting an' gets up t' union. An' when they've got a union they mun hev a strike. For what's t' use o' unions unless you strike, they say? And what's t' use of striking unless you do it when it makes most row? And when's that? Harvest time o' course. So they'll strike.'

'I know,' said Mary. 'That's just it. You put it very well. Why, we're all speakers now in Anderby! I've never heard so much talk in all my life as there's been in the last three weeks. I talk too. You should have heard me on at poor Bert Armstrong! He hardly knew whether he was on his head or his heels by the time I'd done with him.'

Foreman grinned. 'Ay. I heard tell o' that.'

'Well, if the worst comes to the worst, I suppose we can rely on you and Shepherd and Mike. What about those Irish men, foreman?'

'Well, them as is friends o' Mike's will do as 'e says. I don't like t' looks o' Mike these days, Mrs Robson, I tell you straight. It isn't that 'e's drinking worse nor usual. He allus was a good 'un for that. It's way 'e acts when 'e is drunk.'

'What sort of way?' asked Mary, frowning.

How tiresome of Mike to add to her troubles when she had so many things to think about!

'Oh, swearing an' taking on' an' offering to fight anyone

what says a word agin you. And talking about that there Mr Rossitur – saying he was at t' bottom of strike an' all, an' if he hadn't come there wouldn't have been no trouble.'

'Well, that's true in a way, I suppose.'

'Ay, mebbe. But's it's doing no good down i' t' village and it's doing no good to Mike. Waite's like a great mule since 'is row wi' Mike, and Mike's fair crazed over any o' t' union men. I wish ye'd speak to 'em, m'm. There'll be trouble in Anderby one of these days.'

'Oh, there'll be trouble all right. But I don't see what I can do. I'll try and speak to Mike. Is there anything else?'

She returned to finish her tea with John. Poor John! She knew he suffered no less from the changed conditions because he was inarticulate. Sometimes she wondered whether it hurt more to move as he moved, half understanding, among the hostility of a once friendly wold, or to live as she lived, continually estimating and expressing the measure of her own emotions. Perhaps, with her, one pain dimmed the consciousness of another, while John clung steadily to the thought of coming trouble at Anderby.

His mute misery appealed to her desire for action. Besides, it was all part of her plan of life by which she must speak to foreman, she must pacify Mike, she must in short be Mrs Robson of Anderby Wold.

She invented trivial pretexts for working in the kitchen that she might be the first to hear an ominous knock at the door. With her sleeves rolled above her elbows she stood for hours, her hands deep in flour, a self constituted vanguard to repel the attacks of John's enemies.

'You're very busy these days, honey,' he remarked with his

slow smile as Mary rose from the table and began to replace her large white apron.

She was busy with the buttons and for a moment did not answer.

'There's a lot of fruit to bottle,' she said at last. 'Sarah Bannister has sent me some more damsons from the low orchard.'

'Must you do it to-night? you look a bit fagged out.'

He rarely commented on her appearance. She wondered if it had altered lately. That would not be surprising.

'Oh, I'm all right, and you see the fruit was picked in the wet, and will go bad if I don't bottle it at once. Sarah said I should.'

'Didn't you say we were going over there?'

'Yes, Sarah's letter is on the mantelpiece if you want to see it. She asked us to go on Wednesday and stay for tea.'

'She knows I can't get away in harvest.'

'Oh, yes, we can, for the evenings, while we're only reaping.'

He looked up at her drearily.

'Are we going to have any harvest this year, honey?'

'Why, of course. Even if the men do come out for a bit – more fools they – it's only what has happened in lots of places. They'll have to come in again when their savings are gone – which won't be long. And anyway we can carry on with the few who'll stay.'

'Ay. I suppose we'll manage somehow. But do you think we're right to hold out? Willerbys would give in if we would.'

She bent across the table towards him, leaning with her hands outspread on the linen cloth, her strong arms bared to the elbow. The concentrated energy of her quiet voice had gathered to itself all other force and light from the room.

'Are you afraid, John?' she asked.

He shifted in his chair and spoke irritably. 'No, not exactly. But all this tomfoolery and speechifying is a bit too much for me. I'm not a boy to begin all over again getting used to new ideas.'

'A boy! Why, anyone would think you were an old man from the way you talk, instead of being only just over fifty. This is nothing but what's going on all over the country, good gracious! It will be all over and done with in a week or two, and the men will realize how they've been fooled and come back to work and feed out of your hand.'

John produced his pipe and began to fill it with trembling fingers. 'It's all very well for you,' he said at last. I suppose you're right. You always are. But I'm sure I don't know how we're to manage.'

She came to his chair and bent over him with a light across. His helplessness and her increasing care for it engendered in her a new tenderness towards him.

'Why John, be a man! We'll be all right. It'll pass. We've only got to have a firm hand. They may not strike at all when it comes to the point. Don't you worry.'

She left him and went to the kitchen where her pots and baskets of fruit awaited her.

She was glad that John would be content to stand back in the ensuing crisis. She wanted to face the strikers herself, to hit hard and be hit back again, to have people say worse things to her than she said to herself. Somehow she must end this conspiracy of adulation which led every one about her household to tell her what a wonder she was, when all the time she shrank from the thought of herself in loathing, and would have welcomed chastisement with scorpions.

And yet, if it did stop, if she could not hold her position in the village, how was she to live? What was there to live for?

She banged the great stewing-pan on the stove with unnecessary violence.

The carrier's cart drove up to the door and Violet entered with several parcels and a green baize bag.

'Put the groceries away please, Violet, and get me a towel to wipe my hands. Are those the things from the library?' Mary opened the bag and drew forth two novels and a sheaf of newspapers.

'I can't think why we get these things,' she fretted, turning over the pages of the books. 'I'm sure I never have any time to read them nowadays. Take them to Mr Robson.'

'And the papers, m'm?'

'No, no. Give me the papers or leave them there on the table.'

Violet took the books. The newspapers lay among the jars and baskets. Mary resolutely continued her bottling. She did not want to see what David had to say in the *Northern Clarion*. She did not care what he said, not she! She had other things to think about than a mid-summer madness.

Recklessly she splashed the juice of damsons on the table. A crimson spot flared across the newspaper.

Within that wrapper were words he had written. Perhaps as he wrote, some recollection of Anderby and his visit there and her might have stirred him. She had not read one word from him since the letter he had written to her.

It was a pity to stain the paper, though. It would do so nicely for lining cupboards. Carefully she wiped off the juice with her apron. She was holding it so when Mike knocked at the door.

She let him in.

'Foreman said you was wishing to see me, missus.'

'Oh, did he?'

Foreman was an old villain. Still, she had better say something to the man now he was here. She could not quite remember, though, what she was expected to say. It would not do for her to be at a loss – she who was accustomed to kitchen confidences ranging from Sunday collections to illegitimate babies.

'Now, look here, Mike,' she began, 'I want to ask your help.'

Mike grinned.

'If there's anything in heaven or earth I can be doing for you, missus—'

'There is. We've got a trying time ahead of us, both we who are standing together and the men who are standing against us. I know that we can manage here, though, because you and your Irish friends will help us.'

'Yess, indade. There's a few of us won't let any thing happen to you, Mrs Robson. Just you trust Mike. It wasn't for nothing you brought him back to life. No, begorrah! There's many another will wish he had the chance.'

'Yes, Mike, but it's not only working for me. There are other things too. It won't be easy in the village. Now I count on you to help with the other farms as well, will you?'

'Anything you ask Mike, Missus Robson, he'll do.'

'And – and Foreman says you're being very silly about the men who've joined the union. Now, Mike, we mustn't have any fighting. Remember they can't help it. They're ignorant, foolish, driven to do foolish things by men who can talk cleverly but who are really just as ignorant as themselves. They can't help it. They've been fooled by others. Do you understand?'

'Yes, missus, I understand.'

'That's all right, then.'

Believing that she had ensured his peaceable behaviour during the next few days, she let him go.

On Saturday night Hunting came to tell them that the men were going to strike.

Sunday passed in a waiting dream of small comings and goings, the Willerbys driving over to discuss the future campaign in voices sunk to an awful whisper, as though they were in church – Foreman hammering at the door with anxious persistency, quite unbalanced by the necessity for changing the usual harvest routine, Shepherd, grimly humorous, assuring Mary he was ready to run a reaper over the whole farm if need be, John in a state of sulky restlessness like a sick cat.

After tea she fled from the house and went to the gate in the stable-yard.

Westward before her rose fold upon fold of the encircling hills, piled rich and golden beneath a tranquil sky. There was no sound but the crunch, crunch of horses feeding in the pasture.

She locked her hands on the highest bar of the gate and rested her chin upon them. The sunset colours before her paled from golden fields and crimson sky to grey and ghostly corn below faint clouds of primrose.

She closed her eyes and let the cool air blow across her forehead. She must have dozed for a minute, for when she looked up the wolds seemed full of life and movement. From the upland acres came heavy waggons behind great horses that strained and sweated with their golden load. In the harvest field moved the figures of men piling stooks and leading horses and forking sheaves into the lumbering waggons – stooping and lifting, lifting and stooping with a rhythm that swayed atune to the wind across the wheat.

Voices rang out, and laughter from the shadowy hills, as girls passed up the road to greet their homing sweethearts. Empty waggons bound for the hills again rattled merrily past with a load of singing children. The men wore dark loose clothes, quaintly fashioned, exposing their brown throats and sinewy arms. Among them rode the master on a grey cob, laughing with them and they with him as he paused to encourage a worker, and soothe a restive horse.

The light faded. Down the winding road came the last load home, while following in its rumbling shadow the women gleaned fallen straws and ears of corn.

The harvesters passed her, their forks across their shoulders, and as they passed they smiled and saluted her with friendly eyes. The children passed her, carrying garlands of pimpernel and poppies. They waved their flowers towards her, and sang with tired, merry voices. The girls passed, bearing thick brown jars emptied of ale, and baskets brimming with half-ripe blackberries from the hedgerow. The master passed her.

Thus they had harvested at Anderby since those far-off years when the Danes broke in across the headland and dyed with blood the trampled barley. Thus and thus had the workers passed, and the children waved their garlands following the last load home. Thus had Mary and other Mary Robsons before her welcomed back the master of the harvest.

She held out her hands to him with a cry of greeting.

The girls vanished along the road, their dresses fading like pale flowers into the twilight.

The master raised his head to her and for the first time she saw his face. It was not John who rode behind as master of the harvest at Anderby, but David – David with his eager face and smiling lips, riding in triumph behind the singing harvesters.

She called to him. Her voice rang strangely through the quiet air. She opened her eyes suddenly and stared across the empty field to find he was not there. She turned and ran, not looking back till she was in the house.

Outside across the waiting fields moved a quiet wind stirring the grey seas of wheat and barley to plaintive whisperings of sound. Bats flitted below the trees around the garden. In the pasture the horses tore at the dewy grass. One by one the lights vanished from the windows of the house.

The harvest moon rose.

Before six next morning Violet appeared at the door of the room where John and Mary lay waiting for the morning.

'Some men are in the yard. They want to see you,' she said, her small face quivering with distress.

'All right,' answered Mary. 'I'll go. John, you stay in bed. Who is it, Violet?'

'Parker and Deane and Waite and – and Fred Stephens. Oh, m'm, he promised he wouldn't join. On Saturday he promised he wouldn't whatever they did to him.'

'Never mind, Violet. I expect it's all right. We all have to do what the others do these days, it seems. You run along and get your clothes on. We may want breakfast earlier.'

She dressed with deliberate care. It had come, then. She

doubted no longer, and the certainty, after days' suspense, elated her.

John shook off the bed-clothes and thrust his legs out of bed.

'You'd better not come,' she said, braiding up her long hair. 'I'll see the men. The doctor wouldn't like you to get up so early in the morning.'

The dogged look she knew well settled on his face. 'I'm coming down,' he said.

Together they went to the yard door. Mary kept in the background, standing on the kitchen threshold, her hands behind her clasping at the side post of the door. She watched, in the early sunlight beyond John's dark figure, the ring of hostile faces in the yard.

John spoke first.

'Well, men, what is it?'

Parker shuffled forward and spat on the flags by way of prelude.

He was evidently the head of the deputation, a Hardrascliffe man only hired last year and less bound by a tradition of service to his master than were the others. Mary smiled as she realized how the older men made a virtue of necessity by shifting the odium as well as the difficulty of speech on to a comparative stranger. She saw old Deane, who once worked for her father, twisting a greasy cap in embarrassed fingers. They were all there but Mike, Shepherd and Foreman. Waite, who had nothing to do with the farm any longer – even he had come and hovered in the background, manifestly enjoying the situation. Champions of liberty and progress! This was the outcome of David's fine talking. Mary wondered what he would think of them.

It was Parker who finally spoke.

'We ain't going to work to-day, maister.'

'Oh, I gave orders to Foreman on Saturday night that the sixty acre had to be opened up.'

'Ay, you did.'

'Well, then, why aren't you going to do it?'

'We can't make money at this job.'

'Money? What's wrong with your money? Haven't you high enough wages? I've offered ten shillings more than last year.'

Mary, locking and unlocking her fingers, endeavoured to curb her growing desire to push John's lumbering ineffectiveness aside, and herself deal with the envoys of the union. While she fretted Parker found his word, a drifting echo of Hunting's Saturday night oration.

'We want a living wage,' he said.

'Living wage?' repeated John dully. This was an entirely unfamiliar situation, and he was equipped neither by temperament nor training to deal with unfamiliar situations. Mary realized the misery of his hesitation. 'How much do you want?' he asked.

'Three pound,' began Parker.

Waite elbowed him roughly.

'Three pund ten, you fool!' he prompted.

'Three pund ten, maister,' repeated Parker. The 'maister' came scornfully.

John's eyes glanced from one to the other to find a single light of friendliness. One by one the men turned away except Parker and Waite, who looked straight at him, one with surly defiance the other with barely concealed contempt.

'Look here, haven't I always treated you decently?'

John's voice sounded strained and feeble. He ran his hand round the collar of his shirt. Beads of perspiration stood out on his forehead.

Mary could bear it no longer. She came forward and stood by her husband.

'Well, Parker, what have you got to say to that? Well, Deane, you know us better. Haven't we always treated you decently?' She asked sharply.

'Oh, ay.' Old Deane shuffled clumsy boots on the stone pavement.

One of the boys at the back of the little crowd sniggered nervously. Deane glared round for a minute then replied, 'Oh, ay. I haven't nowt to say agin you.'

'You can't, you see. Have either of us done you a single bad turn since you decided to stay on ten years ago?'

'Nay, but—'

'Did my father ever hurt you?'

'Nay, but—'

'And are you treating us decently now?'

Deane looked up with a suspicion of the old twinkle in his eye.

'Nay, missus. We're treating you about as badly as we can. But a man must live. We've got oursens to look to.'

'Oh. And aren't you living now! Which of you has been hungry in Anderby or ill-clothed or ill-fed?' Mary had quite taken her husband's place now, and John, glad to relinquish it, stood back among the shadows of the passage. 'Hearing you weren't satisfied with what we offered we – all the farmers – talked together and are giving you what we can afford.'

'Ay,' broke in Parker. 'An' if ye can't afford more than that we'll go to others who can. Farmers is tyrants, an' you as much as any on 'ere, and we'll have our rights in spite of you.'

'Tyrants, are we?'

The men hung back a little ill at ease. Parker was going too far. What passed for sporting candour in the *Flying Fox* was little to their taste when confronting Mrs Robson at six o'clock on a Monday morning.

'We've got to live,' growled Parker, unable for the moment to think of a more biting retort.

'Oh, you've got to live, have you? I *am* surprised and you prefer to live on strike pay that doesn't amount to more than two or three week's subscription rather than work for your wages, do you? What's come over you all? I've lived at Anderby for twenty-eight years and my father lived here before me, and there's hardly been a wrong word between us and one of you. But now because a glib tongued townsman comes down from Manchester, we're tyrants, are we? Why didn't you speak before, eh? You needn't have come back at Martinmas unless you liked. There were plenty of other places where you could go. Well, if you want to work for us, you can work on our terms or not at all. We'll be masters of our own land, my husband and I, or we'll go somewhere else.'

From the passage came John's beseeching whisper:

'Stop now, honey. Quiet them down a bit and they'll cave in.'

Mary never turned her head. For the first time for several weeks she was thoroughly enjoying herself. A fine glow of righteous indignation replaced the humiliation and uncertainty that had lately assailed her. She felt mistress of the situation at last. Having found an outlet for the pent-up emotions of the summer, she determined to utilize it to the uttermost extent.

'Mr Hunting says we're being crushed by capitalist tyranny.' Parker triumphantly remembered more of his lesson. 'And, by God, we'll have our rights!'

'Quiet 'em down now,' begged John. Even his limited perspicacity had seen that the other men thought Parker had gone too far.

If Mary realized it, she made no sign of conciliation.

'Mr Hunting,' she sneered dramatically. 'And who is this Mr Hunting?'

'Our secretary – man from Manchester.'

'Yes, your secretary, the organizer of the Northern Branch of the Farm Labourers' Union. A man you've seen for two or three weeks and about whom you know nothing. And you've known me for eight and twenty years, and you say I've never done you any harm. I tell you that you're being offered a fair wage. He apparently says you're not. Which are you going to believe?'

She stood in the centre of the doorway, her hands clasping both the side posts, her eyes bright with excitement. She only knew that this was really thrilling and dramatic. Unfortunately, she had omitted to ask herself whether it was necessary.

'We mun do what our secretary says. We mun have our rights.' The old parrot cry echoed monotonously. Having exhausted their carefully learnt phrases, the men had nothing more to say. Deane whispered to Parker. Fred Stephens shuffled and blushed scarlet with perplexity and detestation of anything approaching a scene.

'You stop now, honey. Better offer 'em another ten shillings,' urged John in a hoarse whisper.

But Mary would not stop.

'Yes, you'll have your rights though you don't know what they are. And you'll follow a hot-brained tub-thumper from Manchester, whose business it is to fool you left and right. Don't you know that he's being paid to fool you? Oh, dear, no, not you! You think you're all so clever and modern and you'll be as independent as the miners and have a strike on your own. Very well then, you can have it. We'll do without you. The weather's fine. There are some who have more sense than to be driven off their heads by a red-tied radical. You needn't think you are indispensable. We can manage without you far better than you can manage without us.'

She paused. The men stared at her open-mouthed. This was certainly a new Mrs Robson.

'Well,' she cried. 'Well? What are you going to do? Have you asked your precious union what sort of pay it's going to give you while other men get the harvest in? Why didn't you wait a bit before you started this game?'

There was no answer. The silence infuriated her. She had by this time lost her last vestige of self-control. A shrill note of hysteria rose in her voice.

'You'll be back here soon,' she stormed, 'whining for us to let you in again, and you'll find it too late. Then you'll know who's master. Now you can go. Strike if you like, but don't expect any sympathy from us if it isn't as nice as you think. Go on. Get out of here! Get out, you fools, and never let me see you hanging round the door again. Go to your precious Hunting – and if he can't feed you, then starve! I don't care. Get out of here!'

Not quite sure whether Mrs Robson was mad or angry or merely making a fool of herself, and finding any of these possibilities equally embarrassing, the men began to turn away. Only Waite looked back.

'All right, missus,' he said. 'But you bain't shut on us yet.'

One by one they filed out of the yard. Their footsteps died away along the road.

John faced Mary. For the first time in his life he was really angry with her.

'Well, you *have* done it,' he said. 'What on earth did you want to fly out like that for? I thought you had more sense.'

Mary closed the door.

'And I thought you had more spirit,' she stormed. 'This has got to be fought out or we'll never be masters in Anderby again.'

Her voice was still high-pitched. Her cheeks were flushed. Her breath came in sharp sobs. John looked her up and down, more bewildered than annoyed.

'I think you'd better go and lie down again, honey,' he suggested mildly.

Mary turned on him with fury. Then suddenly as it had come her rage departed. Without a word she turned and fled up the passage her hands pressed to her mouth to check the sobs that seemed to choke her.

John looked slowly after her retreating figure and saw Violet's white face emerging from the pantry door.

'Is this the strike, sir?' she asked tremulously.

'Yes, this is the strike all right,' said John.

17

LADIES AT MARKET BURTON

'What I cannot understand,' said Mrs Holmes, 'is why John ever allowed the man to come near the village at all.'

'Oh, but as far as I can see, he didn't let them come in. That was all Mary's doing.' Ursula pulled a cushion down more comfortably between her shoulders and smiled at the circle of interested faces.

'Mary? Why Mary?' asked Anne, whose round little mouth perpetually opened in search of information, as though she were a bird awaiting a gift of worms.

Sarah Bannister also looked up from her knitting. 'Yes, Ursula, why Mary?'

'Oh, that socialist creature you know – your friend, Sarah. He began it all. Mary brought him to Anderby and rubbed his chest with Elliman's Embrocation because he had a cold, and he started agitating among the labourers – and then the band played. Of course we all know that Mary's awfully well-meaning, and all that, but, really, one would have thought she'd have had a little more sense.'

Since her return from the Hardrascliffe nursing home, Ursula had become an increasingly intimate member of the circle of Robson women. Their 'quaintness' amused her, when the activities of a smarter set of sporting friends proved too strenuous, and her position as the mother of the only male Robson of the rising generation was agreeably important.

'You need not call him my friend, Ursula,' snapped Sarah, who alone was not overcome by the charm of her cousin-in-law's society. 'The young man would have had impertinence enough to argue with Mr Asquith himslf, but he hadn't brains to upset a single creature in the village, I know – not alone, anyway.'

Mrs Holmes shook a doleful head. 'Well, I don't know what we're all coming to, I'm sure. What do you think Emily said to me this morning?'

'Is Emily the cook or the parlourmaid?' asked Anne.

'Emily is the parlourmaid of course – that girl who Mrs Thomson recommended to me and thought was so nice, only she would breathe on the silver before she polished it, which I always think is such an infectious habit, don't you, with all this influenza and germs about? Though, since the doctor at Harrogate told me I ought to spend my winters abroad, I'm sure I hardly dare to think of a germ without swallowing a formamint, nasty though they are. But Emily came to me just when I was having a little dry toast with my tea in bed – all the doctor will allow me during this new treatment – and said to me "Please, m'm, may I go to a dance to-night in the village?" And I said, "Emily," I said, "you can never complain of the way I have treated you, always having the same as we have in the dining-room, and there's no more beautiful food within twenty miles of Market Burton I'm sure. And if it was a question of a night out to go and see your young man's people, it would be a different matter. But a dance!" I said, "This is too much. I will not have any maids learning the same steps as my nieces dance in the Town Hall at Leeds."'

'I don't see that that has anything much to do with it, Janet.' Sarah rose, and began to clear the parish magazines and bound volumes of *Punch*, and baskets of sewing that were piled upon her corner table.

'I can't see why there should be a strike just round about Anderby. It all seems very strange. I'm sure I'm sorry for Mary.' Anne sighed a little, folding up her work.

'As far as I can see, she only has herself to blame,' said Ursula. 'She jolly well asked for trouble, rubbing up the backs of half the men in the village in the way she did. Why, when I was staying there, she had a frightful quarrel with the schoolmaster about some boy or other, and it appears from what Foster says that this man is behind most of the trouble.'

'Foster was down there yesterday, wasn't he?'

'Yes.' Ursula smiled with satisfaction. 'I sent him down to see if there was anything we could do. Of course we are *most* sorry for them both, especially John. For I'm sure, after the way he's worked like a negro, getting the mortgage paid off Mary's farm, the least she could have done was to have made things as easy for him as possible.'

'Did Foster say if John was keeping well?' Sarah would have given much to go herself to Anderby. The consciousness that in John's hour of difficulty no one but Mary was with him, and that she apparently had only increased his troubles, was gall and wormwood to Sarah.

'Oh, he was going on all right so far, I believe. Though of course all this sort of thing must be fearfully bad for him. I really can't imagine what Mary was doing to let it happen. If she had any of the influence you all used to boast she had over the village, I'm sure she could have stopped it. From what Foster gathered, she just was as tactless as she possibly could have been – slanged the men fearfully when they might have come in, and lost her temper absolutely at the end. Really, you know, one sometimes wonders what she'll do next. She either has extraordinary notions of behaviour or very little self-control – though, of course, I always feel inclined to excuse her a great deal, because she hasn't any children.'

'Well, I'm sure if Mary was wise, she would take John away from Anderby,' commented Louisa. She was now helping Sarah, who arranged plates of queen cakes and jam tarts on the corner table as grimly as though she were laying out a corpse. 'After a stroke he ought not to have to face all these new conditions.'

'No, I'm sure.' Janet Holmes sighed sympathetically. 'I know so well what it is for an invalid with shattered nerves to have to face all sorts of changes. When I came back from Harrogate, absolutely exhausted by the treatment there, and found that Lily had given notice, and I had to engage a new cook—'

'Pass me the kettle, please, Anne. Janet, I suppose you are allowed to have a cup of tea?' interrupted Sarah.

'No milk, please – I'm not allowed a drop of lactic matter just yet.'

'You know, what I think is so queer about Mary,' continued Ursula from the sofa, 'is that she always seems so awfully pleased with herself. Of course I'm *very* fond of Mary, mind you, and I wouldn't say a word against her; but you know she really did sometimes seem to think she was God Almighty in that village, and I'm sure she was never quite as considerate to John as she might have been. Though there are some people, of course, who just aren't capable of deep feeling.'

'Well, this must be rather a shock to her,' murmured Anne timidly. 'I'm sure she must be very fond of Anderby. It's such a pretty home.'

'Oh, I don't know. Women with that rather domineering temperament love a fight, don't they? And then it won't do her any harm really, just seeing that every one isn't ready to lick her boots. It's poor John I'm so sorry for.'

The teapot arrived on a silver tray carried by a starched maid, and the ladies put aside their work, and turned their attention to tarts and bread and butter.

'Well, I don't think it would do Mary any harm to hear a little advice—' began Ursula, when the door opened again and Mary walked in.

There was a sudden silence.

'I saw when I passed the window that Millie was helping in the room, so I just came straight in,' she said, drawing off her gloves and coming forward to Sarah. 'John's up the garden with Tom, Sarah. They'll probably like a bit of talk together. I'm glad I've just come in time for tea.'

She took her cup and sat down beside Louisa in the big armchair left vacant for Sarah. She did not know that it was Sarah's chair. She did not know anything except that it was a relief to sit in this comfortable room where life was shaken by such small emotions and crises passed like the ripples made by a draught across the tea-cups.

She stirred the hot fragrant tea and selected with pleasure an iced cake from the dish Louisa passed her. Every one seemed very silent. That was nice. She had talked so much lately. There was too much talking down at Anderby.

'Those were lovely damsons you sent me,' she remarked pleasantly to Sarah. 'I bottled them at once and they were a splendid colour.'

What a blessed comfort to talk of something beside the strike! She took a bite of sugar cake and stretched her long limbs in the cushioned chair. Still nobody spoke.

'It was dusty driving along,' she said.

There was a pause.

'I'm glad you were able to get away,' Louisa ventured at last. 'We were afraid you wouldn't be able to come.'

'Why not? We were busy this morning, but one can generally get away in the afternoons before leading time, and a change is rather nice. Besides, it's a long time since we were here – not since John was ill.'

'But – when things are rather difficult just now?' suggested Ursula.

'Difficult? What do you mean by difficult?' asked Mary irritably. Of course, if they were going to spoil her respite by hinting and fidgeting, she might as well have stayed at home.

'Well, I didn't know if you would be able to leave, now that you are having trouble on the farm.' Ursula stirred her tea meditatively.

'Trouble? Oh, you mean the strike?'

Then the chorus burst forth. 'Yes, of course, Mary.' 'How are you managing, Mary?' 'What is John doing about it?' 'How are you getting the harvest in?' 'How is John?' In a babble of curious voices.

Mary put down her tea-cup, and looked at them all. She seemed about to say something. Then she changed her mind and helped herself to another pink cake.

'Oh, we're getting on quite all right, thank you. How's the great child, Ursula?'

'Thomas is all right, thank you, Mary. But how is John? We've all been so anxious about him?'

'John is quite well again, thanks. How are you, Janet? Did Harrogate do you any good?'

The inquiries had to cease for a little while, until Janet Holmes had given a detailed account of her doctor, her ailments, her domestic problems and her cure. Mary did not think it necessary to listen. She ate and drank with drowsy contentment, the headache that had pursued her during the last fortnight slowly fading under the influence of tea and physical relaxation.

It was restful here, while Janet talked of waters and Turkish baths, and Sarah handed cheese-cakes on fluted dishes, and Anne nervously flicked at her tatting in the corner. Still, one would not like to stay here always – only for a little, until the harvest was in, and the house at Anderby quiet again, and it was no longer necessary to listen every minute for a knock on the back door ... Here it was too quiet though ... too quiet ... a valley, ... trees in a valley ... Her thoughts trailed off to drowsy incoherence. ' ... And so I said "Dr. Merriman, don't dream of it!" And he said "My dear lady, that's just what I should do if I allowed you to continue a minute longer in this dreadful climate."'

Like most of Janet's tales, there seemed no more reason why this should stop than why it had begun. Ursula decided it had continued long enough. She resumed the attack.

'Is it true that you and John are going to retire after this year?' she asked sweetly.

Mary looked up in genuine astonishment. 'Good gracious, no!'

'Well, we thought perhaps that, as John wasn't well and as after a stroke worry and excitement are so bad for people, you wouldn't think it wise to go on farming in Anderby.'

'You see, Mary, he has always been so sensitive from a boy, to any adverse feeling. This must have troubled him terribly,' added Louisa.

Sarah, for the moment, said nothing.

Mary looked round the room upon her relatives.

'Oh!' she whispered softly.

'Of course we quite realize you're not to blame, Mary.' Ursula took up the tale. 'Naturally it was awfully amusing having that young fellow to stay and all that, and hearing his views, so different from anything one gets about here, and, personally, I adore socialists. I've met lots of them in the different places where I've stayed golfing, but in a small village it's hardly wise, is it, to encourage that sort of people?'

'It must have made a difference, John being only just better. You must be very worried about him,' insisted Louisa quietly.

'And, really, there is no need even to sell Anderby unless you liked. You could always rent it to some one. My young cousin, Eustace Darnell, has just left Cirencester Agricultural College and wants a farm. You could get a good rent for it.'

'And there's always Littledale, if John wanted to potter about a bit. I'm sure it would be nice to retire. It's very pleasant here.' Louisa took the tea-cup Mary had emptied, and carried it back to Sarah at the table.

'Of course John's only fifty-two,' continued Ursula, 'and that's early to retire, but he's always been rather old for his age, hasn't he? And now he's had a stroke, I suppose you'll have to be very careful of him. It's really awfully risky, isn't it, keeping him at Anderby at all now the strike's on? It must be rather trying for him.'

Mary looked from one woman to another, in mute amazement.

'Well, really,' she said, 'anyone would think that John had to do all the work himself from the way you talk! Why, at present things are going on as much as usual. We have Shepherd and Foreman and Mike O'Flynn and one or two Irish harvesters who have been with us for several years. The only difficulty will be the leading, and then we've planned to join up with the Willerbys and Glebe Farm people, and get each other's corn in by turns.'

Instinctively she turned a little in her chair and looked back towards Sarah. Sarah was evidently engrossed in the delicate operation of pouring out a second cup of tea for Louisa and paid Mary no attention.

Mary tried to finish her cake. The icing broke off into hard, jagged pieces in her mouth. It was difficult to swallow. Oh, but this was a dreadful place, she thought. What business was it of these women to torment her? Of course they wanted her and John to come and live in Market Burton. They were probably jealous, because she was still young enough to appreciate life at Anderby . . . Trees of the valley, they were jealous of those who stood out upon the hill-tops and battled with the storm. They would try to draw her down, woo her with warmth and ease, and whisper that the fight was too hard, the uplands too bleak –

hold out as a threat the danger to John ... Knowing perhaps, that her conscience was already over-burdened, and that when she thought of her possible complicity in John's illness she lost all sense of reason and proportion.

'Oh, we know of course you'd never let him do *that* sort of work,' smiled Ursula ingratiatingly. 'It's just the strain of working with unfriendly people, and knowing that at any moment there may be more trouble. Of course, when you're down amongst it all, I don't suppose you have quite the same chance of realizing what it all means as we have here. You're very busy, I know – always such a good manager. Naturally you haven't much time for fussing about other things – but we really have been wondering a little how John will stand the strain.'

Mary rose. To herself she said, 'I can't stand this much longer.' Aloud, she laughed lightly.

'Well, you must all remember we've got to get the harvest in somehow – and, after all, Ursula, I have the best opportunity of knowing what's right for John. Sarah, I wonder if you'd let me take one or two tomatoes from your greenhouse. John does like them, and we have none at Anderby ... No, don't bother to come, please.'

She had to escape from the room somehow. It was intolerable, full of jagged glass ornaments, and crude woolwork and tongues that cut like glass. These women would drive her mad. As though she had never contemplated the possibility of retiring!

'I'll come with you.' Sarah spoke to her for the first time that evening.

'No, please don't bother,' begged Mary desperately. 'I really know where they are, and I only want a few.'

Sarah picked up a shawl and followed her from the room without further comment.

The garden was full of slanting amber light and mellow tranquillity. Across the hedge, they could hear the click of mallets on croquet balls, and the intermittent calling of tennis scores from the neighbouring club.

Sarah and Mary walked down the gravel path, between an autumn riot of herbaceous borders and laden apple-trees. For a little while both were silent, and Mary hoped, against all knowledge of Sarah's character, that no further reference would be made to the conversation in the drawing-room. She bent over a tall cluster of Japanese anemones.

'How fine these are this year,' she remarked, 'I never knew such a lot of blossoms. They're so useful for vases too.'

Sarah disregarded her attempted evasion.

'Mary,' she announced abruptly, 'John will have to give up farming.'

Mary began to defend herself with unnecessary vigour.

'Oh, what nonsense you are all talking! John's all right. He is really. Why, think how young he is! You're always saying that your father didn't retire and was killed by an accident, when he was ninety-two. John's better. Really he is.'

'You know he isn't, Mary.'

'Yes, he is. He is really. The doctor said that if he was kept quiet there's no reason why—'

'Exactly. *If* he was kept quiet. Now John has had a stroke, Mary. He's a big heavy man and easily upset. He isn't clever like you.' Mary started at the compliment. 'He'll find it very hard to get used to the new ways.'

'But this won't last long. We're getting along very nicely and the men are bound to come in sooner or later. Things will be just the same again.'

'You know that isn't true,' said Sarah quietly. 'Things will never be the same again. You're deceiving yourself, Mary. You don't like the idea of giving up farming because you're still young and have had a hard time, I know, to set things right at Anderby. But if you keep on, this will kill John.'

'Why, what nonsense! John's quite a young man. What's fifty-two? What should we do, retiring at our age? Settle down here in Market Burton? That would kill him far more likely. Why, the strike will be over before harvest is in. I never heard such a lot of fuss about nothing in my life!'

'And if the strike is over, what then, Mary?' Sarah smiled down at her strangely. 'What about John in the months to come, when every little hitch will seem to mean another strike, and there are new rules and regulations to deal with, and union officials and all that?'

'Yes, but there's me. I can deal with them. John's had hardly anything to do with all this business.'

What right had Sarah to raise all the tormenting doubts and suggestions of the last few days, just when Mary had buried them so carefully deep down in her mind? It was insufferable interference!

'While John is at Anderby, he will always be among it all. You can't alter that, Mary.'

'Oh, of course I know you want to get him back here! You'd like him under your thumb again, as he was at Littledale. You've always been jealous of me, and thought I shouldn't appreciate him properly!'

'Well, Mary, and if I have? Do you appreciate him properly?'

The old brick wall beyond the fruit trees shone darkly red. David's hair was red ... The scent of the flowers was heavy on Mary's nostrils, as their scent had been that afternoon in the cornfield, when the shadow of John's horse had fallen across the wheat ...

'What do you mean?' gasped Mary. 'What do you mean?'

'I don't think you always bear in mind that John gave up his farm at Littledale, and took over Anderby and your father's debts and has worked as though he was your servant instead of your husband ever since he married you. If he hadn't had your mortgage to pay, he'd be a rich man now. If he hadn't worked so hard, he mightn't have had a stroke. If you don't care enough for him to give up your own will on his account, at least you owe it to him after all he's done for you.'

Mary was silent at last. The flush had faded from her cheeks. She stood, white and motionless, the bruised anemones between her hands.

'Mind you. I know this isn't easy. You haven't had such an easy time at Anderby that you can give way now without minding. It's always the things that have been most a burden that are hard to give up; but, if you don't, it'll kill John.'

'I can't do it.' Mary's voice was devoid of all expression now. The hands that held the flowers twisted a little as though in pain. 'You don't know what I've given up to Anderby. You can't.'

Sarah looked at her for a little while in silence. Then she spoke, and Mary had never before heard her voice so gentle.

'Mary, you don't think I've loved my brother all his life, and watched him and you these ten years, without knowing a little about you both, do you? I'm a cross old woman, and not very happy, but that doesn't prevent me from having eyes in my head. You're young and vigorous, and you want to use your youth. It seems dull to you to come and live among a lot of old maids and worn out men and women in Market Burton. Well, it is dull. But it's what we've all got to face sooner or later.'

'But they can't do without me in the village.'

'Can't they? Do you really think that, Mary? How old are you?'

'Twenty-eight.'

'And you think that at twenty-eight – or indeed at any age – you've got enough wisdom to make yourself necessary to a whole village? My dear child, no one's ever necessary to anybody else's welfare really.'

'But it's so cowardly to give up at the first difficulty.'

Sarah smiled again, and plucked an anemone before she answered.

'There are more sorts of courage than one, Mary, and perhaps the rarest kind of all is the courage that can give way graciously when it's too late to fight any more, I couldn't do it myself, but I know.'

'But I've paid for my right to Anderby!'

'And you think because you've paid you can expect your money's worth? Why, I thought you were less of a child than that.'

From the tennis court across the hedge came a girl's clear voice. 'Look out! That'll be a love set if you're not careful, David!'

Mary turned upon Sarah with sudden anger.

'Did you? Well, then, you were mistaken. This is all just a conspiracy. You're all against me because you're jealous. You're out of things yourselves and don't want anyone else to be in them. Well, you'll see. I'll keep Anderby and I'll fight it out and I'll take care of John so that he'll be all right and you'll all see what fools you've made of yourselves. I'm sorry to sound rude, Sarah, but I've made up my mind.'

'Oh, very well.' There was pity as well as bitterness in Sarah's voice. 'But you'll have to change in the end. If you won't give way on your own, things will make you. And that's much worse really.'

'Don't you think,' asked Mary slowly, 'that it's time we got those tomatoes?'

18

GENTLEMEN AT ANDERBY

'Come, ye thankful people, come,
Raise the song of Harvest-home;
All is safely gathered in,
Ere the winter-storms begin ... '

Mr Coast, who filled the double rôle of schoolmaster and organ-
ist at Anderby, attacked the opening hymn of the Harvest
Thanksgiving Service with such violence that he whirled the
congregation along on an avalanche of discordant sound. The
efforts of Miss Taylor, who led the lady sopranos in the choir,
availed nothing, though she quavered gallantly half a beat
behind, hoping that her vocal energy might counteract his
instrumental zeal. But Mr Coast did not care.

He had almost reached the limit of exasperation. In the most
placid of humours, he would have found it somewhat discon-
certing to play harvest hymns with a barley whisker tickling the
back of his neck. Even if Mrs Willerby was rejoicing in the end

of the strike, she might have decorated the organ loft with greater discretion and less exuberance. The scent of geraniums, which Coast abominated, was mingled with an odour of rotting apples, damp prayer books and perspiring humanity from the choir stalls below. Together they involved him in a nightmare of discomfort.

'Wheat and tares therein are sown,
Unto joy or sorrow grown ...'

Precious little joy about it! A record of nothing but failure piled on failure, humiliation on humiliation. Of course, knowing his luck, he ought never to have expected the strike to be anything but a fiasco. After he had taken all the trouble to get Hunting down from Manchester, after he had gone himself night after night to sit in the beer-stifled atmosphere of the *Flying Fox*, trying to drive a little common sense into the bucolic obstinacy of those cursed villagers, wasn't it just his luck that that fool Rossitur should come down and spoil things?

'Grant, O Lord of life, that we
Holy grain and pure may be ...'

Oh, damn! He ought to have played *piano* there! Well, as if it mattered! As if anything mattered very much, when he could see through the mirror that hung before him Mary Robson standing erect and triumphant in the front pew. It was all very well for her to sing hymns when the harvest was gathered in and the men were going back to work next Monday, and her husband had kept well in spite of the gloomy prognostications of the villagers. Well, she had scored again for the twentieth time – and he had to sit on Mrs Cox's best vegetable-marrow and play the tunes for hymns that celebrated his defeat.

That fool Rossitur deserved smothering. He did really. Just when things were going rather well, what business had he to come down and tell the men that after the farmers had compromised by offering £3 a week the strike had gone on long enough for economic purposes, and that its protraction was merely the result of personal enmity?

All that talk about justice and disinterested co-operation was sentimental nonsense. If he told the truth, Rossitur would have acknowledged that the *Northern Clarion* paid him to advertise it among the labouring classes. Any extension of 'progress' implied increased circulation for his paper.

'But the fruitful ears to store
In Thy garner evermore ...'

And, anyway, it had not been as though he, Coast, had done anything outrageous. A word here and a hint there to the men, warning them against premature compliance with a barely concealed tyranny ... Rossitur himself might have done the same. Supposing Coast did dislike the Robsons, to refrain from performing an obvious social duty because its performance exposed him to the charge of personal enmity would have been nothing short of cowardice. Of that, at least, he was certain.

He pulled out the stops for the final *crescendo*. The congregation abandoned all genteel restraint, and unburdened its accumulation of emotion in a flood of exultant song. It was pleasant to know that in spite of apprehensions this business of unions and strikes and progress made very little difference after all. There had been a good deal of talk by the bridge on Saturday nights, and several superfluous pints of beer had been drunk over heated political discussions, and for six weeks a few wives had knitted their brows over unreplenished purses; but all that was over now, and Mr Slater in a clean white surplice was encouraging the wicked man to turn away from his wickedness, as though there had never been any unprecedented scenes in the back yard of the Wold Farm, and no queer speechifyings by a black haired man called Hunting, and a red haired man called Rossitur.

On the whole, Anderby was pleased with itself. Foreman from the Wold Farm and Ezra Dawson, who only deserted the seclusion of the Primitives once a year to climb the hill for the harvest festival, propped their foreheads on their hands and praised the Almighty for His estimable promptitude in restoring order to the village. Violet, wearing a new silk blouse, almost twisted her neck, in her effort to catch Fred Stephens's eye where he stood, white surpliced and chastened in the choir stalls, no longer an enemy of respectability, but a very nice young man with whom anyone might be seen walking out after service. Bert Armstrong flung out his chest and boomed the hymns with tremendous relish. Really, everything was about as satisfactory as it well could be. Some people, of course, did not seem very pleased, but then fellows like Waite never were satisfied about anything. In other parts of the world, strikes might lead to permanent hostilities and riots, and general discomfort. It merely confirmed the conviction of Anderby's superiority to the rest of the world, to realize how quickly and easily it recovered from this decease of industrial enterprise.

Mr Coast, it is true, differed from the majority in his appreciation of Mr Rossitur's intervention. The village could see how throughout the service he had sat huddled on the organ seat, chewing the ends of his moustache. Well, of course, being the chief supporter of the union, even if you couldn't be recognized officially because you weren't an agricultural labourer, it must be rather trying to have your public aspirations checked at their outset.

The sermon was over and the last hymn announced. From the choir stalls, an arm reached out and tapped Coast on the shoulder. He turned irritably. A slip of paper was thrust into his hand. He read the note scrawled on it by the vicar with increasing indignation:

'Dear Coast,

'Would you kindly manage not to go quite so fast with the hymns? I'm sure it's very gratifying to see you know them so well, but the choir cannot keep pace with you.

'Yours,

'E. C. SLATER.'

Well, of all the outrageous impertinence! Coast crumpled it savagely into a ball, and turned to the organ. 'We plough the fields, and scatter' moaned like a funeral dirge, with long-drawn wails at the end of every fine.

The congregation clumped out of church, and stood about the churchyard in scattered groups of threes and fours. Coast began to collect his music with trembling fingers. His head ached intolerably, and he laboured under a strange delusion that the whole village was laughing at him. Every one knew that he had urged the continuance of the strike. Every one would know soon enough that the vicar sent him insulting notes across the choir stalls.

The sexton began to extinguish the candles on the altar, but Mrs Robson still sat in her pew, gazing dreamily before her.

Coast had mislaid the manuscript page of music that fitted in to his psalter, containing the chants for festival psalms. Striking a match he groped among the shadows on the floor.

'Mr Coast,' the vicar's dry voice summoned him from below the seat.

He sat up suddenly, knocking his already aching head on the side of the keyboard.

'Well?'

The vicar was annoyed. 'When I send you a note with a suggestion like that, Mr Coast, there is really no need to caricature my criticism – No? That hymn, that last hymn, it was disgraceful – really quite spoilt, yes, quite spoilt!'

'You asked to have it slow. I gave you what you asked,' snapped Coast, shutting up the keyboard with a bang.

'I don't think that is quite the spirit – not quite the spirit – for you to adopt, Mr Coast. Irreverent work sets a bad example.'

'Well, I don't think there was any need for you to use my pupils to pass your instructions along. At least you might have folded the paper. Half the choir were sniggering – making a fool of me before the boys and then expect the discipline of the school to be good.'

'Well, really, when you will play hymns as though they were polkas yes, polkas, you must not expect me to refrain from some remark. Another time, please play more suitably. Good evening.'

As the vicar passed the front pew, Coast saw him pause.

That damned woman had heard everything then – heard him scolded like a schoolboy by that fool Slater. It was too much.

'Well, well, Mrs Robson' – Coast could guess just how the Vicar rubbed his bloodless little hands – 'I think we have some cause for rejoicing this year – hah? A most trying business, satisfactorily over.'

'Yes,' said Mary. Her weary voice sounded remote and toneless in the shadowed church.

'I think we may congratulate you and Mr Robson – very disinterested behaviour, very. Quite right that you should have stood out for the sake of the small farmers – quite. I was talking to Mrs Armstrong to-day. She said what a help you and your husband had been to Albert. Very commendable.'

Mrs Robson made no reply.

'I hope your husband has not suffered from the anxiety. Is he strong again?'

'I think he will be all right now if he takes care.'

'Quite so, no more strains. But there, you look after him so well.'

'I do what I can, but I can't stop the wind blowing.'

'Ah – of course. We are all in the hands of God's providence. No more talk about your retiring from farming, I hope?'

'Why, where ever did you hear that rumour?'

'I believe your husband said something about it one day at the parish meeting.'

'Oh, I think not. You've made a mistake. He must have meant something else. We shan't retire for years, if ever we do at all – and I don't see why we should. We both hate town life.'

'Of course, of course. I thought perhaps that after your husband's stroke he might find farming a little strenuous after this unfortunate affair.' The vicar coughed discreetly.

'Oh well, now that it's over, I don't suppose we shall have much more bother.'

Didn't she, indeed! Coast on the organ seat smiled bitterly. He could picture in the darkness Mrs Robson's smile of smug self-satisfaction.

'Of course – in your hands – sure to be all right. Very capable. Very.'

They moved away together down the aisle. The sexton limped round the church like a great bat, extinguishing lights and covering brass work with baize hoods.

'Shall I leave the key to you, Mr Coast?' he queried.

'Please.'

Then he, too, went. The schoolmaster sat alone. 'I don't suppose we shall have much more bother ...' Bother about the playing field, bother about the brassocking holiday, bother about taking Jack Greenwood from school before his time, bother about the strike ... All conveniently settled, with the least possible discomfort to herself, Mary Robson. How nice. How truly obliging of the Almighty to arrange the world so manifestly for her advantage!

'Oh, damn the woman! Damn her, damn her!'

There seemed nothing more to say.

At four o'clock the following Saturday afternoon, Coast was walking up the village street on his way to visit old Mrs Armstrong. He had finally been persuaded by the parish council to approach her about her field in the village, which Mrs

Robson had suggested might serve as a playing ground for the school children. The road was full of life that afternoon. Continually bicycle bells chimed and tinkled, and couples rode past to Hardrascliffe. The Saturday after Harvest was always a red letter day at Anderby. Even Fred Stephens, who was due to return to work with his comrades on Monday, had ingratiated himself sufficiently with the Robsons' Violet to escort her, with sheepish humility and the bait of an invitation to the Pictures, along the Hardrascliffe road.

Coast had passed the post office and the bridge, and turned into the street of straggling houses that led to the Wold Farm. A short stocky figure slouched slowly ahead of him. He recognized Eli Waite shabbier and more disconsolate than ever, walking with drooping head, an empty pipe between his teeth.

Moved by a sudden impulse to talk to some one more out of love with life than himself, Coast hailed him with an unusually genial 'Good afternoon, Waite.'

Geniality was hardly Coast's typical manner, so Waite turned round with some surprise. He regarded the schoolmaster as a man of good sense and perspicacity who had played a worthy part in the recent industrial crisis. The nod he gave was less sulky than usual.

'Afternoon, Mr Coast.'

'How's Ethel? Any better? Bad business for her getting ill just now. What does the doctor think of her?'

'He says she ought to get away to a warmer spot, ought not to winter at Anderby, he says. As if I was a millionaire to send 'er off in a first class carriage.'

Waite spat with emphasis on the path.

'Oh dear, that's bad isn't it? What are you going to do about it?'

Coast knew that any other father in the village would have gone for help to Mary Robson, and that she would have found, among the various institutions to whose skirts she clung for the benefit of her protégés, some holiday home for a delicate child.

But there was no such simple solution for Waite's problem.

'There's nowt to do for the likes o' me but wait and let her get better if she can.'

'Let me see, where are you working now?'

Waite gave him one sidelong glance and then broke forth. 'I'm not working. I'm not striking neither. I've been tenting cows for Tommy Dent when he went harvesting. I tell you there are some low down things done in Anderby you'd never hear tell on.'

'Oh. Been out of work since that business with Mrs Robson?'

'Ay.'

'Foolish woman, very. Ah, what's that?'

From the road towards Market Burton came a rumbling clatter. An exultant procession of small boys appeared round the corner of the hedge. Then a column of dark grey smoke rose beyond it, and finally a traction-engine lumbered into view, with its trail of thrashing-machine and elevator.

It drew up beside the Robsons' stackyard gate, where the two men were standing.

'Hello there! D'you know if Robson's foreman is anywhere about?' called the driver.

'I doan't,' growled Waite, 'and I don't care.'

The driver turned to his companion, a mechanic seated on the foot board.

'Here, mate!' he exclaimed. 'This is one of the famous strikers of Anderby, I'll be bound. Where's the Red Flag, mate? Is that your union man?' He pointed a derisive finger at Coast. 'Come on, sonny,' he called to a stout urchin who gazed in rapt enthusiasm at the engine. 'Where's your dad?'

'He's waitin' for you somewheres – wants to get to Hardrascliffe to-night.'

'Well, fetch him along then, for I want a wash up, and a drop of supper at the *Flying Fox*.'

Waite and Coast stood silently by the gate, while a little crowd gathered to watch the delicate operation of manoeuvring the engine and its appendages into the stackyard. Foreman emerged from the Hind's house, already attired in his Sunday best. The 'thrashing man' was an old friend and ally.

'Come on, come in with you,' called Foreman. 'I'm taking missus in tid Hardrascliffe to-night for a bit o' spree like after harvest, and she's had 'er best hat on for last hour waiting o' you. We've got light cart yoked up an' all.'

'Oh, git away with you then. I'll bring in the Rolls-Royce, and drop her gently along side one o' them there stacks for a bit o' rest after the journey like. Whoa there! Back there!'

His hand on the wheel turned with amazing rapidity. The engine snorted and backed, then slowly lumbered towards the gateway, leaving the elevator in the road. There was much backing and twisting, much shouting of small boys and coupling and uncoupling of the thrashing-machine, but eventually it was through, and the engine returned for the derelict in the road.

'You've got a good yardful,' remarked the mechanic. 'How did you come on wi' the strike?'

'Strike? We didn't have no strike – just a few fond chaps taking a holiday through harvest like.'

'Oh, ay. You've got some bonny wheat here.'

'Ay – and yon barley, but the thatching's bad. We missed owd Deane for that. The wet'll get in any day now. That's why maister's all on to have it thrashed an' out of way before weather breaks.'

'It's fine enough now – happen a bit o' wind before morning.'

'Ay. You'd better damp down the fire in yon engine o' your'n. We don't want no sparks flying about with all harvest in. There's not enough water i' t' pond to drown a cat in.'

They were covering the machine now with tarpaulin, fastening everything snugly down for its sabbath's vigil. Coast stood watching them, and noticing how the stacks stood out in firm yellow blocks against the dark background of the wold. The solidarity of their bulging contour depressed him. Of what use was it to attack people who were shielded from poverty and failure by this power of possession? The backwash of progress beat in vain against the solid wall of property that sheltered them. He wondered no longer at the loud voiced communists whom he once condemned as extremists, because they would rob the rich of this destructive potency of wealth. That fellow Rossitur had been wrong as usual, when he declared that, after their taste of independence and co-operation during the strike, the men of Anderby would never be the same again. It would be just the same, the same patronage and injustice, the same complacent prosperity of people like the Robsons, the same heart-breaking rebellion of people like himself. The square grey house behind the sycamore-trees, the close packed sheaves of wheat and barley, the farm buildings astir with the sounds of pigs and horses and cattle, all these testified to the impotence of progress. Oh, the Robsons were safe!

Mike O'Flynn appeared from the stackyard gate that led to the garden of the Wold Farm. He strolled up to the little group where Foreman and the 'machine man' discussed the utility of raising bags of corn by a mechanical invention, instead of swinging them over one's shoulder as in the olden days.

'What's that fellow Rossitur doing up at the house door?'

Foreman turned. 'Nay, Mike, it beats me, but I expect he's gone to see Mrs Robson.'

'Mrs Robson went into Hardrascliffe wi't t' maister this after',' said Shepherd Dawson.

'Well, 'tis no good he's after, anyway, or he'd have gone with Hunting this morning – bad cess to him! And it's glad I am that Mrs Robson was not at home. After the trouble he's given her she'll not be wanting him again hanging round.'

'You off in tid' town to-night, Mike?' asked Ezra, who found Mike's frequent tirades on the subject of David Rossitur somewhat tedious.

'Now, what should I be doing buying squeakers on the sands and going to Pictures? There's a corner seat in the *Flying Fox* that I'd part with for no man.'

The men strolled off. The children still lingered to gaze upon the fascinating complexity of the great machine, and watch the smoke die from its funnel. Coast found that Waite was standing beside him leaning over the gateway. There was still the tiresome business of the field and old Mrs Armstrong to be faced. He must get rid of Waite and go on with his work.

He turned to the figure at the gate.

'Well, I hope your daughter will soon recover.'

'I never have no luck, and Ethel's always been a good girl.'

'Oh, luck can change they say – though I doubt it.'

'Luck's a lousy wench.'

'She's never so queer as when she isn't luck at all, but some person who got their knife into you.'

Waite looked with dawning comprehension at the school-master.

'Ay,' he remarked.

The wind was rising. A little whirl of dust and straw and dried leaves blew along the path at their feet.

'The wind's getting up,' said Coast. He was looking now from the rounded stacks to the man at his side, and a new desire was forming in his mind.

'Ay. I doubt it'll be a blust'ry night,' replied Waite.

'It's been a dry month,' remarked Coast.

'Ay. Pond shows bottom, an' beck's dry.'

'It would be a bad job for Robson if a spark from the engine caught on his straw.'

'Ay.'

'Those buildings are very near the yard, aren't they?'

'Ay.'

'I believe the wind is blowing from the south too. There'll be rain soon.'

'Oh, ay.'

'Did you see in the paper about that stack fire at the other side of Market Burton? They don't know yet whether it was a spark from the engine or whether some one had set it on fire.'

'Here, what are you driving at, Mr Coast?'

'I – I'm driving at nothing. I don't know what you mean. Well, I must be moving. Oh, by the way, do you know that there's a talk that the Robsons may leave Anderby if anything else happens to upset Mr Robson? He's been a bit of an invalid since his stroke.'

'I hadn't heard.'

'Some people wouldn't think it was a bad thing.'

'Ay.'

'Well, good evening.'

Coast strolled on past the garden of the Wold Farm, and the *Flying Fox*, till he came to the Armstrongs' gate.

Then he paused. The light was fading and, beyond the stubble fields, the sky glowed red and stormy. A gust of wind brought the frail leaves which clung to the branches of a chestnut-tree whirling round him. Down in the valley, Anderby village grew dim and grey.

19

THE ROAD TO ANDERBY

'Well,' sighed Mary, 'and that's that.'

She thrust the last parcel into the back of the dog-cart, and walked round to examine the pony's harness. The ostler at the *Paul Jones* had a natural gift of imperfection.

'How many times have I told you to twist the belly-band once round the strap before you pass it under the pony's body?' she inquired with asperity.

While she was attending to this business herself, John lounged into the yard, his pipe in his mouth, and his hands thrust into the pockets of a light overcoat. He stood watching as her strong fingers tugged at the stiff straps and buckles. She gave the ostler his sixpence and climbed up to the driver's seat.

'Just hold the pony's head till we get out of the yard, will you, ostler? Now then, John, are you up?'

'Going to be a rough night, Mrs Robson,' remarked the ostler, as John mounted the step.

Mary looked from the threatening sky to the orange peel and paper bags blown by the wind along the esplanade.

'Yes, but we shall be well home before the storm breaks. With a wind like this, the rain will hold off long enough. That's right. Now let go, please.'

The cart swung out of the inn yard, and clattered down the lamplit street, Mary driving dexterously among the Saturday night crowd.

'I don't much like putting up at the *Paul Jones*, John,' she observed. 'They take such a while to yoke up, and the ostler can't do anything right.'

John made no reply. Ever since his illness he had grown more reserved. The trouble of the strike had stunned him into a lethargy of submission. After his protest on the first morning, when he considered Mary's outburst of temper unjustifiable, he had accepted her judgments without comment. Mary was therefore surprised when, as they drove through the streets at the west end of the town, he volunteered a remark:

'I saw young Rossitur this morning.'

'Oh.'

Of course someone was bound to mention him sooner or later. Ever since she heard of his return to the village, she had prepared herself to face every possible situation. She would meet him somewhere, and be forced to speak with him – or John would meet him, and remember ... But day by day news came of him, of his interview with Hunting, of his impassioned speech to the men of the union, of his final settlement of the strike. And she had never seen him. Perhaps he had avoided her as assiduously as she had avoided him.

She sat silent for a moment, her attention apparently occupied by the reins. Then she gained sufficient self-control to ask, with apparent indifference:

'Did you speak to him at all?'

He knocked the ashes out of his pipe against the splash-board, before he answered.

'Yes, I did. You know, Mary, I don't think we did that young fellow justice.'

'No? Why, John?'

'Well, he always seemed to me a bit of a wind shaker, and there's no denying that if he hadn't been to the village that chap Hunting might never have come down.'

'That's true of course.'

'But you know, I think he must have seen he'd made a bit of an ass of himself, when he saw the strike coming on and all that, at least, so he said.'

'Oh, he said that, did he? Why, John? When did you talk to him?'

'I met him up in village this morning when I went to pay the joiner's bill for mending the reapers.'

'Oh, yes. He was still there then?'

'Ay. He said he was leaving Anderby to-night. Going back to Manchester. He told me he'd wanted to say that as far as the strike had hit us, he was sorry and that when he saw how Coast and Hunting between them were egging the men on to hold out for more money, after we offered the three pounds, he felt he had to come down and stop it if he could.'

'Oh, well, I'm glad he said that. Did he – did he ask after me?'

'No, I can't say that he did. He seemed a bit upset, though

that's not unlikely seeing the way he's treated us. But I will say this, once he made up his mind, he did act like a gentleman. That was a rare speech he made at the meeting in the school room before the men came in. Some one reported it in the *Hardrasclijfe Times*. I got a copy in the market to-day.'

'Oh. I'll look at it when we get in.'

'Ay. Do you remember when you brought him home – last spring, wasn't it? Ah, but that's a while back.'

'Do you remember?' The road was dipping towards the valley where the cross-roads met. All her life, Mary thought, when she passed them, she would see the stoop of slender shoulders, and the back of a red head in a misty circle of lantern-light. She looked sideways at John's bulky figure, lolling on the seat where once David had sat.

'Oh, yes, let me see, that was in the spring, wasn't it?' she replied.

It was strange, how things could happen which seemed to turn the world upside down, and yet the people who saw one every day never noticed.

'... Anyone with my beautiful disposition has to have some physical disability to counteract it.' ... Imagine John ever saying anything as silly as that! John never said anything silly. That was the worst of him.

Then something that she had been wanting to say all day recurred to her. 'John, I was talking to Mr Slater in church last night. He says you mentioned in the parish meeting that you'd like to retire from Anderby. Is that true?'

'Well, I don't know if I said those exact words.'

'But did you mean it?'

'Now, I wouldn't go so far as to say that. But I was talking it over with Sarah Bannister that time she came to see me when I was in bed . . .'

'Oh, I see,' said Mary.

She understood.

'And you know I'm not a young man, honey. And I'm not very clever about these new rules and regulations. And when I have to think about overtime and union secretaries and all that, it strikes me that farming isn't what it used to be.'

Of course. Sarah's very words. It was just what she had imagined. Where John didn't echo her, he echoed Sarah. Well, this time he'd have to echo her.

'Of course it isn't what it used to be,' she said brusquely, flicking the pony with her whip. 'Nothing ever is. We've got to move with the times. It's only when things are changing that it's difficult. In a year or two you'll forget there ever has been a union.

John shook his head. 'I don't know. I feel sometimes it's hard to start all over again, just when I was getting used to things as they were.'

'That's because you haven't been very well lately. You will, though. You'll get used to it. One can get used to anything.'

Again she felt as though there were enemies trying to snatch her kingdom from her, and that she must hold on with both hands in blind tenacity, no matter what it cost her or anyone else.

'Of course I can't hold you here against your will,' she said. 'I'm not going to deny that you came here on my account. Only I do think it would be silly to make a move now, when the mortgage is just paid.'

He did not answer. The wind caught them as they turned

westward along the road to Anderby. It whipped short strands of hair across Mary's face. John clutched at his hat and bent his head to the gale.

'Mind you,' continued Mary, 'I dare say that Sarah is right when she says that any more upset wouldn't be good for you. But now that everything is quiet again, I see no reason why we should worry.'

'Very well, honey. You know best.'

This would be her life, thought Mary. She would always have John's large and ineffective figure beside her. His 'Very well, honey, you know best,' would greet every decision that she made. She would always have long days at Anderby and short hours by the sea, and the homeward road winding before her in the fading light. There would always be the dull absence of expectation that rewards those who have realized their ambitions, and, later, there would be failing energy and old age ... Well, at least she had two possessions which made all that endurable. The kingdom of Anderby was, after all, still hers, in spite of Sarah and John and Coast and Hunting, and that fierce, indefinable power which David called progress. The other thing – she opened her eyes more widely in the windy dusk, and even then the colour rose to her cheeks and her heart beat faster – the other thing was the knowledge that somewhere David was alive and working. Though she might not, no, did not now even wish to see him, yet, from time to time the force of his vitality would quicken her through his writings, through chance news of his activities, through the memories to which she turned again and again when other thoughts were still. She might still amuse herself by pretending to hear his voice offering help again from the darkness of the road, or by rehearsing imaginary scenes to herself, scenes that would follow his return, many years afterwards, to visit her at Anderby. And she would confess what a narrow, complacent fool she had been, and they would laugh together over everything – even that incident in the cornfield, . . . no, perhaps not that. They would never speak of that. All the same, the quiet dream meadow where John had wooed her was driven now from her imagination by the picture of a wheat-field, hot and golden, and the scent of poppies and ripening corn upon the air.

Suddenly she raised her head. The scent of wheat and poppies? This familiar, acrid smell that the wind blew against her nostrils? 'Can you smell something, John?' she asked.

He sniffed the air.

'Ay. Something's burning. Probably they're burning hedge-clippings somewhere.'

'You don't burn hedge-clippings just after harvest.'

A bicycle bell rang furiously just under the horse's nose. He swerved aside.

'Where are your lights?' called Mary. 'It's past lighting time.'

A voice answered from the road. 'That you, Mrs Robson?' Then, almost before she had time to reply, it called, 'Then hurry back. I'm off to fetch t' fire-engine. Your stacks are afire.'

She stopped for no inquiry, but leaning low and plucking the whip from its socket she sent the pony forward at a gallop.

There was only another mile of road to cover before they rounded the Church Hill and the village lay beneath them. Then they would know the worst that was to be known.

The smell of burning grew stronger. The road seemed interminable. The fat pony, overfed and scant of breath, resented this sudden outburst of activity on the part of his mistress. He slackened his pace.

Mary rose from her seat and cut him sharply several times with the whip. It was the surprise of his life. He stopped dead, then started forward and galloped full into the teeth of the gale.

The dark trees and hedges streamed past them as they mounted the rise to the Church Hill, John crouching still and silent, Mary half standing and urging the pony forward with whip and rein.

From the top of the hill they looked down. Below in the village was a glare of red that threw the fantastic outline of roofs and chimneys into black relief, and rose into smoke hiding the outline of the wold and merging into the evening sky.

The fire looked a little too far to the right. For a wild moment of hope Mary thought the cyclist might have been mistaken. As the cart descended the hill she called to a passer-by:

'Where's the fire?'

'Robsons' – stackyard and farm buildings.'

They rattled on. The village street was astir with clamorous commotion. Everyone in Anderby seemed to be out of doors; skurrying black figures moved to and fro in the flickering red light.

Mary drew up outside the stackyard gate and let the reins fall on the pony's heaving flanks. Before her, above a jagged bar of wall, rose the flames from twenty-four stacks merrily blazing. A south-westerly wind swept them towards the farm buildings. The thatch along the covered side of the fold-yard was already alight.

Fascinated, she watched the moving figures of men pass and

repass before the fire. They were leading the horses and cattle away from the stable. Poor things! No wonder the animals were afraid with those horrid sacks tied over their heads. It was a shame, too, that they could not see the pretty fire. For it was pretty. Mary, who loved bright colours, watched the sparks dance upon the wind and trail away in a cloud of smoke like the fireworks at Hardrascliffe during the season.

A sudden jolt of the cart as John clambered down aroused her, but still she did not move. She watched his indecisive movements, his hesitating steps towards the fire, his stumbling return towards the cart.

There was a small crowd in the road. Some one had recognized them now.

'That you, Mrs Robson, that you?'

Even then Mary was glad that it was she to whom they called. 'Yes. We're back. Take the pony to the other stables, some one, and please see that there's a rug put across him. We've come fast. Now then, who's in charge here?'

'Shep's getting the horses out. Foreman ain't back yet. Did you see young Mr Rossitur on the road to Hardrascliffe? He went on his cycle to get t' engine.'

'No – there was a man though, going to get the fire-engine.'

Shepherd approached her, his face grimed with smoke. His blue eyes shone grimly.

'We've got the stock out, Mrs Robson, but I doubt we'll save t' buildings. There's no water in t' pond and we can't get none fra' back till t' fire-engine comes and the hose.'

'Have the far stables caught yet?'

'Not yet, but the wind's blowing right agin' them.'

'Well, we can't do anything about the foldyard, but get some men – anyone, and make a line of buckets and jugs from the pump to the stables, and try and keep the fire off them. Mrs Greenwood, you go and take those other women and get all the jugs and things you can find in the house. Oh, wait a minute. There's the key. Violet's out.'

There was very little that one could do but wait for the fire-engine. John seemed entirely bewildered, not exactly alarmed but stunned and helpless, standing by the wall and doing nothing. That really did not matter because no one could do anything with a fire blazing in a dry stackyard, without an adequate supply of water. She touched his arm.

'There's nothing to be done here,' she cried. 'Not till the fire-engine comes. You'd better go into the house.'

He shook her off irritably, but said nothing and continued to watch the crackling flames and floating wisps of fiery straw.

The onlookers stared at them both with awed curiosity. They wondered what it was like to stand and see one's whole harvest, corn and straw and buildings and all, blazing away like a bonfire on Guy Fawkes' night.

Mary turned to a woman at her side.

'Do they think it was a spark from the engine?' she asked.

The onlooker was Mrs Waite. She stared at Mary with wide frightened eyes.

'Oh, I don't know, I don't know. Eli said it was.'

Louie Watts, roused by unwonted excitement from her usual langour, turned to Mary with the pride of information.

'I heard Mike O'Flynn say it was lit a-purpose. I saw him come from t' *Flying Fox* when news first went round t' village.'

Mary turned to her.

'What did he say, Louie?' she asked.

'He said, "This is the dirty work of that damned skunk,"' repeated Louie, with gleeful recollection. 'And then he ran out of the yard.'

'Oh.' Mary was not really very interested in what Mike O'Flynn had said. It seemed unnecessary for him to run out of the yard when so much remained to be done inside it, but doubtless he must have gone to fetch something ... Because, even if the stacks had been 'lit a-purpose,' some one ought to put the fire out.

She looked at her watch. Eight o'clock. Only about a quarter of an hour had elapsed, then, since she passed the cyclist on the road. That was never David! Why had David ridden for the fire-engine? And, if he had ridden, why hadn't she seen him on the way? Riding at that rate he must have reached Hardrascliffe by now. If he had any sense he would stop at the first telephone call office. She wished that she had thought of that. He passed so quickly.

'Is the policeman here?' she asked abruptly. Constable Burton was usually a most conspicuous figure at village crises. Mary thought that his large stupidity might be comforting.

'He was here a bit back,' a woman replied, 'but some one said something about an accident up street, and he went to see.'

It would take another half-hour for the fire-engine to arrive at the village. By that time, probably, the flames would have reached the buildings to the right of the stackyard. Mary wondered whether she ought to go herself and superintend the fight against the fire. It would be a pity not to do the right thing now. She always had done it ... only somehow, it was so useless, because there wasn't any water ... A dress, the colour of that vivid orange and red, when the flames had caught a pile of loose straw, would be pretty . . . If David rode too fast down the hill into Hardrascliffe, she did hope he would ring his bell before the turn at the bottom . . .

Jack Greenwood stood beside her. His round eyes stared, his wide mouth hung open.

'Oh, Mrs Robson!' he gasped.

'Yes, Jack?' It was so silly that anyone should look so excited. There really was nothing to fuss about. After all, they were her stacks burning and she was quite content to stand watching them. Really it was rather a beautiful sight, so long as one did not stand too near, where the sparks might fall.

'Please, m'm, Constable Burton says I'm to tell you there's been an accident up the street. Some one's hurt and they want to bring him into your house.'

'Of course. I'll go. I can't do anything here. What is it?'

Here at least, was something obvious and familiar to be done.

'Some one's shot that fellow what talked in the village.'

'Shot him? Oh, nonsense! Who do you mean? Mr Hunting?' Thank everything there was to thank that David was in Hardrascliffe!

'No, yon other, with red hair.'

'Oh . . . Is he badly hurt?'

She began to move towards the garden, Jack stumbling beside her, almost running to keep up with her eager stride.

'I doant rightly know. Policeman's there. Mike O'Flynn had a gun and stood agin' him, and kept on saying "I've done 'im in. Praise be to Mary! I've done him in."'

'Mike?'

She frowned a little, as though she did not quite understand.

The garden was dark, with curious flashes of crimson light through the overhanging trees. She reached the backdoor of the house. It swung idly in the wind, but the women who had entered it to search for jugs and pails had gone.

Mary stood in the yard beside it, listening to heavy footsteps approaching up the garden path – the path that led through a wicket-gate into the road on the way to the *Flying Fox*.

She ought to have gone forward into the house and lit the lamps and made things ready. Only it was too late now. It was stupid, of course, to be unprepared, but she wanted to welcome him at the doorway a second time. She smiled to herself. Now, at least, she might have him. She might touch him again. However badly he was hurt she would nurse him back to health. He was young and wiry. Mike was an old soldier, but he probably hadn't shot very straight.

Constable Burton came through the garden door into the yard. She saw his round, solemn face in the flickering light. How silly of him to look so solemn, when he was being kinder to her than ever he had been before … bringing her David, David, David … There was another figure behind him, and something lying between them on a hurdle.

'Oh, do be careful! Mind the step,' she called, as they stumbled into the yard. 'You'll hurt him.'

'We can't do much harm, Missus Robson,' said the policeman.

'Is he badly hurt?'

'Nay. He's dead. Shot right through 'is 'ead. It's a bad job.'

She opened the door wider to receive him.

'Come in,' said Mary.

20

ABDICATION

'Ham, pie, cheese, bread, tarts, a custard and stewed apples. Well, I don't think we shall do so badly. Why didn't you roast a fowl and have done with it, Mary?'

At four o'clock in the morning Sarah Bannister faced Mary across the dining-room table with a smile of grim amusement. Mary looked up from the end of the table. She was abstractedly fingering one of her best netted doilies set under the ham in a moment of mental aberration by the red-eyed Violet.

'Well, I suppose I might have done that without such trouble. I'm afraid one or two have been roasted without any help from me.' She laughed forlornly and pushed back a lock of hair that had fallen across her forehead.

'Where are the men?' asked Sarah.

'I think they've gone to wash their hands. They must all be pretty black.'

'Oh. I'm glad to hear it. You could do with a wash yourself, Mary. There's a smut right across the middle of your nose. No, it's no use dabbing at it with your handkerchief. You'd better by half go upstairs and get tidied a bit. I'll pour out if the men come in.

Mary left the room, and Sarah stood by the table beating a soft tattoo on the back of John's chair. Only five hours ago a cyclist passing through Anderby on his way from Hardrascliffe had brought news to Market Burton of the Robsons' stack fire.

Sarah had asked no questions. She had put on her second best bonnet, roused Tom from his sleep and sent him to hire a car from the garage while she went herself to summon Toby. Sarah never was quite sure why she considered Toby's presence necessary, but a legal adviser might always come in handy and in this final catastrophe John must lack no possible support.

There was a clatter in the passage and three men entered the room: Tom Bannister, flushed and embarrassed, his round eyes wide with sleep, Toby Robson, nervous and loud voiced, wishing himself out of the whole damned show but determined to pass it off with as much joviality as possible, John, pale and miserable, his physical bulk only emphasizing his mental helplessness.

Sarah looked at him anxiously. She wanted, with an intensity that surprised her, to go up to him and put her arms round his broad bowed shoulders and stroke his hanging head and whisper, 'Never mind, John. Never mind, dear John. You couldn't help it. You've done your best. You've given the ten best years of your life to Mary's farm. It isn't your fault it's all spoilt. I'll take care of you. Give it all up and come to Market Burton and we'll all be happy there again.'

Instead she remarked:

'Hum. From the time you've all been away I thought you

must have been having a bath, but now I've seen you I doubt I was mistaken. Tea, John? Tom, hand me the whisky decanter, please. A drop of whisky in a little strong tea won't do any of you any harm.'

She established herself behind the teapot and was pouring out when Mary came in. Quietly Sarah relinquished her place and began to cut the loaf in stalwart slices.

'I wouldn't have any pie on an empty stomach if I were you, Tom. It's a while back since tea and I'm sure after a drive in Collinson's car your liver will be upset for weeks. Give him just a little ham, please, John.'

'Decent fellow that constable of yours, Mary,' remarked Toby, his mouth full of pie. 'Getting his head turned a bit though with two arrests in one night. Murder and arson! It's a bit thick for a village in these parts. You mayn't have much money in Anderby, but you do see life!'

Sarah frowned, but as John seemed to be paying little attention to the conversation she decided that Toby's exuberance was not worth checking. Besides, he had really been quite useful throughout this extraordinary, uncomfortable night.

Mary had been attempting to eat the ham that lay on her plate in limp pink slices. She put down her knife and fork now and turned to Toby.

'What's going to happen to Mike O'Flynn now?' she asked.

'Oh, well, of course, he'll have to be kept safe until the trial. Of course the man's insane. An old soldier you said?'

'Yes, and very excitable. He had pneumonia about two years ago and was quite off his head then for a bit. The men told me he's been drinking a lot lately and getting very worked up. I suppose I ought to have noticed, but I just didn't.'

'Oh, completely mad I should say. Look at the way he never attempted to escape. Just hung about the body till some one fetched the policeman. Why on earth did he do this fellow in, though? Senseless sort of thing it seemed.'

'Oh, I saw him to-night for a few minutes, you know, and he told me.'

Sarah heard Mary's flat dreary voice, sounding as though she told a tale so often repeated that it had become unutterably boring.

'He seemed sane in a way then, but queer of course and not at all ashamed. He said that Mr Rossitur had brought all the trouble to Anderby and when the strike was over he was really furious, but just pretended it was all his own doing. And Mike says that earlier in the evening he saw him hanging round and was sure he was up to some mischief. Then when he heard of the fire he knew Mr Rossitur had lit it to pay us out, and he saw him run off to get his bicycle – really to fetch the fire-engine, but Mike thought he was running away. So he got Foreman's gun, the one John gave him to shoot rabbits with, and ran down the garden path at the back of the house to the *Flying Fox*, and came on Mr Rossitur just as he was getting on his bicycle and shot him point-blank through the head.'

Sarah listened with frowning brows.

Really, now the fire was over, and the police officers interviewed and the Irish murderer and Mary's discharged beastman arrested, it was time to talk about something else. She passed her cup to Mary.

'More tea, please. And, if you have any water, I should like it weaker. My digestive organs are not made of cast iron, and I don't suppose that a heavy meal at this house will exactly improve their condition. Tom, if you've had enough, you'd better go and wake that chauffeur. We'll be moving.'

'Oh, no. You'll stay the night here, please, Sarah,' said Mary. 'Violet's putting some sheets on the spare room bed now. I found her crying all over Fred Stephens in the kitchen, and decided she had better have something else to do. Fred was very tired. He's been splendid to-night. In fact, they all have.'

'Oh, very well. I suppose that man will wait. I'm sure I don't want him to stay, though, if he's going to charge us by the hour, I'd rather he took the car back to Market Burton, and you could give us a lift to the station to-morrow. I hate those nasty, smelly cars, always breaking down just when you want them most. What amazes me is that we didn't have a puncture to-night.'

She straightened the bonnet which she had not yet laid aside, and helped herself to another tart.

It was strange how the memory of another meal haunted her. Last December they had all sat round the table, congratulating themselves on their own cleverness, and Uncle Dickie had made that deplorable speech. Well, Uncle Dickie was dead and there was not much matter for congratulation now. The stack-yard was gone. The farm buildings were reduced to blackened husks. Only the rain, held off too long by the wind to save the stables, had come in time to check the fire before it reached the cottages beyond. And that red haired young socialist lay dead in the back sitting-room. That was bad luck. He was an irrev-erent, conceited young fool of course, but then one was like that when one was young, and doubtless he was rather clever, and had a good many hopes about the fine things he was going to do. It was bad luck, being shot down by a crazy harvester, just when life was beginning. Still, the important thing at the moment was to get John to bed without any more fuss. He looked absolutely worn out. She supposed that even this would not make any difference to Mary's determination to stay on at Anderby. Mary was of the obstinate, selfish type, who insist upon doing good in their own way. If she thought that she was doing her duty there at Anderby, at Anderby she would stay, even if John had twenty strokes and died.

Sarah rose from the table.

'Now then, Mary. What about getting to bed? I'm sure we're all tired, and if Violet has put those sheets on the spare bed we'd better use them.'

'Well, well, it doesn't sound so bad. I could do with forty winks myself,' remarked Toby, with a tremendous yawn.

They trooped upstairs, Mary hurrying first to see that the rooms were ready. In a little while she returned to the dining-room, and found Sarah sitting there. She had not even removed her bonnet.

'Aren't you going to bed?' asked Mary.

'I never go to bed within an hour after a meal unless there is some special reason. Is John in bed?'

'Yes. He went straight to sleep. He must be very tired.'

Mary sat down on a chair near the table, and idly dug little pits in the salt-cellar, raising the spoon and watching the salt stream slowly back into the pot. The fire was dead and Sarah looked from the empty grate to the discarded meal on the table.

'Hadn't you better go to bed yourself? You'll have a hard day to-morrow.'

'I know,' said Mary, but she made no effort to rise.

'You're spilling that salt on the cloth. It'll only be more mess to clear away in the morning.'

Mary's hand was still. She turned and looked at Sarah.

'You were right,' she said at last very slowly.

'Indeed? I usually am. But when do you mean particularly?'

'When you said we should have to give up Anderby.'

'Oh.'

'I was wrong in the garden the other day. And I knew I was wrong all the time. That's why I was so angry, I suppose.'

Sarah raised her eyebrows. This was the first time she ever remembered hearing Mary confess herself mistaken.

'I have not had time yet to talk to Toby, but I will in the morning. About selling the farm, I mean. I think we'll sell and not let it. I shouldn't like the idea of anyone but a Robson farming it while it was still mine. Then we could live at Littledale, or Market Burton.'

Sarah said nothing. Until last Wednesday she had never believed it possible that she could have been so sorry for Mary. The flat, weary voice went on.

'You know, ever since we drove down the hill and heard about the fire, I've had a sort of feeling that if I had given way at once and said we would retire, when everyone thought we should, this wouldn't have happened.'

'Now, you're being sentimental, Mary. You know quite well it had nothing on earth to do with you retiring.'

'I'm not so sure. I think Waite did it to drive us out of the village. If he'd heard we were going anyhow . . .'

'That's all far-fetched nonsense. It's happened and it's a great pity that it's happened. But in a way it might have been worse. After the insurance has been paid, you won't have lost a deal o' money, and you can live quite comfortably somewhere else, and do a bit of farming at Littledale. I certainly think Anderby is a bit too much for John after what's happened, and now he isn't well. He looks done up enough to-night.'

'That's all, then.'

Sarah rose. She was tired herself, and Mary looked tired too. It was quite time that they both went to bed, but something in Mary's face made Sarah hesitate. After all, it was Mary's farm, and she knew it would not be pleasant to be driven out in this way. She wanted to comfort her – at least, part of her wanted to, the other part felt only resentment against the woman whose obstinacy and self-confidence had been so bad for John.

'Hadn't you better go to bed?' she asked.

'I'm coming in a minute. You go. I'm just going to see if the doors are fastened.'

'Mary, is there anything I can do?'

'Nothing, thank you.'

For a moment they confronted one another. There was no sound except the rain, falling in a steady downpour on the house and garden. The wind had dropped. Sarah took a step forward. If Mary had given one sign of emotion, had done anything but stand by the table, with a grey, bored face, Sarah might have tried to console her. She did not move.

'Good night then, Mary.'

'Good night.'

On the threshold, Sarah paused. Mary was still standing contemplating the wreckage of the meal. She was even smiling to herself, a strange, light smile. Now, people hadn't any business to smile like that when they had just made things thoroughly miserable for every one else. Sarah retired to bed.

Mary stood alone in the dining-room. Just through the wall, in John's little gun-room, lay David with a sheet across his face.

It was one of the best linen sheets. Mary was sorry that he was in such an uncomfortable place, but the house had been very full and so many policemen and inspectors and people had wanted to look at him, that it seemed the only thing to be done. It was queer how little anyone seemed to think of him, though, because, really, he was much more important than a stack fire. Mary felt quite angry when she thought of Toby and Sarah comfortably asleep upstairs, while David lay on a sofa in the gun-room. Still, it was a linen sheet . . .

She did not want to go and look at him. It was not fair to go now, when her presence would have embarrassed him so much, had he still lived. There was a note from him in her pocket. He had pushed it under the door that evening after she had driven to Hardrascliffe when Mike thought he was 'hanging about up to some mischief.' He only said he was glad that he had been able to help in settling the strike, and hoped that Mrs Robson would regard this as a more substantial form of apology for his recent behaviour, but that he was just as convinced as ever that Anderby was being worked on a pernicious system of patronage, and it would be so splendid if only she would realize it.

One day, she supposed, she might be glad to have this and the articles he had written, but just now she felt too tired to read – too tired even to think properly, though she was sure that there was something very special she had to think about, if only she could combat that queer, vague feeling in her head that made everything so unreal.

What had happened was all her fault . . . Mike . . . His sudden madness had been her fault in a way, because of something she had said to him in their last interview before the strike. She wasn't quite sure what it was, but she knew that there was something. Then Waite – it had been just his luck that some one should have caught him hiding the paraffin tins in the oil-shed – of course, she might have been less unkind to him ... Then John's stroke, and Coast's invitation to Hunting, and the strike, and the fire, and David's death ... All somehow connected with things she had done or left undone.

She began to move about the room, lifting dishes and placing them on the butler's tray, then putting them back again. But the table refused to become any tidier. She ought to tidy it. Every one would be so busy in the morning. She must do her best to make things easy ...

She had always done her best. Everything, her rule over the village, her saving of the farm, her treatment of John, even her dismissal of Waite ... What was one to do? Was it her fault that all the ideas she had encountered, all the circumstances surrounding her, tended to make her one kind of person?

She must try and get things straight in her head. If she persisted in blaming herself entirely, she would go mad. Besides, it probably wasn't true. If only there was some one to tell her what was true ... David could have done it.

She sat down by the curtained windows and pressed her hands across her aching eyes.

The broad view ... If one could only take the broad view. David had said, it made everything tolerable. There was something he had quoted once in an article in the *Northern Clarion*. 'There comes a time when out of a false good, there arises a true evil.' ... Was that meant for her? David had told her she belonged to a generation that should have passed ... Her work at Anderby might be the best thing of which she was capable, but it was a false good. She looked after people too much. They needed to be taught how to look after themselves, because no one could ever look after people properly. There always came a time when that vicarious strength broke down, ... as with John, or the village after Hunting came ...

Besides, David was dead. David, with his wild ideas for the progress of civilization and the reform of agricultural conditions, could carry out none of them now. He had died, horribly, wastefully, futilely. Such horror and such futility would hardly bear contemplating, because he had been so much alive, so full of purpose, possessing such an ardent desire for work. That was why she must go. Because, if David was dead, it wasn't fair to spoil his work even if one didn't believe in it. If the changes which David desired in Anderby were to come, then she and John must go. For, if they stayed, they would prevent the completion of his work. They could not help it. They were made like that. Whatever they might mean to do, they would slip back at last into the old ways. So, only by going could she in any way make up to David for the folly of his dying, ... and she must go. Market Burton was a dull place, but she supposed there would be work of some kind to be done there. There would always be a girl's club or a nursing association or something – something that couldn't do anyone much harm ...

She smiled a little bitterly. Once she had thought so much of all the good she was going to do to people ...

Of course nothing mattered very much now, but she supposed that one day she would wake up and remember that she was under thirty still, and want again desperately all the things she had missed. David, the smile of the labourers as she passed them by the stackyard gate, the brown, full-bosomed curve of the hills, and the scent of cream and butter in a red-tiled dairy ...

But they were nothing to the things that David would miss. That was why one must remember all the time the things that he had said. Of course it might be consoling to realize that Jack Greenwood and Hunting and Coast and Fred Stephens were the heirs of the future and that by going away quietly she was doing the only thing she could do to ensure them the contentment of proceeding ...

But Mary had seen enough of Market Burton to know that she would find little satisfaction in noble sentiments when her maid gave notice, or the rector altered the date of the missionary bazaar, or Mrs Marly-Thompson wouldn't call.

Perhaps though, even if one did not think of them, even if in one's own limited, unsatisfactory life there seemed no room for them, those fine things were there just the same – courage, service, progress ...

David's courage and service not wantonly wasted, his desire for progress not frustrated, but fulfilled at last because of him – even remotely because of her ...

Just now, though, she must be practical and get to work. The morning was here already and there were policemen and insurance agents to be interviewed and the labourers to be seen and plans to be made for the sheltering of cattle and implements. For a few months until she and John left Anderby she would be too busy to think. Well, perhaps it was just as well and – after that – she might even understand a little better ...

She moved suddenly and flung back the curtains. Outside, the rain had ceased and it was light again. The pungent smell of rain-washed earth came in from the autumn garden, and with it another smell of charred wood and blackened straw. From the church on the hill a bell was ringing for the seven o'clock service. Golden beyond the sodden shrubbery the sun rose slowly over Anderby Wold.

**You can order other Virago titles through our website: *www.virago.co.uk*
or by using the order form below**

☐ South Riding	Winifred Holtby	£8.99
☐ Poor Caroline	Winifred Holtby	£8.99
☐ The Land of Green Ginger	Winifred Holtby	£8.99

The prices shown above are correct at time of going to press. However, the publishers reserve the right to increase prices on covers from those previously advertised, without further notice.

Please allow for postage and packing: **Free UK delivery.**
Europe: add 25% of retail price; Rest of World: 45% of retail price.

To order any of the above or any other Virago titles, please call our credit card orderline or fill in this coupon and send/fax it to:

Virago, PO Box 121, Kettering, Northants NN14 4ZQ
Fax: 01832 733076   Tel: 01832 737526
Email: aspenhouse@FSBDial.co.uk

☐ I enclose a UK bank cheque made payable to Virago for £ . . . .
☐ Please charge £ . . . . . . to my Visa/Delta/Maestro

Expiry Date ☐☐☐☐   Maestro Issue No. ☐☐

NAME (BLOCK LETTERS please) . . . .

ADDRESS . . . .

. . . .

. . . .

Postcode . . . . Telephone . . . .

Signature . . . .

Please allow 28 days for delivery within the UK. Offer subject to price and availability.